EVERY BEAT
OF HER HEART

What Reviewers Say About
KC Richardson's Work

A Call Away

"…the romance between both characters was nice and gave me all the feels by the end. I really think this is the kind of novel you take on holiday and read by the pool. I look forward to seeing what's coming up next for KC Richardson."—*Les Reveur*

New Beginnings

"Pure and simple, this is a sweet slow-burn romance. It's cozy and warm. At its heart, *New Beginnings* by KC Richardson is a story about soul mates that fall in love. …If you're looking for a sweet romance, the kind of romance that you can curl-up with as a fire crackles in your fireplace, then this could be your book. It's a simple love story that leaves you feeling good."—*Lesbian Review*

Courageous Love

"Richardson aptly captures the myriad emotions and sometimes irrational thought processes of a young woman with a possibly fatal disease, as well as the torment inherent in the idea of losing another loved one to the same illness. This sensitively told and realistically plotted story will grab readers by the heartstrings and not let them go."—*Publishers Weekly*

Take one happy and well centered ER nurse add one handsome Cop and the scene is set for a happy ever after. But throw in a life threatening disease and KC Richardson ramps up the angst. …This is a great storyline and felt very well done. While there is a heavy dose of angst, it's justified and well handled."—*Lesbian Reading Room*

"[A]n enjoyable read that doesn't shy away from the realities of dealing with a life-threatening illness."—*Rainbow Book Reviews*

By the Author

New Beginnings

Courageous Love

A Call Away

Taking a Shot at Love

Seasons For Change

Every Beat of Her Heart

EVERY BEAT OF HER HEART

by

KC Richardson

2023

EVERY BEAT OF HER HEART

ISBN 13: 978-1-63679-515-7

This Trade Paperback Original Is Published By
Bold Strokes Books, Inc.
P.O. Box 249
Valley Falls, NY 12185

First Edition: December 2023

CREDITS
Editor: Cindy Cresap
Production Design: Susan Ramundo
Cover Design By Tammy Seidick

Acknowledgments

A huge thank you goes to Radclyffe, Sandy, and everyone at Bold Strokes Books who was responsible for the production of this book. Tammy Seidick, you knocked it out of the park with this cover. Cindy Cresap, my wonderful editor, is so patient with me and teaches me so much about the editing process that makes me a better writer.

My special beta readers, Dawn, Inger, and Rebecca. Thank you for always giving me valuable feedback.

The COVID pandemic led a Twitter friend to me who became such a great friend in real life. It was our mutual love for women's basketball and sapphic romance books that brought Kat and I together. And it was Kat's idea for this story, and she wanted me to be the one to write it. She was instrumental in helping me develop Piper and Gillian as well as the story line. Kat, thank you for the idea, but more importantly, thank you for your friendship.

Thank you, Dr. Amy Cohagan, for answering all of my hospital questions. Any errors that may be in this story are mine and mine alone.

More thanks to my family and friends for their love and support.

Last, but certainly not least, thank you, readers, for continuing to read my books and for your kind words. You make me want to keep doing this crazy thing called writing.

Dedication

To Kat—Ride or Die
To Inger—My heart beats only for you

Prologue

Piper was awakened by a coughing spell that made it difficult to catch her breath. She'd hoped for a good two uninterrupted hours of sleep, but as her disease progressed, that was becoming more unlikely. She reached for the glass of water that was a common fixture on her nightstand. She took a sip to sooth her dry throat and placed the glass back to its rightful place. She closed her eyes again, hoping to reclaim her elusive sleep. Just two more hours might give her more energy to interact with her family today.

Piper's family had been hovering around her more lately, but she understood the reason. Their sister and daughter, the middle child of the family, was dying and she didn't know how much longer she had left. She had no idea how she'd once been an active, energetic woman to now knocking on death's door. She felt the tears form behind her closed eyelids; a single drop leaked out and rolled down the side of her cheek. There was still so much she wanted to do, to see, to experience. Now, all she had the energy for was to pray for a miracle. She heard her bedroom door creak open, and the light from the hallway brightened behind her eyelids.

"Honey, dinner is just about ready." Piper's mom spoke softly, and she sat on the side of her bed.

Piper kept her eyes closed and enjoyed the feeling of her mother's fingers sifting through her hair. She'd witnessed the stress her declining health had on her parents, and she wouldn't wish that on her worst enemy.

"Do you have the energy to sit at the table with the family, or would you like for me to bring you a plate?"

Piper knew this would likely be her last Thanksgiving, and she wanted to spend it with her family. She wanted to make fun of her three brothers and sister. She wanted to laugh with her nieces and nephews. She wanted this to be full of happy memories that her family would be able to look back on with fondness. The smell of turkey, stuffing, and rolls wafted into Piper's room, and it made her dry mouth water. She loved the smell of the house when her mom cooked Thanksgiving dinner. Hell, when she cooked anything at all.

"I'll come to the table, Mom. Could you help me freshen up?" Piper winded easily, and she sometimes needed assistance with the easiest of tasks. "Can you brush my hair for me?" She opened her eyes to see her mom's sad smile, but she nodded. Her mom helped Piper out of bed and into a chair in front of her vanity. Her mom turned on the bedroom light and grabbed the hairbrush from the table.

"You know, I used to love brushing your hair when you were a child. You were always so patient with me when I wanted to do braids or pig tails."

Piper looked at her mom through the mirror. "I loved that too, Mom. It felt like our special time together alone without the other kids around."

Her mother brushed a few more strokes, then placed the brush back on the table. She leaned down and kissed the top of Piper's head.

"Do you have any idea how much I love you?"

Piper nodded and placed her hands over her mom's that were cradling her cheeks. "Probably as much as I love you."

"Oh, no, baby girl. That couldn't be possible. You are my pride and joy."

Piper smiled. "I always knew I was your favorite." Piper tried to laugh but instead was met with a coughing fit.

Her mom smiled. "Don't tell your brothers and sister."

Piper finally caught her breath. "I promise. I can get dressed by myself, so go finish dinner, and I'll be out shortly."

Her mom closed the door behind her, and Piper pulled out her burnt orange sweater and brown slacks—the perfect color combination for Thanksgiving. She would place her melancholy in the back corner of her mind, put on a smile, and soak in the love and laughter that would take place around the table.

She emerged from her bedroom, the same one from her childhood minus the New Kids on the Block posters that used to adorn her walls. Piper had had a well-paying job, her own townhome, and an active social life. But as her health declined, she was unable to work, sold her townhome, and stopped going out with her friends. It was also when her girlfriend decided she couldn't handle seeing Piper so sick, and that it would be better for *her* to leave. It had taken a lot of doctors, a lot of poking and prodding, and a lot of tests to finally give her the diagnosis. At first, she was fatigued, which she attributed to her busy lifestyle. She was young and went out most nights of the week, never one for lying low. Then she started to get out of breath just walking from her car to her office. Occasionally, she'd feel like her heart was skipping beats, but then that became more frequent. When she started having chest pain, she freaked out and went to the emergency room. There she had a series of tests and had seen a few different doctors before she was finally diagnosed with dilated cardiomyopathy. That was eight years ago, just before her thirty-first birthday. Since then, she'd been under the care of her amazing cardiologist, Dr. Donohue, who specialized in women's cardiovascular health. She placed Piper on a ton of medications that had done their job until they didn't. About eight months ago, she began having heart failure and was immediately placed on a transplant list. Piper had a Left Ventricular Assistant Device implanted that was supposed to keep her heart strong enough to pump the blood from her heart to the rest of her body, but then the device malfunctioned, and she had to have it removed. She was currently high on the waiting list for a new heart.

Her parents welcomed her back into their home. She did what she could to help them out around the house—doing chores, helping with cooking, but the past few weeks, even took that from her. She hated being a burden to them, but they kept reassuring her that they would do anything for her.

"Aunt Piper!" Her four-year-old niece with curly blond hair and the same whiskey-colored eyes that Piper possessed came running up to her and threw her arms around Piper's legs.

"Hi, peanut. Wow, you act like you're happy to see me or something." There was a time when Piper would've been able to lift her up and give her a real hug, but now she could barely carry a plate of dinner from the kitchen to the table.

Little Samantha laughed. "I am! Will you sit with me for dinner?"

Piper held Samantha's hand as they walked down the hall to the living room. "I think Grandma and Grandpa want me to sit at the adult table, but I promise to sit with you and your cousins for dessert."

"Yay!" Samantha let go of Piper's hand and ran the rest of the way to play with her cousins.

Piper's siblings and their spouses got up to greet her, giving her gentle hugs and kisses on her cheeks. She missed the big bear hugs that her brothers used to give her. Now they treated her like a glass ornament that would shatter if squeezed too hard. She loved her siblings, their spouses, and their kids. Barring an occasional disagreement, they always had a great time together, and more importantly, they honestly liked each other.

Once the kids were seated with their plates of food, the adults gathered around the table, and held hands to say grace. They'd never been much of a religious family, but the one constant was saying grace before Thanksgiving dinner, even if they were celebrating the day after actual Thanksgiving. It allowed Piper's siblings to join their spouses' families on the actual day, then they all gathered at their childhood home for the family gathering the next day. Even though they didn't consider themselves very religious, since Piper got sick, it seemed they prayed more. It couldn't hurt, right?

Piper's dad cleared his throat. "Heavenly Father, thank you for the food that we're about to eat. We are grateful the whole family is together, and we can enjoy this meal and each other. Please hear our prayers. Amen."

Piper looked around to see sad and watery smiles. She needed to do something to lighten the mood. "Hey, what's a turkey's favorite Thanksgiving food?" The adults at the table all groaned, as they always did at Piper's corny jokes. Samantha yelled out around a mouthful of turkey. "What?"

Piper turned around to look at the kids. "Nothing. It's already stuffed." The kids laughing made Piper turn back to the adults and stick her tongue out at them.

"Stick that tongue out again, little sis, and I'll tickle you until you have trouble breathing."

"Andrew William James! Behave yourself."

"Sorry, Mom." Drew looked over at Piper and winked.

As they were passing around the dishes of food, the house phone rang. Nobody stood to answer it because it was a house rule that nothing interrupted a family dinner. The answering machine—yes, an actual answering machine—would take care of it.

"Hi, this is Dr. Donohue. Piper, if you're there, please pick up. I'll page you."

Drew stood so fast that his chair knocked over as he raced into the kitchen to answer the phone. "Yes, Dr. Donohue, she's right here." Drew's hand shook as he passed the handset to Piper.

"Dr. Donohue? What? Are you serious? Oh, my God. We'll be there soon. Thank you." Piper hung up the phone and held it to her chest. All action ceased as her family stared at her, waiting to hear her news. Tears sprang up in her eyes. "UNOS called. They have a heart for me. I'm getting a new heart."

"Thank you, God. Our prayers have been answered," cried Piper's mom as she raised her hands to the sky.

"I need to get to the hospital right away."

Piper's dad stood. "Mom and I will take you. The rest of you stay here and eat. We'll call you and update you."

Piper grabbed her coat and hugged everyone good-bye. She fervently hoped this wouldn't be the last time she saw them. Just in case, she stopped and looked around the group of both adults and kids to memorize their faces. It appeared they were doing the same.

"I love you all so much. I'll see you all soon."

Samantha ran up to her and hugged her. "I'll save a piece of pie for you."

Thirty minutes later, and a few admonishments from her mother for her dad to slow down, they arrived at the hospital and checked in. Once she was gowned and the nurse got her IV in, her parents were allowed in pre-op to sit with her. They stood on either side of her hospital bed and grabbed for her hands. Piper's mom lifted her hand and kissed the back of it. There was a lot of hustling and bustling in the pre-op area. Piper wasn't the only patient there. Nurses and doctors in scrubs were moving about, and bright fluorescent lights shined above making everything look so sterile. Her parents grounded her and kept her calm amidst the chaos.

"Your dad and I love you so much, baby girl. We have a lot to celebrate today. But we're also grateful that the poor soul who died was an organ donor. That is the most selfless thing anyone can do. While we're praying for you, we'll pray for that person and their family."

Piper nodded. "I feel guilty and selfish. I mean, someone had to die in order for me to live. How am I supposed to handle that?" It was difficult to talk around the huge lump that formed in her throat as the tears formed in her eyes. She rubbed her hand over her traitorous heart then wiped her eyes.

"You get healthy and make your dreams come true. Live life to the fullest, and thank your donor every day. We've been given a second chance at life for you, honey." Piper's dad wiped a tear off her cheek with his thumb.

The curtain opened to reveal Dr. Donohue and Dr. Cohen, the transplant doctor that she'd been recommended to by Dr. Donohue. "He's right, Piper. This is your second chance. Are you ready to do this?" Dr. Cohen explained the procedure, how long it would take, and where Piper's parents could wait.

"Richard, Debra, I have your cell number that Piper gave the nurse. As soon as she's in recovery, I'll call you, but I'll send someone out occasionally to update you."

"I'll be in the OR as well, so try not to worry." Dr. Donohue placed her hand on Piper's mom's shoulder in reassurance.

Piper's dad offered his hand to Dr. Cohen then to Dr. D. "Take care of our girl, Doc. There are a lot of people who love her." Piper's bottom lip trembled when she heard her dad's voice crack.

"I'll do my very best. We'll take you back in a few minutes, so a nurse will be in to take you two to the waiting room."

A moment later, the nurse came by to take Piper's parents to the room they'd spend the next several hours.

"Mom, Dad, try not to worry too much. I got this. I love you both so much."

"We love you too, baby girl. We'll see you when you wake up." She hugged and kissed them both, taking time to breathe them in. Her dad was strong, but when it came to hugs, her mom was the best, hands down. Everything would be right in the world if everyone could get a motherly hug from Debra James.

Piper watched her parents leave, and she started shaking. That could be the last time she saw them. *No, don't think like that. Be positive that everything will be fine.*

"Piper James? I'm Dr. Angel, your anesthesiologist."

Piper snorted then covered her mouth. "Is that really your name?" Nothing like having a comedic break at the time she was about to have a nervous breakdown.

He smiled. "If I had a dollar for every time someone asked me that, I could finally buy a house on the beach. I'm going to give you something to help you relax." He stuck a needle into her IV and administered the medication. "Do you have any questions for me?"

Piper shook her head and laid it back on the pillow.

"I'll see you soon. I promise to take good care of you." The doctor left, and Piper closed her eyes. At least now she'd be able to get some uninterrupted sleep while she was out. She thought about her donor and their family. Was the donor married? Did they have a family that loved them the way hers did? What did they do for a living? What did they like to do? Her ruminations were interrupted by the team that would take her to her new heart. It was finally go-time. They entered the bustling OR, and the first thing Piper noticed was all the machines near the wall. They pulled up along another gurney and helped Piper transfer onto it.

"How are you feeling, Piper?" A large man in light blue scrubs placed his hand onto her arm.

"I'm freezing. How do you all work in this cold room?"

He laughed as a woman also in scrubs placed two warm blankets over her. They felt like they'd just come out of the dryer, and it felt heavenly.

"We have these big lights and big gowns that go over our scrubs. If it wasn't cool in here, we'd be sweaty messes by the end of surgery. I know you've answered these questions many times already, but we need to be sure you're the right person getting the right surgery. What's your name?"

"Piper James."

"What surgery are you having?"

"A heart transplant."

He continued with the barrage of questions. Piper almost felt dizzy with all the people moving around her like a well-choreographed dance. They seemed to know what they were doing, which helped calm her nerves a little. Dr. Cohen came in masked up and asked how she was feeling.

"I'm pretty nervous, Doc."

"That's perfectly normal. The good news is that I'm not nervous."

Piper could see he was smiling by his squinting eyes. "I'm going to go scrub while everyone finishes prepping. Next time I see you will be when you wake up."

Piper nodded.

Dr. Angel stepped close to Piper's head. "You ready, Piper?"

"As much as I'll ever be."

"I'm going to put this mask over your nose and mouth. Take some deep breaths and count backward from one hundred."

Piper got to ninety-six before everything went black.

Chapter One

Two Years Later

Gillian walked through her new-to-her townhome that was about thirty minutes from where she and Kate had lived. She needed a fresh start, and their home carried too many memories and tears that kept Gillian from moving on. That was a lie. She hadn't *wanted* to move on. She wanted Kate back, and she wanted to live the rest of their lives together. That wasn't going to happen though, and in all honesty, the house just felt so big and empty, and it made her feel even more lonely. She had decided to downsize and bought this townhome. Seeing the "Sold" sign in front of her house as she was moving out nearly took the breath out of her. It almost felt like she'd lost Kate all over again, but Harold and Gloria, Gillian's in-laws, were encouraging when she brought up the idea to them, and it was their support that enabled her to list the house and pack up all of their belongings.

She entered her pristine remodeled kitchen with stainless steel appliances, white cabinets with black hardware, and white quartz countertops. It was a stark contrast from their old kitchen. That one had oak cabinets, tile countertops, white appliances—a kitchen that had looked dated back to the eighties. Gillian hated that kitchen, kept dropping hints to Kate for a much-needed remodel, but Kate wanted other projects done first.

Baby, I promise we'll get to the kitchen, but how about we replace the floors instead. The carpet is thrashed. Just think what wood floors would do to the house.

Kate had been right. The carpet was worn down, had stains, and was just disgusting. The house felt cleaner and lighter with the Brazilian koa hardwood they had installed. They just never got around to upgrading the kitchen before Kate had died. After, Gillian couldn't bring herself to change anything else in the home they'd shared for twelve years. Hell, she'd just sort of wandered through life for almost the past two years. It took every ounce of energy for Gillian to return to work just six weeks after she'd lost Kate. The museum director had been very kind with the amount of bereavement time she'd been given. But then again, Gillian had worked for the museum ever since she'd completed her PhD fourteen years earlier and had always been willing to do extra work when it was needed.

Gillian took her cup of coffee back to her bedroom to finish getting ready for work. She stopped at her dresser where she'd displayed a few of her favorite pictures. Her and Kate's wedding picture (she looked so handsome in her tux), one of Kate in her softball uniform, her hat on backward, and a dirt smudge on her cheek, and one of Kate that had been taken just two weeks before she died, sitting on her Harley in her leathers, looking too sexy for words. Gillian picked up the one of Kate on the motorcycle and looked closely, trailing her finger along Kate's face.

"Happy birthday in heaven, baby. I miss you so much, but I still feel you here with me. I'm going to your parents' tonight for dinner, to celebrate you. They're doing okay, going through life as we all are, but thinking of you always. I will always love you."

Gillian kissed the photo before setting it back down and took her coffee into the bathroom where she had the news playing on her tablet, mostly to get the weather report. September in the East could have you bundled in a coat and gloves in the morning and wanting shorts and a sleeveless shirt in the afternoon. Growing up in Virginia had made her an expert at layering her outfits. It wouldn't be long before she'd have to break out her winter wardrobe. This used to be her favorite time of the year, when she and Kate, and almost always Audrey, Kate's best friend, would hop on the bikes and drive along the less-traveled roads in Virginia. Gillian would sit behind Kate, her arms wrapped tightly around Kate's middle, feeling safe with her wife driving. They'd take in the leaves starting to turn fall colors, the reds, yellows, and oranges, flittering in the breeze. They'd stop for lunch at a diner, then continue their ride. Sometimes they'd go apple picking or stop at a place where they could take a short hike.

Gillian shook her head to bring herself back to the present. She took a quick glance at the clock and noted she was running late. She hurriedly finished her makeup and dressed before grabbing her briefcase and heading out the door. Normally, she would take the Metro into DC to get to work, but since she was going to her in-laws' for dinner that night, she'd decided to drive. Traffic could be iffy so she wanted to give herself some extra time. If she arrived early, she'd be able to stop at the coffee cart and pick up a muffin for her breakfast. If not, well, she'd just have to settle for a protein bar that she had stashed in her desk drawer. She parked in a nearby parking garage, checked the time on her watch, and realized she still had twenty minutes. She took a deep breath and let it out slowly. She had plenty of time. She grabbed her briefcase, locked her car, and headed to the sidewalk that would lead her to the museum.

As she approached the coffee cart that was a fixture not too far from the entrance of the museum, Gillian smiled at the older gentleman running the cart and filling an order. She patiently waited in line until she reached the front.

"Now, there's a sight for sore eyes. What can I get you, Dr. Phillips?"

"Lou, I've told you a million times to call me Gillian." She added a wink to let him know she wasn't upset. "And I'll have a black coffee with a blueberry muffin, if you have it."

"I saved the last one for you." He reached below and pulled out a plastic-wrapped muffin and handed over her coffee. She gave him a ten-dollar bill.

"Keep the change, Lou. Have a great day."

"You too, Dr. Phillips."

Gillian chuckled as she left. She'd known Lou for over eight years, and he always addressed her as "Doctor." One day, when there were no other customers around, and she was on break, she had a nice conversation with him. He'd told her he had retired from his job as a school janitor, but it was bugging his wife to have him underfoot constantly. He was bored so he decided to start his coffee business. He'd been doing it almost every day since. He wasn't a fool though—he took winters off, and in the summer, he added iced coffee to the menu.

Gillian had a good day at work, a quiet day, which she appreciated from time to time. As a curator for the Smithsonian Museum, most of her days were busy, some were long. She didn't mind putting in extra work, especially since she no longer had anyone waiting for her at home. She took some time to walk through her latest exhibit after lunch. She loved the smell of the museum, the architecture, the paintings and sculptures, the sound of her heels tapping on the marble floor. It was familiar, comforting, like her home away from home.

One nice surprise that'd happened that day was her assistant brought her a small plant in memory of Kate's birthday. Gillian mostly had her emotions under control these days, but this small act of kindness choked her up. She felt the lump in her throat and her bottom lip tremble before she hugged Maya. She managed to say thank you before she playfully kicked her out of her office and told her to get back to work. She placed the plant on her desk near a framed picture of her and Kate.

"Wasn't that thoughtful of Maya, honey? She remembered your birthday."

Gillian had set her alarm for five thirty p.m. so she remembered she would have to leave shortly after. She cleaned up her desk, powered down her computer, grabbed her briefcase, and headed back to her car. The sun was setting, and she recalled a trip she and Kate had taken to Provincetown, Massachusetts, one year for Women's Week. One evening, they sat out on their balcony overlooking the harbor, watching the sun set and drinking wine. Gillian could almost smell the salt water and hear the ripple of waves in the harbor. Kate had looked over at Gillian and told her how beautiful she was and asked how'd she become the luckiest person on earth to have a woman like her as her wife. Gillian had been thinking the same thing except she was the lucky one to have Kate as her wife. That had been one of their favorite vacations, indulging in seafood, cocktails, and nightlife. They spent the rest of the night making love with the drapes billowing from the breeze floating off the water.

Gillian arrived at her in-laws' with a bottle of Pinot Noir in her hand. She walked in to the aroma of pot roast filling the house. It had been Kate's favorite meal, and they always had that for her birthday along with mashed potatoes and gravy, and cooked carrots. She walked into the kitchen to see Gloria at the stove. Gloria's shoulders were hunched as if she was carrying the weight of the world.

"Smells good in here, Mom."

Gloria jumped and turned around, smiling at Gillian.

"Hi, honey. I didn't hear you come in." She walked over to Gillian and took her in her arms, giving her a long, tight hug.

"That doesn't surprise me. You looked like you were far away."

Gloria laughed. "I was. Forty-six years back in time to be exact. I was just thinking about when I was in labor with Kate. She was so stubborn, wanting to stay inside my belly while I was ready to get her out so we could finally meet her."

Gillian smiled and handed over the wine. "She always said it was so warm in there and too cold in the outside world."

Gloria chuckled as she opened the wine bottle. "She wasn't wrong about that. I would have done anything to keep her warm and safe." Gillian didn't miss the sadness in Gloria's voice, and she knew exactly what she meant.

"Where's Dad?"

"He's taking a shower. He'll be down soon. How was your day?"

"It was fine. Wished Kate a happy birthday this morning, had a nice, easy day at work, and Maya gave me a gorgeous plant in honor of Kate."

"She's a sweet girl. You're lucky to have her as your assistant."

"Don't I know it." Maya wasn't from around these parts. She was a transplant from California, so from time to time, she'd had her over for holiday meals with her in-laws and Kate for the past few years before Kate died. Maya had been her assistant for five years, but she was also working on her PhD to become a curator herself. Gillian had taken her under her wing to be her mentor, and in doing so, she'd also become a friend.

Harold came down the stairs, dressed in khakis and a button-down shirt, wet hair slicked back, and smelling like Irish Spring soap.

"There's my favorite daughter-in-law." Harold hugged Gillian and kissed her on the cheek.

"That would have more merit if I wasn't your only daughter-in-law, Dad." She squeezed him and kissed him back.

"Gilli was just telling me that Maya gave her a nice plant in honor of Kate's birthday. Wasn't that sweet of her?"

"She's a good kid."

Gillian laughed. "She's thirty years old, Dad. Hardly a kid."

"Listen, since I'm almost seventy, all of you are kids to me."

"How's the new place, honey?" Gloria asked as she was moving the food to serving dishes.

"It's fine. I'm still unpacking, but I like the neighborhood. I haven't had much time to explore the area, but there seems to be a lot of cute shops and restaurants within walking distance. The Metro is only a quarter of a mile away, so I can walk there easily."

They all brought the food to the table, and there were four place settings. They always had a setting for Kate, as if Kate was joining them. Harold poured the wine as Gloria dished the food onto their plates. Once they were all settled, Harold raised his glass.

"To our Kate. May she always be watching over us, and waiting for us with open arms when our time comes."

They clinked their glasses and wiped away their own tears. As they ate, they all told charming and funny stories about Kate. After all, they were celebrating her birth and her life on this earth. Kate had a way of making everyone love her. She was kind, thoughtful, inquisitive, and loving. And she was funny. God, she was so funny.

Eventually, they had tears in their eyes, this time from laughing recalling Kate's shenanigans. Their stories could have gone on for hours, but they would be told often, as they should. After dinner, they had red velvet cake with cream cheese frosting (Kate's favorite) and coffee while continuing with their stories, most of them told many times over. Gillian helped clean up, hugged her in-laws good-bye, and headed home to her empty townhome. Except it didn't feel so empty that night. People might call her crazy, but Gillian felt Kate's presence with her all day and night.

She climbed into bed and talked to the picture of Kate on her nightstand. "I had a nice time with Mom and Dad tonight, baby. I'm sure your ears were burning with all the stories we told about you. I'm not sure how long I'll be feeling this deep ache inside my heart and the deep hole in my life I've had since you left, but it eased for a short time tonight. That's something, isn't it? I love you so much, my sweet wife. Forever and always."

Gillian kissed the photo and turned out the light. She was hoping she'd get to dream of her beloved.

CHAPTER TWO

Piper and her friend Mallory snagged a table close to the bar for their weekly happy hour gathering. It was the one day a week she allowed herself a glass of red wine, with permission from her doctor. Since she'd had her heart transplant, she maintained a healthy lifestyle with eating, drinking, and exercise, with the exception of an occasional indulgence. Mallory wasn't much of a drinker, so they tended to make their one glass of wine last an hour between catching up, gossiping, and laughing. Piper had always been healthy, even before she went into heart failure, so her lifestyle change wasn't much of a change at all. It had been almost two years since her transplant, and all had gone according to plan. Her doctors were pleased with her progress, she was religious about taking her medications, and she'd continue to do everything needed to live a long life.

"How's the shop doing? Steady traffic coming in?" Piper and Mallory had been friends and colleagues for about ten years when they both taught art at the community college. Mallory was the one friend who made an effort to stay in contact and visit when she got sick. The others, Piper assumed, didn't know what to say or how to act when Piper's health declined so much, that they probably just thought it would be easier to drop off than try to be actual friends.

Piper took a sip of her wine as she nodded. "It's good. Having art classes to offer also helps."

Once Piper had recovered from surgery, her brother Drew and his wife, Kelly, partnered with Piper to open an art supply store in a new development that offered apartments above the stores. The area was a good mix of shops, restaurants, and a couple of bars, and a short distance from the Arts District. Piper lived in the apartment above their store, and the area was very convenient for her. Almost everything she needed access to was within walking distance. Kelly wanted to be involved in the day-to-day activity of the shop, which Piper greatly appreciated so she could teach art classes. They ended up both teaching classes and tending the counter with an occasional part-time worker. Besides, Piper loved Kelly as if she was her sister by blood. Drew had definitely married up.

"That was a really great idea you had, and it will definitely increase the traffic in the store."

"Yeah, and the fact that Kelly is an artist too makes working with her even more fun." As Piper got older, she turned her artistic interests more toward sculpting and pottery. She taught classes in those two disciplines, and Kelly taught sketching and painting. Between those four classes, that made up close to fifty percent of their revenue.

Piper checked her watch and was surprised to see they'd spent an hour drinking a glass of wine and sharing some appetizers. Piper had never been much of a drinker, more social than anything, but before she got sick, she'd probably have been on her third glass by now. At the very least, she would've finished two glasses and started on a glass of water. But she didn't need alcohol to have a good time, especially when she was with Mallory. She had a great sense of humor, and they always had stories that made them crack up.

Piper and Mallory walked out of the pub and hugged each other good-bye, Piper turning left and Mallory turning right. As she walked down the sidewalk past bustling restaurants and stores closed for the night, Piper took the opportunity to breathe in the cool late summer night air and appreciate the second chance at life she'd received. There wasn't a day that went by where Piper didn't think of her donor and their family. By someone dying, Piper was able to live. She'd had plenty of guilty feelings about that, which her cardiologist said was normal for transplant recipients. She prayed to her donor every morning and night, thanking them for their very special gift and wishing them an eternity of peace.

As she approached her store, she saw a woman standing in front of the large floor-to-ceiling window looking into the dark space. Piper took in the woman's profile and liked what she saw. The woman was shorter than Piper, dark hair to her mid back. It was difficult to tell the exact color under the yellow glow of the streetlamp. Piper slowed her pace, not wanting to startle the woman. She took her hands out of her pants pockets to seem less threatening.

"Hello," Piper said when she was a few feet away, and the woman jumped. So much for trying not to scare her. Piper held her hands up. "I'm sorry. I didn't mean to scare you."

The woman placed her hand over her heart. "It's okay. I was just lost in thought and didn't see you approach."

"Is there something I can help you with?" Piper hooked her thumb toward the large window. "This is my store. Are you an artist?" Even under the streetlamp, Piper could see the woman blush, and it hit her how beautiful the woman really was.

"Me? Oh, no. I mean, I love art, but I'm not very good at it."

"Well, if you're interested, we give lessons and classes in sketching, painting, sculpting, and pottery."

"I don't know. It's not anything I've ever really thought of."

Piper noted that the woman's smile was sad, and she wondered why. For some reason, Piper wanted to know everything about her. She offered her hand. "I'm Piper James. I own this store with my brother and sister-in-law."

The woman took Piper's hand, and despite the slight chill in the air, her hand felt warm in Piper's. "I'm Gillian Phillips. I'm new to the neighborhood, so I thought I'd take a stroll to see what's here."

"Hey, that means we're neighbors." Piper pointed up. "That's my apartment up there. How long have you been here?"

Gillian chewed the inside of her cheek, looking like she was trying to decide if she was going to answer or not. "Just about a week now."

"Where did you live before?" Piper saw Gillian shut down. The window shade had been pulled down. She realized she was being nosy. "I'm sorry. You don't have to answer me, a complete stranger," Piper pointed at herself. "I tend to be a bit curious, and my family has told me more than once that I need to tone it down, that I can be too much sometimes."

Gillian appeared amused, so at least that was something. Piper pulled out her wallet and gave Gillian her business card. "Here, if you need any art supplies or lessons, keep us in mind. I promise not to be so nosy next time."

"Thank you. Have a good evening." Piper watched Gillian walk away, a little stiff-bodied if Piper had to describe her. She'd always been an inquisitive person, but was even more so since receiving her new heart. It was as if a switch had been flipped on, and Piper suddenly wanted to know everything and everyone. She didn't know how much time she had left on earth…one day, one month, thirty years. But then again, nobody knew. What Piper did know was that she wanted to live life to the fullest. She didn't have endless funds to do everything that cost money, but she could learn, and that didn't cost anything.

Piper walked up her stairs behind the building and entered her apartment to her very loud, very displeased cat, Agnes. It was like she was being yelled at. By her cat.

"What are you so upset about? I told you I would be back later, and I even fed you before I left."

More meowing by Agnes had Piper throwing her arms up in the air. "Well, I don't know what to tell you. I left the TV on Animal Planet for you. Did something upsetting happen?" She bent down, picked up Agnes, and kissed her on the head before putting her on one of her many perches around the apartment. "I'm sorry, kitten. Let me get ready for bed, then you can tell me all about it."

Piper did her nightly routine, donned a surgical face mask and gloves before cleaning out Agnes's litter box, and filled her water dish, then climbed into bed. She had talked to her transplant doctor before rescuing Agnes six months ago regarding anything she should avoid. Since she didn't have anyone to clean out the litter box, he advised her to wear a mask and gloves, then wash her hands. She would have done anything he told her so she could have her cat. Despite Agnes being disgruntled at times, she did bring a lot of joy and helped keep Piper's anxiety at bay. Agnes laid down on her chest, and Piper started her nightly cat-loving routine by stroking her thumbs back and forth on the sides of Agnes's face.

"So, I met a very pretty woman before I came home. I saw her looking through the window of the shop, but I don't think she's interested in taking any classes." She continued to pet Agnes as she purred. "She said she's new to the area. She seemed kind of, I don't know, sad maybe. She wasn't very talkative, and you know how I can get going, talking about anything."

Agnes meowed.

"I know, but I can't help it. You know how friendly I am. I adopted you, didn't I?"

Another meow.

"Okay, fine. You adopted me. Can't you even sometimes pretend that I'm the boss?"

The meow actually sounded like "no." Agnes moved to her own pillow, and Piper turned on to her side, turned out her lamp, and closed her eyes. "Fine. You're the boss."

❖

Gillian locked her door and placed her keys and purse on the table in the foyer. She removed her coat and threw it over the back of the couch on her way to the kitchen. She poured herself a glass of wine then went to the living room and turned on some jazz. She sat on the couch and looked at the three boxes in the corner that needed to be unpacked. Mostly books and knickknacks that normally adorned a living room. There was a mantel over the electric fireplace and nondescript white walls surrounding her. She mentally began to decorate her new home. She'd place a couple of pictures on the mantel, including her and Kate's wedding picture. There were a couple of paintings they'd bought at a gallery in New York that she could hang on the walls. Maybe we would get some plants and stands to place by the window. Not we. She. She was no longer part of a we. She took a big swallow of her wine. Even after two years, she sometimes said we. After over a quarter of a century being a "we," it was a difficult habit to break. She stopped decorating in her mind and thought back on her day.

It had been an unremarkable day at work, and she arrived home with a little daylight left. She'd changed out of her work clothes and put on a pair of jeans and a casual shirt. She heated up some leftover spaghetti in the microwave for dinner and sorted through her mail. She was feeling a bit restless, and after she ate dinner, she grabbed her sweater and purse, and went for a walk.

The closer she got to the main street, the louder it got. A lot of the shops were closed, but a few were open, including an ice cream shop and a candy store. A lot of the restaurants had patio seating, and Gillian discovered much of the noise was coming from lively conversation. Customers were taking advantage of the gorgeous late summer night. She could appreciate that. In fact, she missed that. A lot. When Kate was alive, they would often get their closest friends together once a month for dinner and drinks. Each friend was responsible for picking the place when it was their turn. She should restart that tradition. In fact, she'd call Heidi, Amanda, Jen, and Audrey to invite them to dinner. She stopped in front of an Irish pub and restaurant for a couple of minutes. It was busy, there was a live band, and everyone seemed to be having a great time. This would be her first choice when they would resume their monthly gatherings.

On her way home, she stopped in front of a shop that was closed for the night, but she noticed the sign above. Rainbow Arts. *Rainbow* was lit in rainbow colors, and it caught her eye. After all, rainbows were recognized as gay. Maybe it was gay-owned? She was starting to read a notice taped on the inside of the window that talked about art classes they offered, when the woman who owned the store approached her. There was a vague familiarity about her, but Gillian couldn't place where she might know her from. She wasn't certain she'd seen her before, since she'd just moved to the area, but something about her got to Gillian. She was sure it would come to her at some point if she'd known her.

Gillian loved art but did not have an artistic bone in her body. But did that mean she couldn't learn? Drawing and painting were out, she already knew that. But maybe she could learn pottery. Make a bowl or a dish or something. At least it was something to get her out of the house. Maybe meet some new people, possibly make a friend or two. One couldn't have too many friends. The past two years consisted of going to work, going to her in-laws', or going home. She'd visit with her friends, but usually a potluck at one of their homes. She did nothing for herself, by herself. Maybe it was time for Gillian to start living again. She knew Kate would've been upset with her for taking so long to rejoin the living.

Gillian enjoyed her stroll through her neighborhood that night. She felt safe, and she looked forward to discovering more of the charming town. When Kate was alive, they lived in a town only a thirty-minute drive from Alexandria, but she never paid too close attention to all the different shops and restaurants except for the one they were going to. She had a feeling there'd be plenty for her to do in the area. She could walk along the Potomac River, visit the Arts District, walk the neighborhoods, maybe take some pictures. With more excitement than she'd felt in the past two years, she went to bed, looking forward to more exploration of her new neighborhood.

CHAPTER THREE

Gillian and her crew, as she liked to call her friends, finally found a date and time where they could all meet for drinks and appetizers. They had agreed to the Irish pub close to Gillian's house, as they could walk to the establishment and not worry about finding parking. They'd started at Gillian's for a glass of wine, beer for Audrey. Gillian's friends had helped her move, but tonight was the first time they'd been there with everything put away and fully decorated.

Jen raised her glass. "To Gillian and her new home. May you have only wonderful times and happy memories here." The rest of the crew raised their drinks and clinked.

Gillian could feel her blush forming. "You all are the best friends I could ever ask for. The past couple of years have been so hard," she looked at Audrey, "for all of us. Kate will never be far from our hearts or our thoughts. Do you think she would've liked this place?" Gillian knew Kate better than anyone, and she knew Kate would have loved it here, but sometimes she needed validation. There were times when she could feel Kate with her, especially as she figured out the places she wanted to display pictures of her. Gillian would look around her new home, wishing Kate was with her, but deep down inside, she knew she was.

Audrey smiled. "She would've loved it. Especially being able to walk to the restaurants and to the river."

"Speaking of, let's head out before it gets too late."

Audrey offered her arm to Gillian, and she took it as they walked toward Old Town.

"Kate would've loved living in this area, Gilli. And she would've loved the new place. I did notice you didn't have many pictures of her up in the house."

Gillian leaned her head on Audrey's shoulder. "I have my three favorite pictures of her in my bedroom and our wedding picture on the mantel. How many do you want me to put up?" Gillian laughed. "I talk to her all the time. Just because I don't have her pictures displayed all around the house doesn't mean I've forgotten her."

"I didn't mean to imply otherwise, Gilli. I'm sorry I said anything."

Gillian kissed her cheek. "Don't be. I just wanted you to know that not a day goes by that I don't talk to her or think of her."

When they arrived, they all decided to eat on the patio. The weather was pleasant, and there was another band playing that would make it difficult for them to talk. On the patio, they'd still be able to enjoy the music without having to yell. By the time their food arrived, they'd finished their first round of drinks, and they ordered another. Gillian was a pretty mellow person, but when her friends got together, she let loose. The alcohol didn't hurt, as well as the back and forth between Amanda and Heidi. They all loved each other, but Amanda and Heidi had a camaraderie that consisted of friendly trash talking, one-upping each other, telling hysterical stories that had everyone at the table nearly screaming and crying with laughter.

Gillian wiped her eyes and took a sip from her refreshed glass of wine. She looked across from her, over Heidi's shoulder, and she spotted the woman she'd met a couple of weeks ago, the one who owned Rainbow Arts. Heidi looked behind her then faced back to Gillian.

"What are you looking at?"

Her friends looked in the direction where Gillian was looking. "Just someone I met a little while ago. And way to make it obvious by all of you looking."

They all looked at her with their eyebrows raised. Gillian looked at each of them. "What?"

"You met someone?" Audrey asked, rather accusingly, it sounded to Gillian.

"Not like that!" If she'd been sitting next to her, she would've slapped her arm. She looked at Heidi, who was sitting next to Audrey, and she slapped her arm for Gillian.

Before Audrey could say anything, Heidi told her the slap was from Gillian.

"She didn't even say anything." Audrey continued to rub the spot that had been assaulted by Heidi.

"Listen. One, stop being a baby. I didn't hit you that hard. And two, Gillian's like the other half of my brain. She doesn't have to actually say words for me to know what she's thinking." Heidi looked at Gillian and blew her a kiss. "You're welcome."

They all laughed with the exception of Audrey, who was still rubbing her arm. Heidi was right; Audrey could be a baby sometimes.

"I met her one night when I was taking a stroll in the neighborhood. She owns an art supply store that offers art lessons. I just happened to be looking through the window when she was on her way home, and she introduced herself." Gillian took another sip of wine, and her friends remained quiet, staring at her. "What? That was it. She asked if I was interested in taking a class."

"Uh-huh. I just bet she'd love to teach you something." Amanda smirked. She was sitting next to Gillian, so she did smack her arm.

"Hey, show some respect. Gilli's not interested in that kind of lesson," Audrey said. "Are you?"

Gillian laughed. "I most certainly am not. I'm not interested in seeing or sleeping with anyone. My one true love is gone, and I'm not interested in having another relationship."

"Ever? You're only forty-six. You can't be alone forever." Jen was one of the quieter ones in the group, and the most sensitive, so it was an unlikely comment to come from her. Gillian reached across Amanda and took Jen's hand in hers.

"I'm not alone. I have you four and Kate's parents, not to mention my friends at work. I was lucky to have been with her for so long, and every moment we had, I will always cherish. There's just no way I'd be able to replace her."

"Not replace her but at least date. You never know." Jen sure had some opinions on Gillian's dating life, but she couldn't be upset with her. Jen was one of the kindest people she'd ever met, and Gillian knew that whatever Jen said, it came from the love she had for her friends.

"I love you all, but let's get off this subject."

They'd spent the rest of their time drinking, eating, talking, and enjoying the traditional Irish music coming from inside. They'd split the bill, as they'd always done, and headed back to Gillian's. They spent the next hour eating a carrot cake she'd baked earlier and drinking decaf coffee to give everyone time to make sure they were sober to drive. It was always a rule that if they'd had too much to drink, they'd stay over. But by the time the cake and coffee were finished, everyone felt fine and able to drive home. Gillian walked them out to their cars and gave them all hugs. She wrapped her arms around herself to ward off the small chill as she watched the taillights disappear around the corner. She went back inside and basked in the love and laughter she'd shared with her friends. The food and music at the pub were fantastic, except for the little sidebar of discussing Gillian's potential dating life. She just wasn't ready to start thinking about dating anyone and didn't know if she'd ever be ready. The entire night had been uplifting to Gillian's heart, and she'd promised her friends to think about other possibilities, including dating.

Chapter Four

Piper looked at her phone for what seemed like the hundredth time since she'd slid under her covers an hour earlier. She and Mallory had gone to the pub to listen to some music, and they were lucky to grab a table for two at the window overlooking the patio and street. She had taken a drink of her sparkling water when she'd looked outside and saw the woman she'd met outside her store a couple of weeks ago. Piper couldn't remember her name, but she remembered her face. The woman's face would periodically pop into her head, and although she was unsure why, it made her smile. She nearly choked and sprayed the water out of her nose. Mallory laughed at her as she handed her a napkin. Piper had told her that the liquid went down the wrong pipe, but she said nothing of the woman having dinner with four other women on the patio.

The woman looked a lot happier than she did when Piper first met her. To see her smile and laugh made Piper's heart feel lighter. It also struck Piper how pretty she was. For the next hour or so, Piper would sneak glances out the window, careful to not let Mallory see her. Piper didn't want to explain why she kept looking at a woman she didn't even know. Silly? Of course, it was. But she felt the pull and was drawn to her inexplicably. Piper turned over and fluffed up her pillow. It was going to be a long day tomorrow if she didn't get some sleep.

After five hours of restlessness, Piper finally gave up and got dressed. Agnes watched her the entire time, and she meowed when

Piper gave her a little scratch on the chin after she'd placed her food dish onto the floor next to her water dish. She took the inside stairs down to her shop and turned the light on in the back room, closing the door to the shop so any crazy person who might be up at this ungodly hour who might be walking by wouldn't see the light on. She donned her smock, grabbed a three-pound wad of clay, and filled a bowl of water before taking a seat at the wheel.

"Alexa, play smooth jazz." Music started with sounds of saxophone and piano. Piper took a deep breath and let it out slowly, then applied pressure to the pedal. Piper cupped the clay with her wet hands and helped form the clay into a cone before pushing it down. As the clay widened out, she slowed the wheel and placed her thumbs in the center to start the bowl she wanted to make. As time went on, and it started to take the shape Piper wanted, she dipped her hands in the water and returned to the clay. She pulled the clay out then smoothed the unevenness before wetting her hands and the clay again.

Times like this, Piper could get into a trance and lose herself in the feel of the wet clay taking form just by her hands and fingers. She used various tools to etch designs on her creation, giving them each a unique design that would hopefully catch someone's eye. By the time she was done, she asked Alexa what time it was. When she learned it was just after six a.m., she frowned. Today was going to be a long damn day. She placed her bowl on the shelf that would be placed in the kiln later, then removed her smock. She turned off the light and returned to her apartment, feeling satisfied with what she created. Agnes greeted her at the door and kept meowing at her, like she was asking Piper where she'd been all night.

"What's your problem? You sleep all day long while I'm at work. Are you hungry? You know, you have a whole bowl of kibble on your condo shelf. Not to mention the fact that I actually fed you canned food before I went downstairs."

Another meow and this time, she pawed at Piper's leg. "Fine, I'll dish out your canned food again. You are so impatient." Piper picked her up and gave her a smooch on top of the cat's head. It was a miracle that Agnes wasn't a thousand damn pounds at this point between her food and her treats. Once Agnes was happily eating her wet food, Piper had to decide if she should crawl into bed for a couple of hours, or should she just suck it up, shower, and stay awake until it was time to go to work. She walked back into the kitchen to put the coffee on. That answered her question. While it brewed, she stripped out of her dirty clothes and stepped into the hot shower, letting the spray wash away the tension she felt in her shoulders. She washed her hair and scrubbed the dried clay off her skin with her loofa and bodywash that advertised it would keep her alert and awake, as opposed to the other bottle that would help her sleep. By the time she toweled herself dry, the smell of coffee drifted through the apartment, and her mouth watered. She was excited for that first taste of her favorite decaffeinated French roast. She dressed quickly, poured herself a very large cup of coffee, and sat on the couch looking out the window as the sun slowly rose in the sky, casting a light purple glow. Delivery trucks were parked in front of businesses unloading the goods that would make their respective businesses ready for the day.

The first scalding sip caused Piper to curse, but she blew on the hot dark liquid and quickly took another sip. She had another two hours before she'd open the shop. Kelly would arrive an hour after opening and teach her first class, and after lunch, Piper would teach a couple of sculpting and pottery classes. She loved teaching, seeing the students concentrating on what she was saying then trying to replicate it with the clay. It was times like these, when she was alone and able to reflect on all her blessings, she thanked her heart donor for her second chance at life. The donor's selfless act enabled her to live a life she loved. She also said a prayer for the donor's family and loved ones.

Piper went down to the shop, turned on the lights, and unlocked the door, ready to welcome customers into her store. Not being far from the Arts District certainly helped the flow of traffic, especially on the weekends. Anyone from students, to novice artists to experienced would come in for paints, brushes, sketch pads, canvases, and clay. Rainbow Arts also offered memberships for artists to come in and use the studio anytime during business hours, particularly for those who want to use a pottery wheel or kiln. Already, after just an hour, there'd been a steady stream of customers coming and going. At one point, she thought she'd seen the woman who had been infiltrating her thoughts lately, but she couldn't be sure. She didn't have time to look with a line of five people waiting to pay for their supplies.

❖

Gillian wandered through her townhome while sipping her cup of tea and eating a slice of dry toast. Her stomach had been turning since she'd decided she would step outside her safe little box and sign up for a pottery class, just to try it out. She stopped at a photo of Kate displaying her trademark smirk that Gillian loved so much. Last night after her friends left, she decided to add a couple more photos of Kate, and one of her in-laws to the living room. Once completed, she'd discovered it made her home homier.

"Do you think it's silly that I'm going to sign up for a pottery class, baby? I mean, I work with brilliant pieces of art almost every day, but I have no artistic ability whatsoever."

Gillian could almost hear Kate telling her that it was just one lesson, and she might actually be good with some practice.

"I know. It's possible I can make a little coin dish or a small bowl, but it'll probably be trash-worthy. The important thing is I'm getting out and doing something different, something for myself, right?"

Gillian finished her tea and toast, rinsed out her cup, and grabbed her purse before she stopped back by the picture of Kate she'd just been talking to.

"Wish me luck, honey. I love you and miss you every day."

She blew a kiss before leaving. She put on her sunglasses to block out the already glaring sun. The morning was a little cool, but according to the news, temps would be warming up to a pleasant day. Maybe she'd take a walk along the Potomac River later and wander through the neighborhoods and look at the Brownstones. When Gillian entered the shop, there was quite a line at the register, so she decided to look around. There was a wall with shelves that captured her attention full of pottery vases, bowls, and mugs that were so vibrant and colorful, it was difficult to tear her eyes away. Except on the wall next to the shelves were smaller canvases of abstract art that Gillian felt were worthy of an exhibit. She looked at the price tags and gasped. The paintings were way underpriced in her opinion. They could easily get ten times what they were listed at. She went back to the pottery to check those prices. Again, in her opinion, way underpriced. The vase that first got her attention was listed at fifty dollars, but she would've easily paid two hundred. She shook her head as she cradled the vase in her arms, protecting it like a newborn child, and carried it up to the line to the register. She recognized the woman ringing up items as the one she'd met in front of the shop weeks ago. When it was finally her turn, the woman behind the counter startled.

"It's you."

"I'm sorry?" Gillian almost laughed at the odd greeting.

The woman gave a noticeable shake of her head. "We met before. In front of the store. At night." The woman closed her eyes, and an adorable blush flushed her cheeks. "Let me start over. We met about a month ago when you were standing in front of the store when I was on my way home. I'm sorry, I can't recall your name."

"Gillian." She took in the woman who owned the store, brown hair pulled back in a ponytail, maybe a shade lighter than her own. Her nose was crooked, like it had been broken previously and never set quite right. Her eyes looked like the color of Kate's favorite Scotch whisky, but they were sharp and almost sparkling. She didn't look anything like Kate, except for maybe her crooked nose, but there was something else familiar about her. She just couldn't put her finger on it.

"Right. Gillian. I'm Piper. So nice to meet you again."

Gillian was quite amused by Piper's stammering, but she had a serious question to ask.

"Is this vase really fifty dollars?"

Piper's eyebrows scrunched together. "Well, I suppose I could let you have it for forty."

Gillian shook her head. "Not less. More. This is a beautiful piece, and I was thinking it should be more like two hundred dollars."

Piper laughed. "I wasn't sure if anyone would buy it if I priced it over fifty. Besides, it didn't take me long to make it."

"You made this? Piper, it's gorgeous, and I'd love to buy it, but only if you charge a fair amount."

"Thank you. How about a hundred dollars?"

Gillian shook her head. "Two hundred."

"No. That is way too much. You know, the customer usually tries to get the price down. I've never had anyone try to pay me more than the listed price of my pieces. Maybe I should hire you to reprice the pottery and paintings." She laughed and blushed simultaneously.

"Fine, one hundred dollars. And I already have a job, but you really need to reconsider how much you're listing these beautiful pieces. If this store was in the Arts District, these would go for four times as much." Gillian handed over her credit card.

Piper ran the card through the machine then handed the receipt for Gillian to sign. She watched Piper intently as she assembled a box and wrapped the vase in bubble wrap.

"I only made them so people could see what they can do with pottery. When I teach lessons, we work with much smaller balls of clay, but it gives the students an idea of what they can create. The paintings on the wall next to the pottery were done by my sister-in-law, Kelly, who's my business partner. She's in the back teaching sketching right now, but she also teaches painting. She's married to my brother, but I don't hold that against her. He definitely married up." Piper took a breath, and Gillian laughed at the rapid-fire stream of words that came out of Piper's mouth.

"Sorry. I've been told more than once that I talk too much and ask too many questions."

Gillian shook her head. "Don't apologize. If you don't ask questions, you don't learn what you want to know." She thought it was adorable, but no way would she voice that opinion. She returned her credit card to her wallet as Piper taped the top of the box closed. "I remember you told me you teach pottery, which is why I'm here. I've been told I should get out of the house more and try new things, so I decided to sign up for your class."

"Really? Fantastic. I teach pottery Thursdays, Fridays, and Saturdays. The weekday lessons are taught in the evening, and the weekend classes are taught in the morning and afternoon. Which day would you like to start?"

"You don't happen to have today available, do you?"

Piper frowned and shook her head. Piper seemed disappointed. "Today is booked, but I have a slot available next Saturday. Or Friday if you prefer."

"Next Saturday will be fine. Shall I pay now, or when I come to class?"

"When you come to class will be fine. Make sure you wear clothes that you don't mind getting dirty."

Gillian saw a new line starting to form behind her. "Great, I'll see you next Saturday. Thanks for boxing up my vase. And if possible, I'd like to meet your sister-in-law. Her paintings are beautiful." Gillian picked up the box, and Piper waved good-bye.

With her unexpected package, Gillian went home and immediately unwrapped her new vase. She walked into her living room and looked around for the perfect home for the vase that was glazed in different shades of yellow and orange. It reminded her of the colors of the fall leaves that she and Kate used to see on their motorcycle rides through the country.

"Isn't it beautiful, honey? I went to sign up for the pottery lessons, and I start next Saturday. In the meantime, I looked around the store and found some wonderful art made by the owner and her sister-in-law. I bought this vase because it reminded me of our fall road trips.

Gillian held on tight to Kate's waist as they rode the scenic road on the Virginia/Maryland border. Even with her leathers on, she could feel the chill in the air. The trees on either side of the road were bursting with brilliant fall colors, and when Gillian didn't think they could get any more vibrant, a new grove came into view, causing her to squeeze Kate tighter. How could she feel so much love and not have her heart explode?

After two hours on the road, Kate pulled into a small diner parking lot. Kate dismounted first, as always, to help Gillian off the back of her bike. They removed their helmets, Kate's hair looking wild and sexy. Gillian threw her arms around Kate's shoulders, feeling the happiest she'd ever felt. The smell of Kate's hair gel mixed with the cold damp earth and leaves made Gillian's heart pound.

"I love you so much. Thank you for this day trip."

"You know, Gilli, there's no one I'd rather be with more than you. Feeling your arms around me as we lean into a turn, well, there's no better feeling. Let's eat, refuel, then I have a special place I want to show you."

After lunch, they climbed back on the bike and continued on their adventure. She wasn't sure how long they'd ridden. Time seemed to stop when she was with Kate. Kate had turned onto a side road, pulled into a turnout, and turned off the bike. When they took off their helmets again, Kate grabbed Gillian's hand and started walking along a narrow trail.

"Where are we? Where are you taking me?" Gillian's curiosity and excitement ramped up. She wasn't sure where they were headed, but she'd go anywhere with Kate.

Kate looked back at her with a devilish smile. "Somewhere special, baby. Don't worry, it won't take long."

Gillian could hear water in the distance, sounding almost like a trickle. They broke through the brush to see a small waterfall making its way down moss-covered rocks. She stepped forward to admire the scene then turned to see Kate on one knee. She covered her mouth and felt her eyes widen.

"Gillian, I've loved you for so long, I can't remember my life before you. The first time I saw you in the hallway in high school and you looked at me, I knew instantly I was going to marry you. Even though we've been together for many years, now that we can legally marry, I want to put a ring on your finger officially. I promise to love you, honor you, and do the dishes every single day for the rest of our lives."

Gillian burst out laughing through her happy tears. "I'm going to hold you to that dishes promise."

"Baby, will you marry me?"

Gillian pulled the glove off her left hand and held her hand out for Kate to slip the engagement ring onto her left fourth finger. Kate had given her a ring many years ago after they'd graduated high school, and Gillian had always considered that her "wedding ring." Kate kept reminding her that it was a "promise" ring, and that one day she'd replace it with a proper one. Gillian didn't care about showy, shiny diamonds. Her simple gold band meant everything to her.

"A million times over, I'll marry you."

Kate wrapped her arms around Gillian and swung her around in a circle. Kate was her dream come true, and they were going to have an amazing life together.

Gillian wiped an errant tear off her cheek and smiled at her memory.

"You will always be mine, my love."

Chapter Five

O kay, Agnes, I'm going out for a while. You have plenty of food and water, and your litter box is clean." Agnes laid on the back cushion of Piper's couch, purring, and gave Piper one slow blink. Piper swore that Agnes knew exactly what she was saying. Piper leaned down and gave Agnes a kiss on her head and a little scratch under her chin before grabbing her small backpack with her essentials—phone, earphones, wallet, keys, and a zip-up hoodie. She locked her door and headed down the stairs to the sidewalk. She put on her aviator sunglasses, took a deep breath of the crisp morning air, and strolled to the Blue Line platform to wait for the next car. Piper tried not to get too hopeful that the Metro would arrive on time, as the one thing everyone in the DC area knew was that it always ran late. The shop was closed on Mondays, allowing her to venture out to do something fun, or just hang around the apartment and get some chores done. Today, she was headed to the National Mall.

Once she sat down, she put in her wireless earbuds and tapped her New Orleans Jazz playlist. She fell in love with that style of music when she'd gone to New Orleans her one and only time. She'd gone to the famed Preservation Hall, and there began her love affair with the music. The Metro pulled away, and Piper spent the rest of the trip looking out the window. She loved living so close to the Blue Line—it was a cheap and easy way to travel to DC, and she did so often, less in the winter and summer, but more in the fall and spring. The scenery out the window was nothing to write home about, but that would change as she got closer to the nation's capital.

She disembarked when they'd reached the Smithsonian Station, and she returned her earbuds to their case. Piper followed the signs to street level and headed east toward the museum she wanted to visit. She could've transferred to another line that would've dropped her off under the museum, but she still had some time before it opened. Besides, the day was too nice to not enjoy the outside.

Piper followed the concrete path that would lead her to the front entrance. She pulled open the massive glass door and walked through after tossing her empty water bottle in the receptacle. The museum had more employees than guests walking around at that time. It was a benefit of visiting on a Monday rather than on the weekend. Most people were at work, and Piper felt she could roam the museum and take her time appreciating all that was on display.

She inhaled through her nose and closed her eyes. She tried identifying the different smells—stone, fabric, and a hint of cleaning solutions. Piper grabbed the glossy map that informed her of the various exhibits and their locations, and she stepped to the side to be out of the way while she perused the floor plan.

She took her time entering the rooms with art displays, reading the placards under or next to each piece hanging on the walls. By the time she'd seen the entire first floor, her stomach growled, and she was surprised when she'd looked at her watch to see she'd been there for two hours already. She found her way to the café and looked at the menu, deciding on a turkey sandwich and cup of chicken noodle soup. Once she paid for her food and bottle of water, she went looking for a place to sit. She nearly dropped her tray when she spotted a familiar face. She took a deep breath as she made her way over to the table.

"Gillian?"

"Piper. Hi. What are you doing here?"

Piper nodded to the empty chair. "May I?" She placed her tray on the table and sat when Gillian held her hand out. "I had the day off, so I decided to come check out the new exhibits. What about you?"

"I work here."

Piper nearly spit out the drink of water she'd just taken. "No way! What do you do?"

"I'm a curator, one of many here," Gillian said with a laugh.

"That sounds amazing," Piper said before she took a bite of her sandwich.

Gillian covered her mouth as she finished chewing her food. "It is, and I really love the people I work with."

"I thought about working in a museum when I was in school, but then I realized how much schooling there was to be a curator, and that was the end of that." The crowd had lessened so Piper felt like she could concentrate fully on Gillian. She was very pretty with her medium brown hair layered that fell just below her shoulders. Her dark eyebrows were arched and expressive, at times serious, other times, playful and maybe a bit mischievous.

"Not a fan of school?" Gillian took another bite of her salad that was mixed with cucumber, chickpeas, beets, and grilled chicken. It all looked good to Piper except for the beets. To her, they tasted like dirt.

"No, it wasn't that exactly. When I was in college, I discovered I liked creating art instead of studying it."

Gillian set her fork down with enough force that it caused a loud clank that startled Piper.

"You don't think a curator creates art? I have to decide what kind of exhibit I'll create, then I have to secure the necessary pieces for said exhibit—"

Piper held up her hand to stop Gillian's tirade. "I didn't mean to imply that. I'm fully aware of how creative curators are. What I meant was that *I* fell in love with sculpting and then with pottery."

Gillian stood and gathered her things. "I have to get back to work. Good-bye, Piper."

Piper watched Gillian walk away, toss the remains of her lunch in the trash, then leave the café, as if she couldn't get away from Piper fast enough.

"She's feisty. I like it." Piper nodded then finished her lunch and moved on to the second story of the museum to continue her day.

She hoped that Gillian would keep her pottery lesson appointment on Saturday. Just the thought of Piper insulting Gillian made her feel a little sick to her stomach. The last thing she'd want to do was hurt Gillian, and as soon as she saw her again, *if* she saw her again, she'd apologize.

❖

Gillian strode to her office with the sole purpose of putting as much distance between her and Piper. She probably was a little too defensive with her in the café, and if she had been in her right mind, she would've known that. Gillian knew Piper hadn't meant anything negative about what she'd said. For some reason, Gillian felt a little off kilter around Piper today, but who knew why. They barely knew each other, but there was also something familiar about her, and even though Gillian was adamant about not dating, she felt an attraction there. It was small, but it was there. Piper looked nothing like Kate, and she had been the only other woman she'd been attracted to. There must be something else about Piper that drew Gillian's attention.

Gillian rubbed her forehead and closed her eyes. She remembered that she was supposed to take a pottery class from Piper on Saturday, and she'd just stormed off from having lunch with her. She rubbed her forehead again and knew she needed to apologize.

When Gillian returned to the café, she glanced all around looking for Piper when she found their table abandoned. She went to the gift shop to see if she'd gone in, but again, no Piper. Gillian didn't have the time to be searching all over the museum for Piper—she could be anywhere, and it could take hours to find her. There were phone calls and emails she needed to complete before she left for the night. After all, she was at work, and duty called.

Back in her office, she tried to rid her mind of the look on Piper's face when Gillian left her sitting alone at lunch. She dropped her head and pursed her lips together as she recalled Piper's frown when she looked back at her. Piper looked confused and maybe a little hurt, and Gillian was ashamed of herself. She picked up one of the pictures of Kate on her desk and studied her face. God, she missed her so damn much.

"I'm so embarrassed, honey. Why did I act like a complete bitch to Piper? I know she didn't mean that being a curator wasn't artistic, so why did I take it the wrong way? I wish you were here to say it was just a misunderstanding and everything would be fine."

Gillian placed the frame back on her desk when Maya walked in.

"Everything okay?"

"Sure. Why wouldn't it be?"

Maya sat in the chair in front of Gillian's desk and took a moment to look at her. "You look sad."

Gillian gave Maya a gentle smile, touched at her concern. "I'm fine. Just missing Kate right now."

Maya nodded and looked thoughtful. "The anniversary of Kate's passing is coming up. I can't believe it's been almost two years."

"Yes, in about six weeks or so. There are times that feels like she's been gone forever and times where it feels like it just happened. I don't know which is worse, to be honest."

Maya reached her hand across the desk, and Gillian took it.

"Are you sure there's nothing I can do? I know I ask you a lot, but sometimes I feel like I'm not doing enough for you. Besides being my boss, you're also my friend."

Gillian squeezed Maya's hand before letting go. "You know, when I hired you to be my assistant, I didn't realize you would become my friend, as well. You do an amazing job at both. I promise, if I need anything, I'll let you know. In the meantime, I have a few more calls to make, so get out." Gillian slightly smirked when she admonished Maya.

Maya laughed and saluted. "Yes, ma'am."

Later that night, as she nursed her glass of wine, she tried to think of nothing but happy times with Kate. There were occasional flashbacks to when Kate died that would slither their way into her thoughts.

Gillian had pulled the green bean casserole out of the oven a little early so she could cook the sweet potato casserole. Her in-laws were bringing the turkey, stuffing, and pies over for dinner. There was a salad cooling in the fridge and corn in a pot on the stove. She looked at her watch, then ran upstairs to change her clothes. Where was Kate? She should've been home by now. She had barely pulled her sweater over her head when the doorbell rang. She ran back downstairs and ran her fingers through her hair, trying to give it a little body. She opened the door to see Kate's parents, arms filled with the rest of their dinner.

"Hi, Mom, hi, Dad. You can take everything into the kitchen." She kissed them on the cheek as they passed her. She stepped outside to see if there were any signs of her wife, but there was nothing, not even the faint roar of her Harley in the distance. She closed the door and joined her in-laws in the kitchen to finish putting dinner together.

"Where's our daughter?" Gloria asked as she placed the pies on the counter.

"She went for her last motorcycle ride before the weather got too bad. She should be home anytime now."

Harold took a few crackers from the platter on the table. "I don't like her riding that bike. I worry about her."

Gillian hugged her father-in-law. "I know you do, Dad, but she's a very good driver and always very careful."

"It's not her driving that I'm worried about. It's the other people on the road."

A knock on the door interrupted the conversation. Harold went to answer the door while Gillian and Gloria continued with dinner.

"Gillian!"

Gillian and Gloria ran to the living room to see Harold with the doorknob in his hand and a police officer on the front stoop. There was a loud whoosh in her ears, and she felt like her legs would give out.

"Are you the family of Katherine Phillips?"

Gillian wiped away the tears that fell steadily down her cheeks and gulped down the rest of her wine. There were times when she recalled that day that it felt like her heart would stop beating, and it was difficult to catch her breath. She'd wake up in the middle of the night, certain she was having a nightmare, but then she'd reach over to touch Kate and would find the sheets cold.

"That was the worst day of my life, sweetheart. I can't believe it's been almost two years since you've been gone. I miss you every minute of every day, but I feel you are always with me. I love you, and only you."

Kate took her glass to the kitchen and turned off the light before heading to bed. She was convinced that she'd be able to forsake all others and remain married to Kate for the rest of her life. She just couldn't see herself loving anyone else. No one else could take the place of her beloved wife.

Chapter Six

Piper hopped off her stationary bike after thirty minutes and developing a good sweat, and picked up some dumbbells to work on her arms and shoulders. The weights weren't heavy—she wasn't trying to bulk up, only keep her muscles toned. That was her everyday routine, more so since she'd had her heart transplant. Prior to her getting sick, her workouts were occasional, whenever she felt the mood strike her. But since the surgery, she'd been almost obsessive about it. She knew that it would help prolong her life. She finished her morning workout with a few yoga poses to help stretch her out and calm her mind. She gulped down a small bottle of water while Agnes sat in the corner cleaning herself and showing no shame. Once her skin cooled down and her color returned to normal, she threw her sweaty clothes in the hamper and headed for the shower.

Piper went down to the shop early to prepare the back studio for the day's classes. She loved having the shop but loved even more teaching people the art of pottery and sculpting. There was so much creativity involved, and sometimes it was fun just to get your hands dirty. She set up five wheels and stools for her students and herself, gathered the tools they might use, although probably not that day. That was for more advanced students. She also filled bowls with water and sponges. Satisfied the room was set, she went into the store to straighten the shelves and check the supplies. Piper replenished some paint brushes, paints, and canvases. She did everything and anything to keep her mind off one particular student she hoped to see later. After Gillian's minor outburst at the museum, she wasn't sure if she was still going to come. A little flutter caught her attention, but rather than it being in her chest, she felt it in her stomach. Sure signs of nerves that made Piper laugh and shake her head. Yes, Gillian was attractive, and Piper was certainly attracted to her, but she'd already decided that she was going to stay single for the rest of her life. It wasn't fair to fall in love, and have a woman fall in love with her, if she couldn't guarantee a long life together.

Piper knew in the back of her mind that her reasoning was ridiculous given the fact that nobody knew how much time they had to spend on earth. But the fact that she was living with a donor heart meant decreased survival years. She was also doing everything her doctor told her to do. She was eating right, limiting her alcohol intake, and exercising. She had no stress, thanks to Drew and Kelly. She showed up to work, sold supplies, taught art, and Drew and Kelly took care of all the bills and financials. It was like a dream come true.

"Hey! Whatcha doin'?"

Piper jumped at the surprise announcement by Kelly.

"Jesus! Don't scare me like that! Want me to have a heart attack or something?"

Kelly pointed at her and scowled. "Don't joke. I came in early to prepare for the day, but I see you already beat me to it."

Piper shrugged after hugging Kelly. "I had some restless energy, so I thought I'd come down and get an early start."

Kelly placed the back of her hand on Piper's forehead. "Are you okay?"

Piper playfully slapped Kelly's hand away. "Knock it off. I'm fine. Just…you know." Piper shook her hands and let out a deep breath. She felt under scrutiny with Kelly's hard gaze. "Fine. Okay. There's a woman who I met recently who's supposed to be in my pottery class this morning. I ran into her when I went to the museum on Monday. She's a curator there, and we ran into each other in the café. Apparently, I said something to offend her, and she left me alone in the café. But I haven't heard from her, and she hasn't canceled her lesson, so I have no idea if she's going to show up."

Kelly tried to suppress her smile, but Piper knew her too well. "I'm talking really fast, aren't I?"

Kelly nodded. "Is it possible that our little Piper has a crush on this woman?"

"Kel, I'm forty-one. I'm hardly little, and I'm a little too old to be having a crush, don't you think?"

Kelly put her arm around Piper's shoulders and pulled her close. "I've known you since you were twenty, so you're still my little sis. And in my opinion, you're never too old to have a crush. Also in my opinion, you've been single for way too long. It isn't fair to all the women out there that you're not making yourself available."

Piper could feel the heat envelop her face and she busied herself straightening the already straightened shelves. The possibilities of potential relationships had crossed Piper's mind over the last couple of years, but then she'd swept them to the furthest corner of her mind. Prior to her illness, she'd had a girlfriend, she taught art at a community college, and had a very fulfilling social life.

"Piper, you're going to have a very long life. You've been given a gift. Hell, we all have. Don't live afraid. Live life to your fullest. It's the least you could do for your donor. If it wasn't for them, you wouldn't even be here."

"Ouch!" Piper clutched her chest to fend off the harshness of Kelly's words, but she'd never been known to pull punches. And Piper knew she was right. It would be insulting to her donor to not live life to its fullest—that included being open to the possibility of love.

Piper thought of her donor every day, giving thanks to their generosity. She knew nothing about them. Did they have siblings? A spouse? Parents who loved them? After her transplant, she wrote a letter to her donor's next of kin, telling them about herself, how she grew up, the love of her family, and how she would give thanks to her donor's selfless act every day, and she had.

"You're right, but is it fair to ask someone to love me when I can't promise them forever?"

Kelly looked sympathetic for a whole second before she rolled her eyes. "That's the dumbest thing I've ever heard. Nobody knows how long we have to live. Hell, I could die tonight, and do you think Drew would regret loving me or marrying me?"

"No." Piper could feel her face and ears heating up, and she looked down at the floor, not wanting to look Kelly in the eyes.

"You need to get out of your own way, Pipes. Even if this woman *you have a crush on* isn't the one for you, then there are plenty of other women. Why would you not want to have the love of a wonderful woman who'll love you and laugh at your stupid dad jokes."

Piper knew what Kelly was saying, but maybe it would be easier just to agree with her so she'd get off Piper's back. Also, her jokes were fucking hilarious, not stupid.

"You're right, Kel. I promise I'll keep an open mind from now on." Piper just hoped Kelly didn't know she was crossing her fingers behind her back.

A short time later, they opened the store and prepared themselves for the day. Piper had thirty minutes until her pottery class started, and since the studio was ready for her students, she decided to hang out at the register with Kelly.

"Are you going to the parents' house for supper tonight?"

Piper smiled at a customer who just came through the door. "Of course. I'm not about to miss Dad's grilling. I wonder if there's a special reason, like an announcement or something."

Piper laughed at how wide Kelly's eyes got. "Maybe Beth and David are pregnant."

Piper's youngest sister and her husband of three years have been trying, unsuccessfully, to get pregnant. Beth was the baby of the family, almost ten years younger than Piper, who was the middle of five siblings. Piper swore that her parents kept trying for another girl after Jon, Piper's younger brother, was born because she desperately wanted a sister. When her parents brought Beth home, Piper immediately took over the big sister/mother role with her. At the time, Piper was too young to realize that she'd eventually have three other sisters when her brothers got married. Of the five siblings, Piper was the only one who wasn't married. All three of her brothers and their wives had kids, giving Piper two nieces and three nephews. Piper would love to have a few more.

"That would be amazing. A whole new audience to tell jokes to."

Kelly groaned and it made Piper laugh. Her niece Samantha was still young enough to laugh at corny jokes, but she was the only one now.

Piper looked to the door when it opened, and the fluttering returned. Even in a pair of jeans, sweatshirt, and with her hair in a ponytail, Gillian still looked amazing.

"Hi. You made it." Once the words were out of her mouth, Piper knew she sounded surprised.

Gillian's eyebrows raised. "Of course, I did. I signed up for the class, remember?"

Piper waved her hand to get Gillian to meet her at the end of counter, away from Kelly's prying eyes and ears. She lowered her voice so only Gillian could hear her.

"I know, but after Monday, I wasn't sure if you'd still come. I'm sorry if I hurt your feelings. That wasn't my intention at all."

Gillian sighed. "I know, and I wanted to apologize for that. I jumped to conclusions, and I shouldn't have. I know you didn't mean anything by what you said."

Piper hurriedly shook her head. "I really didn't. In fact, I'm in total awe of the creativity curators have to produce exhibits."

"Thank you. And not that it's an excuse, but I was feeling out of sorts that day. I was bitchier than I normally am."

Gillian's smirk made Piper laugh. "I doubt you're always bitchy, but occasionally it happens to all of us." Gosh, Gillian was so pretty, and Piper felt no matter how bitchy Gillian might get, it wouldn't do anything to dissipate her beauty.

Gillian laughed. "Yes, well again, I'm sorry."

"Apology accepted. You excited about getting your hands dirty?"

"You know? I actually am. It wasn't even on my radar until you told me about it, and then I saw your wonderful pieces, and I've been looking forward to what I'll be able to create."

"Come with me." Piper led Gillian into the studio, and she pointed to the far wall. "You can hang your purse on one of those hooks. Grab a smock on the other row of hooks and pick a wheel.

Obviously, you're the first to arrive, but we'll get started in about ten minutes. We're expecting only a few more people. Take a seat, and I'll be right back."

When Piper returned to the shop, and out of sight from Gillian, she placed her hands over her stomach to help quell the butterflies, and she let out a deep breath. Wow. Her mouth was dry, and she'd give anything for a bottle of water. "Oof." She looked over at Kelly to see her staring back, an amused grin on her face.

Piper held up her hand. "Shut up."

Kelly laughed. "What? I didn't say anything."

"Your face said it all." Piper walked away and pretended to be attending to the supplies on the shelf.

"She's very pretty."

Piper jumped and placed her hand over her heart before turning around. "Jesus, Kel. You nearly gave me a heart attack again. Stop sneaking up on me." She took the bottle of water Kelly handed her, as if she knew Piper's wish, and she chugged it down, then handed the empty bottle back to Kelly.

Kelly waved her hand like she was shooing a fly. "Pfft. Who was that you were talking to? Is that the lady you have a crush on?"

"Geez, give it a rest. She's just a pottery student."

Kelly squinted her eyes and stared at Piper. But she would hold strong and not let Kelly see her squirm.

"Mm-hm. I'm not through with you, Pipes." Kelly made a "V" with her index and middle fingers, pointed them at her eyes then pointed them at Piper. "I got my eyes on you, little sis." She laughed as she walked back to the counter.

"You don't scare me," Piper mumbled under her breath while she went back to the studio. She found her three other students sitting at their wheels talking with Gillian.

"Oh, good. You're all here. Let's get started."

❖

Gillian listened to Piper explain how the wheel worked, the different tools sitting in a cup, as well as a bowl of water and a sponge, and what they're used for. She could tell that Piper was enthusiastic about teaching by the inflection in her voice. Piper sat at a wheel herself and proceeded to demonstrate how to hold their hands, to use their thumbs to start the opening. Once she had the clay formed to how she wanted it, she took a tool out of her cup and made designs on the outer part. She made it look so easy.

"Okay, your turn."

Gillian and the other students looked at each other like deer caught in the headlights, making each other laugh. Gillian shrugged, got her hands wet, and started the wheel. At first, the slimy feeling of the wet clay grossed her out a little, but as she got used to it, she began enjoying it. She cupped the clay with her palms and placed her thumbs together to make the opening of her...what. Was she trying for a bowl or vase? She decided to stick with a bowl, as a vase seemed way too advanced for her novice hands. She felt the top of the bowl collapse and she took her foot off the pedal that controlled the wheel.

"Ah, damn it."

Piper was at her side in an instant, chuckling. "Don't worry about it. Happens to everyone."

Gillian nodded at the other three students. "Not to them."

Piper smiled, and why did Gillian feel warm all of a sudden? She hadn't had that feeling for the past two years, so it was extremely unfamiliar to her.

"Not yet," Piper said with a wink. As if she was psychic, one of the student's clay collapsed. "Wet your hands again and roll the clay into a ball. Once it's nice and round with no cracks, put it back on the wheel and try again."

Gillian watched Piper move on and gave encouragement to the other ladies. She paid attention to Piper's facial expressions and noticed for the first time the slight cleft in her chin and shallow dimples in both cheeks when she smiled. And there was that damn warm feeling again. She shook the thoughts of Piper out of her mind and resumed balling up the clay to start over. She focused her attention on reshaping her bowl and tried again. When the class ended, Gillian took the knife to get her so-called bowl off the wheel.

It looked like a third grader made it, but she was actually proud of herself for stepping out of her box and trying something new. And she made it with her own hands. That was something, wasn't it?

Gillian washed her hands after placing her bowl in a box with the others that Piper would fire up in the kiln later. She returned her smock and grabbed her purse, ready to leave when Piper called her name.

When she turned, she found Piper standing just a few feet away, hands tucked away in her back pockets of faded jeans that had rips that exposed her knees. She looked a little shy, a little fragile, and a lot cute. Just because she wasn't in the market for dating didn't mean that she couldn't appreciate the complexities of a woman. She had to admit that Piper was really cute.

"So, what did you think of the class?"

Oh, so that was it? Piper wanted to know if Gillian would come back for more lessons? She didn't know why she felt that Piper wanted to ask something else.

"Well, it's a lot harder than you made it look." Piper blushed and Gillian smiled. "But it was a lot of fun and something I want to try again."

Was that relief that flashed across Piper's face? Maybe pleasure? Whatever it was, it looked adorable on her.

"That's wonderful. Let's get you set up for the next class."

They started to walk out of the studio, and Piper placed her hand on Gillian's arm, stopping her in her tracks.

"Would…I mean…maybe…" Piper looked down, let out a deep breath, then looked back at Gillian. "What I wanted to say is that I'm glad you decided to try it." Gillian again felt that there was more Piper wanted to say, but she let it go because honestly, she didn't want to invite more. She was the pottery student, Piper was the teacher, and Gillian was just fine with that.

"I'm glad too."

Once Gillian signed up for next week's class, she waved good-bye and walked home, surprised to discover herself smiling. On the walk home, Gillian felt lighter in her chest, like the weight of the world had been lifted off her shoulders. She was proud of herself for trying something new and doing it alone. Until Kate passed, everything she did was with her, not because she couldn't do anything alone, but because she loved spending every second with her. Since she'd passed, Gillian had been reluctant to go anywhere alone to be social. If she went out, it was with one or all of her friends. She realized she needed to put on her big girl underwear and start doing things on her own, or she'd be spending a lot of time alone in her new home.

She enjoyed the company of the other three students, and she really liked the way Piper taught. She was funny, modest in her skills, and Gillian would be lying if she didn't notice how cute Piper was. But that had nothing to do with anything. Gillian was lucky to have found the love of her life, unlucky that they wouldn't grow old together. She wasn't convinced that Cupid would strike twice, so she'd be grateful for the love she'd found with Kate, and she'd enjoy her time with her family and friends.

She walked into the living room and dropped her purse on the coffee table before taking Kate's picture off her mantel.

"You would've been so proud of me, baby. I went to the pottery class today, and I met three other women there. They seemed nice and fun, and we're all meeting next week to take another class. Piper is the instructor and owns the shop with her brother and sister-in-law. I think I told you about her. It's funny, but today there was something familiar about her, like I've known her, but that's crazy because we've just met recently. I did notice that when she's thinking hard about something, she rubs her chin like you used to, so maybe that's it. Anyway, I miss you and love you so very much."

CHAPTER SEVEN

Piper arrived at her parents' house just as Drew and Kelly exited their car, and she waited at the front door so they could walk in together. She nodded at the covered Tupperware bowl her brother was carrying. "What'd ya bring?"

"Pasta salad. You?"

"Same." Piper burst out laughing at the exasperated look on Drew's face. "Just kidding. I brought potato salad."

"How in the world did you have time for that? I just saw you an hour and a half ago, and you didn't know what you were bringing." Kelly had her hands on her hips, ready to call Piper out.

"It's called going to the deli and paying for six pounds of the stuff then putting it in my own bowl so Mom thinks I made it."

"Mom knows you can't cook so I don't think your secret's safe." Drew bumped Piper's shoulder as he pushed past her and opened the door, announcing their arrival.

"Where are the boys?" Piper asked Kelly as they followed Drew into the house.

"Caleb and Andy are at the high school football game. They'll be over after."

"Makes life a whole lot easier now that Andy has his driver's license, huh?"

"Yes, in that I don't have to cart them everywhere. No, in that my mind is always worried there'll be an accident. Andy's a good driver, but there's always the other guy, right?"

Piper patted Kelly's shoulder because she wasn't wrong. You couldn't control other's actions. All one could do was drive defensively and watch out for the other guy.

"There are my girls." Piper's mom greeted them in the kitchen with warm hugs and cheek kisses.

"Hi, Mom. I slaved over this so I hope you like it." Piper handed over her own Tupperware bowl.

Her mom lifted the lid then closed it. "Tell Cecil I said thank you."

Piper laughed when her mom mentioned the deli owner from whom she procured said potato salad. She'd never been able to pull one over on her mom. Piper lowered her voice so just her mom and Kelly could hear her. "What's the deal for tonight, Mom? Is Beth pregnant?"

Kelly slapped Piper on the arm, and she grabbed the spot. "What the hell, Kel?"

"That was just silly talk between us." Kelly shook her head and looked at Piper's mom. "Don't listen to her, Debra.

"Can't I just have my children and their children over for a cookout? Stop being so suspicious."

Piper's mom shook her head and turned her back on Piper and Kelly. Piper didn't miss the smirk that turned her mom's mouth upward. She pointed at her. "Mom knows something. I know it and you know it, sis."

"Y'all just hush and go see your dad. He's outside with your brothers."

Piper and Kelly knowingly smiled at each other as they headed outside and took in the wonderful smoky smell of the chicken and brisket on the smoker. They each took a bottle of beer from Rob as Kelly headed to where Rob's wife, Julie, was sitting with Piper's youngest siblings, Jon and his wife Laura, and Beth and David. Piper hugged her dad and Rob, her second oldest brother.

"So, are we here for an announcement?" Piper took a drink of her beer and hit her bottle neck to Rob's.

Her dad flipped over the brisket and chicken breasts, and notably did not make eye contact.

"I don't know what you're talking about." With a family as big as theirs, it was impossible to keep a secret.

Rob took a swig of his beer. "I hear you have your eye on someone, Pipes."

Piper turned to Kelly and glared at her. She should have laughed when Kelly put her hands up, acting like she didn't know what Piper was talking about, but she hated when her family knew everything about her life.

"Where did you hear that? I don't have my eye on anyone." She shot Kelly a look who stood and started to make her way toward them, a look that warned her not to say anything.

"Oh, really? There's not a student in your pottery class that you find attractive?"

Piper backhanded Kelly's shoulder. "What have you been saying?" There was nothing more she wanted to do in that moment than climb into the biggest hole she could find so she could avoid that conversation.

"Don't blame Kelly. Drew is the one that told me."

"And Kelly must've told Drew because how else would he know?"

"Aha. So, there is someone."

"God damn it!"

"Language," Piper's dad said as he smiled while he tended to the meat. "I don't know if anything said is true, but it's time you find your woman, Piper."

"Dad! Et tu?"

"I'm just sayin', sweetheart. You've been alone long enough. It's time for you to find someone to spend your life with." He said all of that while pointing his beloved tongs at her.

Piper looked around until she found her youngest niece, her soul child, Samantha. She needed a distraction from her inquisitive family. "Sam!"

"Aunt Piper!" The six-year-old came running and jumped into Piper's arms.

"I have a question for you. Why can't you give Elsa a balloon?" Piper knew Sam would love that joke since she'd seen *Frozen* no less than a thousand times.

"Why?"

"Because she'll let it go."

Sam's six-year-old giggle contrasted with her hard eye roll. "You're silly, Aunt Piper."

Piper set Sam down on the ground and walked over to Beth and David, and she hugged them both. "How's it going, baby sis?"

"You tell me. I hear you have the hots for someone."

"Jesus. Does everyone know?" Piper threw her arms up in the air, frustrated but also feeling very loved that her family was looking out for her happiness.

"So, it's true?"

"Are you pregnant?"

"What?" The red blushing Beth's cheeks was her answer.

"I'll answer your question if you answer mine."

Beth slapped Piper's arm and winked. Why was everyone slapping her today? "Please let me announce it."

Piper hugged Beth and whispered in her ear. "I'm so happy for you and David. And to answer your question, yes, I have a small crush. I'm not sure if I'm going to do anything about it though."

"Well, I think you should ask her out. The worst that can happen is that she says no. But what if she says yes?"

Piper sat at the dining table, taking in the conversation and faces of her siblings and their spouses, her mom and dad, and across the room at the kids' table that held all her nieces and nephews. The Jameses were a raucous bunch, but they were all hers. She flashed back to almost two years ago, how she was convinced that would've been her last Thanksgiving with her family. But she was given the gift of life at the consequence of someone losing theirs. She felt a nudge to her left arm and she looked that way. Drew leaned close. "You okay, Pipes?"

She smiled and nudged him back. "I'm good, bro. Just acknowledging how lucky I am."

"You're not kidding. Anyone would be lucky to have a brother like me."

"Yeah. If not for you, I wouldn't have Kelly and the boys. Good to know you're good for something."

"I'm also good for this." Drew's fingers started tickling her and Piper screamed, trying to block Drew's assault.

"Hey, you two. Enough roughhousing," their mom yelled from the opposite end of the table, causing the kids to laugh.

"Ooh, Uncle Drew and Aunt Piper are in trouble. Don't mess with Grandma."

Later, Piper was in the kitchen on dish duty with her brother Rob while Beth put away the food, and Jon and Drew dried. They talked and worked while the spouses organized the kids to play games. It wasn't long ago that Piper wished she was in with the kids, but now she appreciated the time she had with her siblings. Well, that was still up for debate when Jon asked her about her love life.

"How many times do I have to tell you? I don't have a love life."

"What about that woman Kelly told us about? What's her name again?"

"Gillian," Drew offered. "Piper's her teacher."

A chorus of oohs came from all of them followed by laughter. Piper's whole face felt like it caught on fire. "I'm not really her teacher. She's just taking a pottery class from me."

"Oh, I see a *Ghost* image in my mind. Piper sitting behind Gillian, their hands sculpting the clay." Beth supplied the group with quite the image.

"Thanks, baby sis. I appreciate your input. I thought us girls were supposed to stick together."

"If I can't tease my big sis, who can I tease?"

Piper waved her arms around the kitchen. "Your big brothers?"

Beth threw her arms around Piper's shoulders. "I'm just thankful you're still here for me to tease." Their brothers stopped what they were doing and surrounded Piper in a group hug.

Drew, the oldest of the siblings, and the one Piper was closest to, spoke. "We might not talk about it, maybe because we don't want to think about how close we were to losing you. We're all so grateful that we're all here, especially you, Pipes."

Piper wiped a tear that was about to fall over her lower lid. "Don't make my eyes sweat, guys. Geez!"

Rob rubbed the top of Piper's head, messing up her hair, and breaking up the kumbaya moment. "Now that the mushy stuff is over, let's get down to the serious topic at hand. Are you going to ask Gillian out?"

Piper shook her head at the relentlessness of her siblings. "I don't know. I'm thinking about it."

"What's stopping you, Pipes?"

"I don't know." She turned around and leaned up against the light gray quartz countertop. "I think she might be out of my league. She's a museum curator, absolutely gorgeous with thick wavy brown hair and warm brown eyes. Sooo sexy." She looked around the room at her brothers and sister, who were paying close attention. Piper knew she was a good person, but since she'd gotten sick and came so close to dying, she questioned her strength and ability to be someone that a woman would be comfortable being with, *wanted* to be with.

Jon stood next to Piper and slung his arm around her shoulders. "Listen to me, big sis. If anything, you're out of her league. You're smart, kind, funny."

"You forgot pretty," Piper said as she batted her eyes.

"Yuck. You're my sister. But yes, I suppose you might qualify as pretty."

Piper elbowed him in the ribs, and he burst out laughing.

"Jon's right. You have a lot going for you. Don't forget amazingly talented in pottery."

"Do it, Pipes. Do it! Do it! Do it!" The chorus from her siblings grew louder until their mom came in.

"What on earth is going on in here? The people in the next town can hear you."

"Nothing, Mama. We're just encouraging Piper to ask someone out."

"Gillian?"

Piper threw her arms up in the air. "Is there anyone out in the world who doesn't know about Gillian?"

"I don't think Mr. Jenkins on the next block over knows, but I can go tell him."

Piper backhanded Drew in the stomach. "All right, fine. I'll ask her out."

Cheers erupted that brought the rest of the household into the kitchen, including the kids.

"Why is everyone yelling?"

Piper pulled Sam over to her and kissed the top of her head. "Your aunts and uncles convinced me to ask someone out."

Sam looked up to her with her large eyes sparkling. "Gillian?"

Piper dropped her head in defeat while everyone else laughed.

❖

Two years ago

"Are you the family of Katherine Phillips?"

Gillian felt arms come around her waist. They must have been Gloria's. She couldn't move. It was like her feet were stuck in cement and her brain in a fog.

"We're her parents, and that's her wife. What's going on?"

"I'm sorry to tell you, but she's been in an accident. She's been taken to the hospital by ambulance.

A small voice next to Gillian's ear spoke. "Is she all right?" Weird. It sounded like Gloria's, but it was shaky. She normally had a strong, unwavering voice.

"I don't know, ma'am. It was pretty serious."

When the officer told Harold what hospital Kate had been taken to, Harold told Gloria to turn off everything in the kitchen while he got Gillian in their car.

"Dad? What's going on?" Harold helped Gillian into the back seat and Gloria got in next to her.

"Kate's been in an accident, sweetheart. We're going to the hospital to see her."

Gillian couldn't comprehend anything that had happened since the police officer came to the door, and the trip to the hospital was a blur. Next thing she knew, Harold and Gloria were on either side of Gillian with their arms around her.

"We're here to see Katherine Phillips. We were told she's been in an accident." Gillian's father-in-law was in control, holding steady, holding them together. They were directed to a private waiting room

where they sat in hard plastic chairs. There was a television on in the corner with low volume. The bright fluorescent lights helped increase Gillian's headache, along with the smell of antiseptic and cleaning solution. Gillian looked at Gloria who had her eyes closed, lips slightly moving, and hands folded in her lap. Harold was pacing and it was driving Gillian a little mad.

"Dad, please come sit down."

Just as he sat next to Gillian, the door opened and a doctor came in. "Katherine Phillips's family?"

"Yes. How is she?"

The doctor pulled over a chair in front of them and took a seat. "I'm Dr. Katz with the trauma team. Katherine has been in a serious accident."

Gillian found her voice. "Kate."

"Excuse me?"

"She goes by Kate. I'm her wife, and she hates it when people call her Katherine."

Dr. Katz closed his eyes and nodded. "Kate's injuries were extensive, and she's suffered severe damage to her brain. She's currently on a ventilator to help her breathe and initial tests conclude there is no brain activity."

Harold and Gloria were sobbing now, and Gillian was annoyed. "Wait. She'll get better though, right? I mean, she's a healthy woman. She can come back from this."

"We're still running tests, but initial test reveals brain death. At this time, only the ventilator is keeping her alive."

"Are you absolutely sure she's brain dead?" Harold looked up with red eyes and a pleading look on his face.

"We will run more tests in six hours that will give us confirmation."

Gillian covered her eyes with her hands and dropped her head. How could this be happening? They should be at home eating Thanksgiving dinner, not at a hospital being told her wife is being kept alive artificially. No. Gillian had to see her, then she could make up her own mind. The doctor had to be wrong. "Can we see her?"

"Of course. I'll have a nurse bring you back. Do you have any questions at this time?"

Gillian could only shake her head. She had to see Kate, her wife, the love of her life that shouldn't be leaving her a widow.

"We'll bring you back to see her in a few minutes."

They were led to the trauma room where Kate lay on a gurney, a large machine with a tube that was inserted into Kate's lungs, helping her breathe. Gillian approached her wife's side while her in-laws remained at the foot of the bed. Gillian almost didn't recognize her—there were cuts on her swollen face, both eyes were black, and her head was wrapped in gauze. Gillian picked up Kate's hand and kissed it. It was warm. That had to be a good sign, right? Gillian turned when she heard a knock on the door.

"I'm Dr. Walker. I'm a neurologist and part of the trauma team."

"I'm Harold Phillips, my wife, Gloria, and our daughter-in-law, Gillian. What's going on with our daughter?"

Dr. Walker went to the opposite side of Kate's bed from where Gillian, and now Harold and Gloria were. He checked the screen on the machine then pulled out something that looked like a pen with a light. He opened each of Kate's eyelids and flashed the light across her eyes then returned the pen to his pocket. "As you know, Kate has suffered devastating injuries to her brain, and it appears it has stopped working and cannot possibly recover. I understand Dr. Katz informed you we would run more tests later to confirm this."

Gillian wiped away her tears and held Kate's hand to her cheek. "She's still warm though. That means she's still alive, right?"

"It means that she's being kept alive by the ventilator. If the next round of tests confirms brain death, she will be declared medically dead. I'm sorry to bring this up, but I'd like you to consider organ donation. A decision doesn't have to be made right now, just something for you to consider. If you do decide to donate Kate's organs, I can have someone from the organ donation organization come talk to you to explain how it will work. I'll leave you to have time with Kate, and I'll be back later to check on her. Again, I'm very sorry."

Once Dr. Walker left the room, Gillian, Harold, and Gloria hugged each other and cried. This couldn't be happening. Her Kate couldn't be gone. They were supposed to grow old together. This couldn't be happening.

The anniversary of the worst day of Gillian's life was coming up in less than two months. Last year, she was still too numb and depressed to really acknowledge the day, but this year, she was hoping she could do something special to recognize the day she lost her wife. A sweet remembrance perhaps.

For the first year, she had nightmares of the accident. Night terrors where Kate would appear in her mangled body. Some where she'd appear whole and healthy then fade away. Over the past year, though, she'd begun to have more pleasant dreams of Kate, where they'd been on a date in a restaurant, on a drive through the country, or even just taking a stroll through the neighborhood. The more pleasant dreams started when Gillian would talk to Kate daily, whether she was describing her day, or had a problem she had to work out. It might have sounded silly, but it made her feel like Kate was still with her. Not in the physical form, but spiritually. Gillian imagined Kate looking after her and her parents. It made her feel better.

Gillian thought about all the different ways she could honor Kate. Her townhome had a small yard, so she thought about planting a memory garden, but that would have to wait until spring. She opened her laptop and did a search for some ideas. She thought about donating a brick or plaque on a park bench in Kate's name. Something she could do now was make a scrapbook. She had the entire week of Thanksgiving off from work, something she'd planned in advance to devote the week to doing Kate's favorite things. She didn't have her own motorcycle, not that she'd get on one without Kate anyway. But she would drive the backroads in her car to look at the fall leaves, visit the spot where Kate had proposed. She was having Thanksgiving dinner with her in-laws, but on the next day, she'd have them and her friends over for Kate's favorite meal. They would tell favorite stories just like they did on her birthday, and celebrate the life she lived, and the gifts she gave once her life was over.

Excitement overwhelmed her, filling her with an enthusiasm she hadn't felt in almost two years. She would never find another love, for that, she was sure. But it was time to start living and stop mourning. She would always miss and love Kate, and she would give anything to have her back again, alive, full of dreams for the two of them. But that was impossible, and she would dishonor Kate if she didn't continue to love and find joy in life, just as Kate had. Gillian wasn't sure what brought on this exuberance to turn her world around, but she knew if she didn't return to living life, she'd die herself.

She went to the guest bedroom and pulled down the boxes of pictures she had of Kate from when she was a baby until the last year of her life. Mementos of their shared life together—tickets from shows and concerts, receipts, magnets from different places they visited. She spent the rest of the day sorting through everything. There were plenty of tears, even more laughter, and as the sun started to set, Gillian had a plan of what needed to be done over the next several weeks before she went to her in-laws' and celebrate Thanksgiving and Kate.

The next day, Gillian woke up full of energy and with a plan for the day. She was full of enthusiasm with a plan to execute. She dressed, drank her coffee with half and half, no sugar, and used it to wash down her peanut butter toast. Once she finished, she set out to the local arts and crafts store and spent what felt like hours walking through the aisles, putting scrapbooks, shadow boxes, alphabet letter stickers, and other fun stickers she could use on her scrapbook pages in her cart. She'd thought about taking up scrapbooking years ago when it was really popular, but between working and going to school for her PhD, she never had the extra time. That wasn't exactly true. The little extra time she did have, she'd wanted to spend with Kate. They'd go out to dinner, or to a movie, or order in and watch a movie on TV. But as with pottery, it was never too late to start.

She arrived home and dropped all of the packages on her dining table and poured herself a glass of wine. It was five o'clock somewhere. But in Virginia, every day was an essential happy hour...except Sundays. But what the hell?

She'd start with a scrapbook for her in-laws—pictures of Kate as a baby, as a toddler, a child, pre-teen, then finally a teen. With decorated paper, fun stickers, and a few funny comments, she was pleased with the outcome. Next came a book of their life together.

Kate and Gillian met during their sophomore year in high school, and Gillian knew almost immediately that Kate would be the love of her life. It took a year of friendship, secret glances, and daydreams for Gillian to work up the nerve to tell Kate how she felt, that she liked her more than a friend, which was honestly the bravest thing sixteen-year-old Gillian could've done. They were able to keep their love a secret for almost a year before Gillian's parents found out about them and immediately disowned Gillian as their daughter. Kate's parents welcomed Gillian into their family with open arms, and she started her life as a Phillips. When she became an adult, she legally changed her last name to Phillips, even before she married Kate. Gillian no longer had communication with her birth family, but her chosen and married family meant more to her than anyone else.

She included pictures of her and Kate's high school graduation, Gillian's graduation pictures of her undergrad and graduate degrees, their wedding, honeymoon, and the rest of their lives together. Fortunately, there were enough photos to fill two books—one for her in-laws and one for herself. Gillian filled shadowboxes of their many experiences and trips together. She knew the exact places on her hallway wall leading to her bedroom that she would hang them.

The grumbling of her stomach made her look at the clock on the wall, and she was surprised to see it was way past dinner time. She really didn't want to stop, but she hadn't eaten anything since breakfast. She suddenly had a craving for fish sticks and French fries, one of her favorite comfort foods. Her air fryer cooked them quickly, and she was able to satisfy her hunger. She worked for a few more hours until her eyes started to cross and burn. After she finished getting ready for bed, she slid under the sheets and grabbed Kate's photo off her nightstand.

"Baby, I had such an amazing day today. I'm putting together scrapbooks to honor your life and our life together. It's been almost two years since you left, and I still miss you so much, but I know you'd be upset if I kept mourning. I decided I'm going to celebrate you from now on." Gillian kissed Kate's photo. "I love you, baby. Always and forever."

CHAPTER EIGHT

Piper's heart raced and her mouth had been dry ever since she woke that morning. Gillian would be coming in later for her class, and by some unknown power (or known aka siblings' pressure), she had decided she was going to ask Gillian out for dinner. Or lunch. Maybe she should stick with coffee. That was less intimidating, right? Then, if Gillian had any questions whether it was a date, Piper could play it off as the start of a friendship. She was hoping for more though. Since the first time she'd met Gillian, Piper was smitten. There was something about Gillian that first night that made Piper want to wrap her arms around her and make her feel that everything would be okay.

There was more though. The following encounters she'd had with Gillian were more of the same. The run-in at the museum where Gillian had been short with Piper and left abruptly. Then the next one when Gillian showed up for her pottery class, vulnerable, apologetic, unsure of what she was doing there. But she'd kept her eye on Gillian during class. She'd seen her interaction with the other ladies in class, could see her drop her shield, and she'd started enjoying herself, and the interaction with the other students. By the end of the class, Gillian was ready for more. And Piper was the one who wanted to offer that to her.

"You ready to ask out Gillian, or are you going to chicken out?"

"Jesus, Kel." Piper placed her hand over her heart. "You have *got* to stop sneaking up on me."

"Who's sneaking? You're standing at the counter, and I'm here to start my shift."

Piper checked her watch and realized Kelly wasn't wrong. "I'm not chickening out. I'm just trying to work out how I'm going to ask her out."

"How about this? 'Hey, Gillian. Would you like to have dinner with me?'"

Piper smirked and acted like she was busy straightening up the counter that happened to be meticulous. "That just goes to show you how long you've been out of the dating game, dear sister. The kids nowadays tend to keep things more casual."

"Yes, as a mother of two teenagers, I know exactly how they're running things now. However, you're forty-one, not a kid. You are an adult with adult vocabulary. Use it. Today. With Gillian."

Piper waved her hand as if she was shooing away a pest, and that pest's name happened to be Kelly. "I know. Stand down, sis. I got this."

"Really? Is that why your hands are shaking?"

Piper shoved her hands into her front pockets. "I don't know what you're talking about."

A little while later, Piper was in the studio with Gillian and the ladies who made up the class the previous week.

"Okay, ladies. Let's throw some clay."

The students wet their hands, used the foot pedals to start the wheels, and went to work producing their works of art.

"Gillian, sit closer to the wheel and anchor your elbows tightly against your body. Great, just like that. When the clay complies, squeeze the clay and cone up."

"Like this?"

Piper smiled. "Exactly. Great job. Now both hands should be touching. Take your hand like this"—Piper placed her hand over Gillian's—"and press down." That flutter in Piper's belly threatened to make her hand shake, but she held strong and didn't think of how wonderful Gillian's shampoo smelled like coconut and apricot. She mentally patted herself on the back for not getting closer to smell Gillian's hair.

Piper helped Gillian through the rest of the steps with the control of a saint until she formed a nice-looking bowl. "Look at that. Just like a pro."

The smile on Gillian's face would forever be imprinted in Piper's mind. *God, she was in trouble.* Once Piper had given herself permission to ask Gillian out, she had been thinking about her a lot. She'd wondered what her favorite food was, what music she liked, what her home looked like. What did Gillian like to do for fun?

An hour later, Piper's students finished up their projects which were greatly improved from the week before. Especially Gillian's. Piper tried to spend equal time with the four ladies, but she spent extra time glancing Gillian's way. Her focus and determination were evident as her eyebrows made a V and the tip of her tongue would barely poke out between her luscious lips. Piper felt herself grow warm a few times, and she wondered if Gillian was aware of the tongue thing. Because now Piper was *very* aware of the tongue thing. Holy moly. It was all so innocent, but it really ratcheted up the heat deep in Piper's stomach.

Piper caught Gillian before she had a chance to leave. There went nothing. She shook off her nerves and took a deep breath before diving in the deep end.

"I was wondering if you'd like to hang out sometime, maybe grab coffee?"

Piper's heart pounded when she saw the look on Gillian's face, like a deer caught in headlights. *Think of something to say. Anything.*

"Um, I'd like to talk to you about working at the museum and art in general. I don't have many friends who are interested in that except for Kelly and my friend Mallory." That sounded plausible, and not like she was asking Gillian on a date.

Gillian visibly relaxed. Okay, obviously Gillian wasn't interested in dating Piper, and that was okay. Piper could always use another friend, and she'd rather have that than nothing at all. Although she couldn't ignore the ball of disappointment in the pit of her stomach.

"Sure, I'd like that."

"Great. Do you happen to be available later this afternoon? Or we could get together later this week if your schedule allows it." Was she being too eager? Piper tried to internally rein it in.

Gillian hesitated again, making Piper want to find the closest hole in the earth and climb in, never to be seen again.

❖

"I don't have any plans later, so if you want, we can make it dinner. What time are you off work?" What was Gillian doing? She was about to decline Piper's offer when it sounded like Piper wanted to go on a date. Now she was suggesting they grab dinner, which sounded a lot like a date, for Pete's sake. Besides, Gillian wasn't looking to date anyone. Kate was her true love, and Gillian wanted no other. Right?

"Sure. I'm off at five. Want to meet me back here at five thirty? We can walk down the street and find a place to eat."

"Okay. I'll see you in a little bit."

Gillian walked the two blocks to her home having a very long conversation with herself. What she knew of Piper, she liked. She seemed normal enough, not like some of those crazy women Audrey had told her about that she'd dated through some of those apps. But this wasn't a date. It was a gathering of sorts between new-ish friends that involved food at a restaurant. It was fine. She was fine.

Gillian made herself busy when she got home with cleaning house and doing laundry. One, it would mean she could just take it easy on Sunday. Two, it kept her mind off how she would be having dinner with a woman who wasn't her wife and not quite a friend. Maybe she should just call the store and tell Piper she wasn't feeling well. She picked up her phone to call and cancel when she heard Kate's voice in her head.

"Just go and have fun, Gilli. You need to get out and have some fun." Kate was always her voice of reason, and it seemed like that hadn't changed since she wasn't physically there anymore. In a weird way, it made Gillian feel better to think Kate was still looking after her. In reality, it was probably her imagination that Kate would say those words, but whatever. Gillian would hold on to everything that comforted her.

Fine. Gillian put her phone down and went to get ready to have dinner with Piper. It would be fine. She would be fine.

Gillian locked her front door at five fifteen to walk the two blocks to the store where she would meet Piper. She pulled her black puffer coat closed and tucked her hands into the pockets. It was mid-October, chilly out, the sun getting ready to set with winter right around the corner. The air smelled clean and crisp, and almost cold enough to burn her lungs when she took a deep breath in. Halfway to the store, she'd wished she'd thought to wrap a scarf around her neck or pull a knit cap over her head—anything that would keep her warm.

Five minutes later, she entered the store and shivered. She wasn't sure if she shivered from nerves or that she was finally warm. A friendly-looking blonde behind the counter smiled. Gillian had seen her before at the shop.

"Hi. Gillian, right?" At Gillian's nod, the woman continued. "I'm Kelly, Piper's sister-in-law. She'll be right down."

"Thank you." Well, that was odd. Kelly knew her? Did Piper talk to Kelly about her? Gillian used the extra time to peruse the store, including the pottery that Piper had created. She did everything she could to keep her mind off the fact that she was about to have dinner with a woman other than Kate. Piper was so incredibly talented that Gillian wondered why Piper was working in this shop rather than producing her art. She'd easily be able to make a living selling her creations. A few moments later, Piper appeared at Gillian's side.

"Hi. Sorry to keep you waiting. Are you ready?"

Gillian nodded, and they walked the sidewalk, passing shops before they reached the restaurant portion of the block.

"How about this place?" Piper stated they had American fare, a little bit of everything. They entered and got a table immediately, being it was early on a Saturday evening. They gave their drink orders, a glass of Chardonnay for Gillian and a glass of Merlot for Piper. They spent a few minutes looking over the menu, not talking or looking at each other. A little awkward, but whatever. Once Gillian decided what she'd order, she closed her menu and placed it on the edge of the table.

"I haven't been here before. How is it?"

Piper closed her menu and placed it on top of Gillian's.

"It's pretty good. Sometimes I order something to pick up from one of the restaurants and take it home. This is one of my go-tos. It's not fun to cook for one."

"I know what you mean. Depending on what time I get home, I'll make a sandwich or pop a frozen dinner in the microwave."

"Do you like to cook?"

"I used to. If I have my friends or family over, I love to cook. I figure if it's just me, what's the point?"

"I'll bake occasionally, especially if my parents are having a shindig. Cookies are my favorite, but I've been known to bake a cake or pie."

"Is that so? What's your favorite cookie to bake?"

"Duh. Chocolate chip." Piper winked at Gillian making her smile.

The server delivered their drinks and paused their conversation. "You ladies ready to order?"

Gillian looked at Piper who offered her hand, indicating she could go first.

"I'll have the grilled salmon, please. I'll take a baked potato with sour cream and chives."

She looked at Piper who was staring back, a wide grin on her face. "It's funny, but somehow I knew that's what you'd order." She turned her attention to their server. "I know this might sound weird, but I'd like mac 'n' cheese with a dill pickle on the side."

The server paused, giving Piper a weird look, then continued writing her order.

❖

Gillian's face lost its color like she'd seen a ghost.

"Are you okay? Do you need some water?" Piper was concerned for Gillian and what made the color drain from her face.

"You ordered macaroni and cheese with a dill pickle."

"Yes. I know it's quirky, but I love it. I normally eat healthier, but the cold weather makes me want to order comfort food."

"I've known only one other person who liked dill pickles on their macaroni and cheese, so it took me by surprise that you ordered that. That's an unusual combination."

"Do you want to tell me about it? I mean, obviously it upset you, so I'm willing to listen."

Gillian waved her hand. "It's fine. So, you wanted to talk about my work?"

Piper hesitated, unsure of how to proceed. She wanted to know more about Gillian's person who ordered what she did. Piper bit her tongue though, and she began her inquisition of Gillian's work.

"What made you want to become a curator?"

Piper saw Gillian relax, like the weight of the world was just lifted off her shoulders. They were now in safe territory, and Piper would do her best to keep them there.

"I love art and what it evokes. Art means something different to everyone, and if I can put together an exhibit that will bring people in, talk about it, think about it, then I'm helping open people's eyes to the beauty of it. I'm helping expand their minds.

"I was a young girl when I saw my first exhibit, maybe around nine years old. My fourth-grade class took a field trip to a museum, and while the chaperones were trying to keep all the kids together and behaving, I was studying every piece of art and trying to figure out what it represented. From then on, I was hooked."

Piper laughed. "I could almost picture you as a nine-year-old wandering the halls of a museum, taking in the paintings on the walls."

Gillian held up her glass to Piper. "You pictured it correctly."

"Some of my favorite field trips involved trips to the museum, as well. Unlike you, I was drawn to the sculptures on the pedestals. I knew early on I wanted to be an artist."

"You're brilliant at the pieces you've made, so obviously you made the right decision. But I have a question. Why don't you do it full-time? You could make a lot of money."

Piper shrugged and remained silent for a moment, wondering how much to reveal. She decided to keep her prior illness to herself for the time being. She'd learned early on that people looked at her with pity when they learned what she went through, and she didn't want to see that from Gillian. Besides, they were getting to know each other, and that wasn't how she wanted to start things off.

"My sister-in-law Kelly wanted to do something for herself now that her boys are teenagers and are busy with their own lives. She asked me if I wanted to partner with her and my brother in the store, and we could teach art lessons. Kelly and Drew take care of all the financials, so it's a pretty stress-free job for me. I sell some of the pottery and sculptures I make and earn a little extra money. But I really love teaching my passion to others and watching them develop their talents."

Their conversation was halted when their food arrived. Piper took her time cutting up the pickle into bite-sized pieces. Then she dumped them into her macaroni and stirred it all in. She looked up to see Gillian watching her with guarded eyes. Piper wished Gillian would tell her the reason for that.

Gillian shook her head and took a bite of her salmon. Piper had a feeling she'd blown it already. Maybe she should have ordered something normal like a grilled chicken sandwich. Truthfully, the pickle thing was fairly new to her, and it bewildered even her. About a year ago, on a rainy day, she'd made some mac 'n cheese, and it was like a voice in her head that said, "Hey, you know what would taste amazing? Diced dill pickle mixed in." And, sure as heck, the voice was right. She'd been doing it ever since. Another quirky habit she'd picked up around the same time was eating and finishing one side dish before moving onto the next, and she'd eat her main course last. She didn't know why, and it wasn't something she'd always done, but that was now how she ate a meal.

It had been a quiet meal, each of them commenting occasionally on how good their food was, and Piper was running out of time with Gillian. On the walk home, Piper felt like she should apologize.

"I feel things turned awkward when I ordered my dinner, and I feel like I should apologize, but I'm not sure for what. Is my weird dinner choice a game changer for our friendship?"

Gillian took a deep breath and let it out while continuing to look ahead. "My wife used to eat her mac 'n cheese with diced dill pickle, and it's not something I'd ever seen before."

"Okay, now I am sorry. I didn't realize you were married."

Gillian detoured to sit on a bench, and Piper followed her. They were far enough away from the restaurants that it felt like they were all alone. Piper placed her hands in her pockets to keep them still. After a moment, Gillian spoke again, still not looking at Piper. "My wife passed away two years ago. You're the first woman I've had a meal with who hasn't been part of my best friends' group. Tonight kind of felt like a date, even though we didn't call it that, so I've been in a weird mood since we talked about having dinner. Then the whole pickle thing happened." Gillian then looked at Piper and a small grin graced her lips.

Piper placed her hand on Gillian's arm. "I'll admit that I'm attracted to you, and I'd hoped we could go on a date. But if that's not what you want, or you're not ready to date, I'm perfectly fine being just friends. I like you, Gillian, and I hope we can get to know each other better and be friends."

Gillian covered Piper's hand and smiled. "I like you too, and I would like to be friends. I'm not sure about dating. I'm not sure if I'll ever be ready to date someone else."

"I can appreciate that." Piper nodded and pursed her lips. "I'm down for being friends. How long were you with your wife?"

Gillian laughed and leaned into Piper. "Too long to count. I thought we'd be together forever, but fate had different ideas."

Piper felt Gillian's sadness like a curtain that covered her. If they were only meant to be friends, then Piper felt like that would be a good outcome. "Come on, I'll walk you home."

They spent the little time they had left on their walk talking about the pottery class and how much Gillian was enjoying it. When they got to the front door, they smiled at each other.

"Thank you for tonight. And thank you for understanding."

"My pleasure. Would it be okay if I gave you a hug?"

"I'd like that." Gillian stepped closer and they wrapped their arms around each other. It may have lasted only five seconds, but it was long enough that Piper would be replaying this night over and over in her head.

Chapter Nine

I need you all to come over for dinner tonight. If you already have plans, it's fine, but I need my friends.

Gillian sent out the group text early Sunday morning after a night of tossing and turning. She enjoyed her time with Piper the night before, but the hug at the end? She felt something, and she wasn't sure what it was. She needed to talk it out with her girls so they could tell her it was nothing. She was relieved when they all responded they'd be there. But now she had eight hours to kill before they arrived. Her house was clean, her laundry was done, and she didn't watch football. She decided to go to the market to pick up items for dinner. On a chilly night, she would make chili. She chuckled to herself at the play on words.

Once she was showered and dressed, she drove to the nearest store and got all the necessary ingredients for chili, including cheese, onion, and Fritos corn chips. She grabbed a few different bottles of wine for her, Heidi, Amanda, and Jen, and some beer for Audrey. When she was almost to the checkout line, she spotted Piper already checking out. Gillian felt her face flush, and she headed in the opposite direction, away from the checkout, away from Piper. She knew she was being a chicken, and she and Piper were becoming friends, but the fluttering she felt deep in her midsection the previous night during their hug good night had Gillian's mind all messed up. She needed to figure out what that was about before she could talk to Piper. Hence, the dinner with her friends.

After fifteen minutes of pretending to look at items she didn't need, she figured enough time had passed that Piper was long gone. The relief she felt when Piper was nowhere to be seen allowed Gillian's breathing to return to normal. She thanked the checker and bagger, and she took her cart out to her car to store the bags in her trunk. Coming straight toward her was Piper, making Gillian's breathing become erratic again.

"Hey, you. What's going on?"

Gillian reminded herself to smile and use her words. "Oh, hi. Having some friends over for dinner. Chili. Um, I'm making chili." *Come on, Gillian. You have a PhD. Act like you know how to have a conversation with someone.*

"That sounds really good. There's a place on King Street that has all kinds of chili dishes, as well as the most amazing fried pickles."

Gillian laughed. "You really love pickles, don't you?"

Piper shrugged and grinned. "Guilty. We should go there sometime. I mean, if you'd like to hang out again."

If Gillian was reading the room correctly, it seemed that Piper might seem unsure whether Gillian wanted to continue to be friends. Which she did. She just had to get her feelings under control, whatever those feelings were.

"That sounds like fun." They stood in the parking lot, looking at each other, smiling, clearing throats. "Well, I better get going, get ready for my friends."

"Right. I'll see you Saturday?"

Gillian nodded. "I'll be there." When she reached her car, she looked back and found Piper looking at her still. Piper waved and turned to go back into the store. Gillian felt the smile on her face as she placed her groceries into the trunk.

Once she got home, she browned the meat, then threw it in the slow cooker along with beans, veggies, and seasonings. To keep her mind off Piper and fried pickles, she told Alexa to play Pink as she prepped the rest of the food. As music came through the device, she danced around the kitchen in between chopping onions and grating cheddar cheese. Since no one was watching, she let loose and by the end of the song, she was out of breath. Damn, that felt good. She felt less stress, and dare she say, maybe a little happy? That was an emotion she hadn't felt in two years. Gillian and Kate would often dance to loud music on the weekends while cooking or cleaning house, but she hadn't done that since Kate left this earth. She'd muddled through life since Kate died, but ever since she resolved to celebrate instead of mourn her, she'd been trying to allow herself to smile and mean it, laugh and have it sound joyous, be happy to greet the sun in the morning instead of wanting to cover her head under the covers. She didn't expect to change everything overnight, but she could certainly take steps toward achieving that goal, and be patient with herself if she happened to slip.

She poured herself a glass of wine and continued dancing in her kitchen, getting ready for her friends to arrive. The house smelled like cooked ground turkey, onion, and chili powder. She poured herself a glass of water after dancing to three songs, and continued to dance to Pink, letting her body go, celebrating the lyrics of her favorite song, and singing at the top of her lungs. She jumped when the song ended, and she heard applause. Her friends were standing at the kitchen entrance smiling and laughing. If Gillian was looking in a mirror, she surely would've seen her face red as a lobster.

"We knocked, but apparently you couldn't hear us over your concert performance. Did you forget to tell us you were going on a world tour with Pink?"

"Ha! I'm a legend in my own mind. Thanks for coming, loves. Help yourself to wine. Audrey, your beer is in the fridge." She continued to dance when the next song came on. She saw her friends look at each other, probably wondering when Gillian had gone off the deep end. That didn't last long though, and they held their drinks up and started dancing with her. A few more songs, and they were trying to catch their breath. They refilled their drinks and went into the living room.

"Well, that was fun for a Sunday afternoon." Heidi held up her glass and the rest followed suit, clinking their glasses and bottle.

"As much fun as that was, do you want to tell us what's going on with you? Are you all right?" Audrey took a long gulp of her beer.

Gillian took a deep breath then a healthy swallow of her wine. She looked at all of her friends, expectant looks on their faces. She chewed her lower lip as she thought of how to start the conversation.

"I had dinner with a woman last night. A new friend."

The wide eyes and open mouths of her friends indicated they were dumbfounded by the new development.

"You're dating?" Audrey's face was red, her voice accusatory.

"No, not exactly. I had dinner with my pottery instructor, Piper. She's an artist and wanted to know what it's like to be a curator and work in a museum."

"Okay, but what does the 'not exactly' mean?" Audrey was acting strange, and Gillian had never seen her like this. She would have to talk to her privately to find out why she was being defensive.

"It means…damn it. Let me back up. Piper asked if I wanted to grab coffee to talk about art. I suggested dinner. But she ordered a dill pickle to chop up and mix into her mac 'n cheese."

Heidi, Amanda, and Jen scrunched their noses, but Audrey's eyes widened. As Kate's best friend and riding buddy, she understood the inference.

Gillian nodded. "I know, Audrey."

"What's the meaning, other than it sounds disgusting?"

Gillian placed her glass on the coffee table. "Kate used to eat it that way. I've never heard of that combo until Kate came up with it. But Piper ordered it."

Audrey slammed her beer bottle on the end table next to the easy chair she sat in. "So, because of that, you want to date this chick? What the hell, Gilli?"

"Hey! Stop right there, Audrey. What makes you think you can talk to Gillian like that? You better watch yourself." Heidi had been Gillian's friend since childhood. She'd known her longer than anyone else in the world, and with that, she was an overprotective sister. At Kate's funeral, it was Heidi who ran interference between Gillian and "well-wishers."

Gillian stepped out of the limo and joined Gloria under the umbrella. It had been raining since the night before. Gillian saw it as a sign of God crying for the loss of a beautiful life. They walked with Harold to the tent covering the rows of white fold-up chairs and the hole in the ground that would soon welcome her wife's ashes. The funeral director guided them to their seats—Harold on the aisle, Gloria next to him, and Gillian next to Gloria. Gloria took Gillian's hand and held tight enough that she might lose feeling. Gillian felt someone approach from her right and was relieved it was her best friend, Heidi, and her other two closest friends, Amanda and Jen, right behind her. Audrey took her place next to Jen, wearing her Ray-Ban Aviator glasses even though the sky was dark. Gillian knew Audrey was trying to be strong and hide her eyes that were probably red from crying. Gillian let out a sigh of relief, knowing her friends would take some of the pressure off her to be social.

"How are you holding up, honey?" Heidi sat next to Gillian and put her arm around her.

Gillian dropped her head onto Heidi's shoulder and sighed. "About as should be expected. Do me a favor and stick close to me. If you see anyone taking up too much of my time, run interference. I don't think I have the energy or the patience for people telling me what a great person Kate was."

"Don't worry about that. We have your back."

Heidi looked at Gillian after staring Audrey down. "Go ahead, sweetie."

Gillian sat on the chair arm next to Audrey and took her hand. "I was taken aback by the menu ordering and the feeling that she seems familiar to me. But Piper is a really nice person and an extremely talented artist with pottery and sculpture." She pointed to the fireplace mantel where the vase she'd bought from Piper sat. "She made that. I told her a little about Kate. I told her I didn't know if I'd ever be ready to date again, and you know what?" Gillian squeezed Audrey's hand so she'd finally look at her. "She was okay with that. She said that if all I could offer was friendship, she'd be happy with that."

Gillian moved back to her own chair on the other side of the living room so she could see all her friends.

"She walked me home and asked if she could give me a hug good night. I felt safe enough with her to give her permission. I haven't been able to think of anything since. Trust me when I say I didn't have this on my bingo card."

"Welcome back, lady."

Gillian scrunched her eyebrows, confused at the acknowledgement from Amanda. "What do you mean?"

"I mean, it's been two years since Kate died. But now you've finally returned to the living."

Jen smacked Amanda on the arm. "What she means is that Kate wouldn't want you to live the rest of your life alone. If situations were reversed, would you want Kate to stay single for the rest of her life?"

"Of course not. I wouldn't want her to forget me, but I wouldn't want her to be lonely either."

"Gillian, are you listening to yourself? Do you think you could ever forget Kate?"

Gillian felt her hackles rise. "Of course not. She's the love of my life."

Amanda pointed to her. "Of course, you wouldn't. But do you think she'd want you to be alone for the rest of your life, or would she want you to find someone who could make you laugh, make you feel safe, treat you with love and respect?"

Gillian finished off her glass of wine. She normally didn't drink so much, but tonight seemed to be a special occasion, and that occasion was trying to keep her calm.

"Hold that thought." Gillian refilled her glass. "No, she wouldn't want me to be alone. But don't you think it's too soon? She's only been gone for a couple of years."

"How long is appropriate?"

Gillian held her hands up, causing some of the wine to splash out of the glass and into her lap. "Shit. I don't know." She wiped her hand on her pants to dry them. Great. Now she'd smell like a winery.

"Nobody does, honey. There's no rule or law that you have to wait a certain amount of time. Whenever you're ready is probably the correct answer to that question."

Gillian could feel her eyes well up, and she covered them with her hands. "I'm not sure if I'm ready yet." She felt multiple arms around her, and she opened to find her friends gathered around her.

Heidi wiped away Gillian's tears. "Then just remain friends with Piper. She already said she'd be fine just being friends, so it's not like she's putting any pressure on you."

Gillian shook her head. "And she wouldn't. She's very sweet."

"Good. Then just play it by ear. Get to know her better. If all that happens is that you remain in the friend zone, so be it. Just remember who your best friends are." Heidi winked and squeezed her shoulder.

"Like I could ever forget my tribe. Who's ready to eat?"

"I could eat." They all laughed because Audrey could always eat, like she had a bottomless pit for a stomach.

"Good, because I bought Fritos just for you."

Audrey clapped her hands together. "Now you're talking."

They spent the rest of the evening eating and talking about Gillian's new interest in pottery. Once she'd talked it out with her friends, Gillian felt much better about her blossoming friendship with Piper.

Later that night, when Gillian got into bed, she picked up Kate's picture and used her index finger to trace Kate's face. Since Kate had died, Gillian spoke to her every night. It made her feel like Kate was just on a trip, that she'd be back eventually. It made her feel less lonely even though she knew that Kate would never come back. As long as it made her feel less lonely, she'd continue their nightly chats. "The girls told me tonight that you wouldn't want me to be alone for the rest of my life, and I already knew that to be true. But I still miss you so much. How am I supposed to date someone when you still have my heart? It's weird though because she reminds me a little of you with her dill pickles mixed in with her mac 'n cheese, and she rubs her chin when deep in thought. I do like her though, so maybe we can just be friends. I love you so much, baby. Good night."

Kate replaced the picture and turned off her table lamp, feeling much more at ease than she did just a few hours ago, and also a little buzzed from all the wine she drank. Tomorrow morning, she'd pay for tonight's indulgence.

Chapter Ten

For some reason, Gillian woke Tuesday morning thinking of Piper and fried pickles. How completely ridiculous of her. She didn't even like pickles, for crying out loud. As her day went on, she would think about her dinner with Piper a few days ago, then she'd look at Kate's picture and guilt would wash over her like a tidal wave. What was she doing? She wasn't ready to date anyone, but Piper did offer friendship. When she exited the Metro Tuesday night, she took a slight detour to Rainbow Arts. She just wanted to say hi to Piper. She shook her head, knowing damn well she wanted to see her, not just say hi. She opened the door and was greeted by Kelly.

"Gillian, hi. What can I help you with?"

"Hi, Kelly. I was wondering if Piper was around."

"Sure, she's in the studio."

"Oh, I don't want to disturb her class. Please tell her I stopped by." Gillian turned to leave, disappointed that she wouldn't see Piper after all.

"Wait, she's not teaching. She's in there by herself. Go on in."

Oh. Gillian hesitated then walked slowly to the entrance where she stood for a moment observing Piper sitting at a wheel, the look of hard concentration as she held a tool Gillian had seen in the cup during her lessons. She was using it to etch designs into her vase. Gillian realized that it wasn't the pottery itself, but the designs she created in the clay that upped her artistry exponentially. She could've stood there all night watching her create, but her slight movement caused Piper to look up. She placed the tool down and smiled.

"Hey. How long have you been there?" She stood and wiped her hands on her smock as she moved closer to Gillian.

"Not long. I didn't want to disturb you creating your latest masterpiece." The closer Piper got to her, the more her nerves kicked in. She was really pretty, even with her hair in a messy ponytail and smudges of clay on her cheek.

"Ha! Funny. Not that I'm not happy to see you, but what brings you by?"

"Well, I was wondering if you'd like to grab dinner, but I see that you're busy."

"No, no. That sounds great. I was almost done anyway."

"Can you show me how you use the tools?"

"Of course. Come over and sit by me."

Gillian took a seat by Piper, and she picked up the tool she was using. The quiet space mixed with the smell of wet clay somehow calmed Gillian's insides.

"I'm using this one to carve out long diamond shapes in the clay."

"It almost looks like a tool a dentist would use."

Piper laughed, and it made Gillian smile and feel light-hearted.

"You're not wrong about that. Depending on what I want to make will determine the tools I use. I'm using this one that looks like a dental pick to make thin lines and small nicks that might not seem like much, but they can really add to the design. If you want, I can show you more at a later time. But I do believe you said something about eating, and my lunch was too many hours ago. Let me clean up here and then come up to my apartment so I can take a quick shower."

Piper opened a door in the studio that Gillian hadn't noticed before that opened to a staircase with one big ceiling lamp above. When Piper opened the door, they were assaulted by the very loud meowing of a long-haired gray and white cat that seemed very angry about something.

"This four-legged annoyance is Agnes, and in case you don't speak feline, she's telling me that she's hungry, she's upset that I've been downstairs all day even though she's been passed out on my pillow the entire time, and if I don't want her to claw me within an inch of my life tonight when I go to sleep, I must feed her now."

"She said all that with just the meows?" Gillian was thoroughly amused by both Piper and Agnes. She reached down and held her hand in front of Agnes who rubbed her cheek against it then swatted her hand away. She'd never had any pets when she was growing up, so she wasn't exactly sure what to make of that furry creature.

"It's all in the inflection of the meows. You'll catch on." Piper opened a can of food and dished it out on a small plate, placing it on the kitchen floor next to a water bowl. "Now that she'll be quiet for a while, can I get you anything to drink? I have some sparkling water or grape juice."

Gillian barked out a laugh. "Grape juice? You drink grape juice." She said it as a fact rather than asked a question. "I don't hear of many people drinking grape juice anymore" She didn't say out loud that that was one of Kate's guilty pleasures. "I'm fine, but I'm getting hungry, so go take your shower so we can go eat."

"Right. Have a seat and make yourself comfortable."

Gillian made her way around the open apartment that was very much a home. So many pictures of what Gillian assumed to be Piper's family. A few different paintings hung on her walls, a couple of landscapes, one abstract. She looked closer at the abstract painting that drew Gillian to it like a magnet. The colors of purple, blue, and yellow were so vibrant, inspiring, and fascinating, and it seemed to fit Piper's personality. It was perfect for her home. Once she'd looked at every picture, every painting, every knickknack in Piper's living room, Gillian took a seat on the couch, and holy cow, was that the most comfortable couch in the world, or what? She felt the light gray microfiber cushions envelop her like a big bear hug. She leaned her head back and closed her eyes for a few minutes until she was startled by a big fluff ball jumping in her lap and making herself at home.

"Was your dinner good, Agnes? Your mommy feeds you the good stuff, doesn't she? Do you play with all the toys that are scattered all over the floor? You sure are lucky to have a mommy like yours." Agnes answered with a slow blink and a meow that sounded like "yeah." Gillian stroked her fingers through the cat's fur, and she started purring. Gillian had never been around cats for any amount of time, so the vibration from Agnes fascinated her.

"I see you made a friend." Piper grinned when she walked into the room.

"Yes, we're nearly best friends now. By the way, I love your place. That painting over there," Gillian pointed at the wall to her left, "who painted that?"

"Kelly. Isn't it great?"

"Kelly? Your sister-in-law, Kelly? Wow. I mean, I saw some pieces in your store, but that one really caught my attention. Has she done any shows?"

"No. She and Drew have two teenaged boys, so she's spent the past sixteen years being a mom. She'll paint occasionally, but she didn't want to be a prisoner to having to paint. She says owning the store and giving lessons are more her speed."

"I get that. I imagine it could be very stressful having to produce a certain number of pieces or being commissioned."

Piper picked up Agnes from Gillian's lap, and that was the closest their faces had been. It wouldn't take much to go just a bit further and taste the lipstick on Gillian's lips. Their eyes locked for just a moment until Gillian was the first to look away. Piper stood upright with Agnes in her arms and took her time putting her cat on the floor. Whew, that was a close one. Piper needed to slow down since Gillian hadn't expressed interest in anything more than being friends, and Piper would respect that.

"You ready to go eat? My stomach is about to rumble."

They walked a block west, then two blocks north to the restaurant that Piper claimed had the best fried pickles. She would indulge in the pickles, but have a healthy dinner. It was all about balance. She held the door open for Gillian and nearly ran into the back of her when Gillian had stopped just inside the door.

"This place is so great." There were classic metal posters interspersed with old western photos hanging on the walls, a red brick floor, and a large neon jukebox in the back playing country music that sounded a little like swing, blues, and Dixieland music. Piper shook her head and swallowed a laugh while watching Gillian take in the funky joint. Not only was the food delicious, but it was the décor that drew Piper to that restaurant. The hostess led them to their table where they were immediately brought ice water in mason jars. Piper watched Gillian look around the restaurant, clearly amused with the décor as she kept pointing out different pictures and posters.

"Pretty cool, huh? If you like chili, you're gonna flip your lid when you see all the choices."

They took a few moments to look at the menu. When the server came by, they were ready to order, but only after Gillian asked Piper about a few dishes she couldn't decide on. Gillian ordered a bowl of chili over cornbread smothered with cheddar cheese, tomatoes, onions, and sour cream. Piper ordered the teriyaki grilled chicken with a side of steamed vegetables and a cup of vegetarian chili. And of course, she ordered fried pickles for their appetizer.

"That's a pretty healthy meal you ordered, Piper."

"Believe me, if I could get away with ordering what you did, I'd do it every day. I've had a lot of different dishes here, and they're all delicious."

Gillian took a sip of her wine that she'd ordered with her dinner. "Why can't you get away with it? You look like you're in pretty good shape."

"Uh." Piper blushed and took a drink of her water to buy her some time. Did Gillian like the way she looked? Sure, she worked out, but she had a love-hate relationship with it, and she was diligent with it to keep her heart healthy. She didn't want to tell Gillian about her heart just yet. She didn't want her feeling sorry for her because there was no reason to. "I'm trying to stick to lean proteins for the most part. The fried pickles are my indulgence tonight."

The pickles with ranch dip were delivered, and Piper clapped her hands and let out a little squeal, making Gillian laugh.

"Take a bite, and you'll understand why I'm so excited."

Gillian shook her head, took a fried pickle chip, and dipped it in ranch before taking a bite. Her eyes grew wide and nodded. "I see why you love them so much." Gillian licked a little drop of ranch off her lip, exposing her tongue.

Oof. Piper's desire, which had been dormant since she got sick, flickered to life. She needed to think of anything other than Gillian's tongue and what it was capable of doing to her. She needed to tell a joke. "What's green and has two wheels? A motor pickle."

Gillian legit laughed at Piper's corny joke, and she felt quite pleased with herself. "Usually only my six-year-old niece laughs at my jokes, so thanks for indulging me."

They spent the rest of their meal talking art and pottery, keeping conversation on safe ground. They walked down the sidewalk shoulder to shoulder until a gust of wind sent a chill through them both. Gillian hooked her arm through Piper's, possibly to ward off the chill, but Piper didn't care about the reason. She just wanted to remain physically close to Gillian, occasionally catching a hint of her sweet, flowery perfume. They were getting close to Piper's apartment, but she wanted more time with Gillian, even it if was spent in comfortable silence. Piper felt Gillian start to slow down, but Piper turned to her and smiled.

"I'll walk you home."

"You don't have to. Don't you want to go inside and get yelled at by Agnes?" The lilt in Gillian's laugh warmed Piper's insides, and it made her want to keep making Gillian laugh. It had been music to her ears.

"I didn't realize you had a hidden camera in my apartment. I really don't mind walking you home. Gives me more time with you." And Piper couldn't think of anything she wanted more at that very moment.

Gillian squeezed Piper's arm and thanked her.

"It smells so good out here. It's my favorite time of the year when the air smells crisp with a hint of firewood burning and wet leaves." The noise from the restaurants and bars dimmed as they got closer to Gillian's, and it felt like they were the only two people in the world. Regrettably, they reached the front door, and Piper knew the enjoyable evening was coming to an end.

"Would you like to come in for some coffee?"

Well, that was a nice development, and Piper seriously considered it. But she felt there might be a chance for more if she took it slow with Gillian.

"Can I take a rain check? I don't want to keep you up too late if you have to go to work in the morning."

Gillian looked at her watch, then back to Piper. "I hadn't realized how late it was. Where did the night go?"

Piper shrugged and smirked. "Time flies when you're eating chili and fried pickles."

"You make me laugh, Piper. Give me a hug and get going so Agnes doesn't claw you in your sleep for leaving her for so long."

Piper stepped into Gillian's arms and held her. It sounded like Gillian sighed, but it may have been her. Piper could've sworn that Gillian would be able to feel her heart pounding. They swayed back and forth before stepping back and breaking their hold.

"Thanks for coming by the store and having dinner with me." Piper slowly walked backward, slightly stumbling before regaining her balance, not wanting to stop looking at Gillian. "Have a great day tomorrow, and I'll see you Saturday."

Gillian waved and closed the door behind her, severing their contact. On her way home, Piper recalled their evening. Gillian had made the first move by coming by the shop and suggesting dinner. It felt like they were getting closer, but going slow, and Piper was just fine with that. It wasn't that long ago that she balked at the idea of having a relationship with anyone, and although they were far from having a relationship, for the first time in a long time, Piper felt hopeful. Her question now was when she should tell Gillian about her medical condition?

CHAPTER ELEVEN

Gillian closed the door and leaned back against it, sighing. She thought she'd never be interested in another woman, but Piper was starting to make her way into her periphery. She took off her coat, hung it in the coat closet, then went into the living room, grabbing their wedding picture before curling up in her chair.

"Baby, I'm so confused about Piper. We had dinner tonight, and I had a really good time. I never thought I'd want to be with another woman since you were the love of my life. But I also know you'd never want me to spend the rest of my life alone. I think if you were still alive, you'd be good friends with Piper. I had fried pickles tonight, and they were so good. I'm almost starting to see the lure of pickles you had. I don't think I'm ready to tell Mom and Dad that I might be interested in dating Piper. I don't know how they'd take it." Gillian paused, looked to the ceiling, and let out a deep breath. "You're right. They'd be fine with it. But whatever happens between Piper and me, or anyone really, I'll always have you in my heart. I love you so much."

While Gillian slept, she dreamt of Kate, but eventually Piper's face would replace Kate's. They weren't sexual dreams, just the nice ones she'd had over the past year. The fact that Piper had been inserted into her dreams where Kate had been had her discombobulated when she woke the next morning.

When she got to work, she sat at her desk and tried to organize her thoughts. She made a list of things she needed to do that day, then called Maya in to see where she was in looking at art to procure for the next showing. With Maya handling things on her end, it left Gillian time to send some emails and make some calls.

When she took some time for lunch, she had a quick salad in the café then went to the section of the museum that held abstract art to remind herself of what was hanging on the walls. She spent an ample amount of time looking at the different paintings by Pollock, Kandinsky, and Malevich to name a few of their more famous artists. She then recalled the painting in Piper's apartment that was done by Kelly. Her work, in Gillian's opinion, was comparable to the greats. She thought about calling an acquaintance of hers who had a gallery to see if she'd be willing to show Kelly's paintings. Of course, she wouldn't do that until she asked Kelly's thoughts about it. Piper told her Kelly didn't want to be tied down to *having* to get paintings done. But she had enough hanging in her shop, maybe some extras at home. She'd swing by the store on her way home to talk to her. Bonus? She'd get to see Piper.

Later that evening, she entered Rainbow Arts and saw Kelly working the counter and cash register.

"Hi, Gillian. What's going on?"

"I'm actually here to see you. Do you have a moment?"

"Uh, sure." Kelly looked around the shop, as did Gillian, to find it empty.

"I saw your painting in Piper's apartment."

"You were in Piper's apartment?" The smile on Kelly's face was so wide that Gillian was tempted to snap her fingers to bring her back to the present. Also, what was with the massive smile?

"As I was saying, I saw your painting and the ones hanging in here in the shop, and I was wondering if you'd be interested in showing your work."

Kelly looked to the studio door, maybe to summon Piper.

"If you're not interested, it's perfectly fine. But I think you have so much talent that it's a waste not to show it off to a larger audience. I have a friend who owns a gallery, and if you're interested, I could talk to her about showing your work. I'm not making any promises, but I didn't want to call her before talking to you."

"Wow, I don't know what to say."

"Say you'll think about it. No pressure." Gillian smiled. "Is Piper in the studio?"

"No, she's in her apartment, but you can go on up if you want."

"Are you sure she's not busy?"

Kelly took a moment to look at Gillian, studying her is what it felt like. "I'm sure. I'm just wondering what's going on between you two. Forgive me for being nosy, but Piper is very special to me and her entire family. We don't want her getting hurt or stressed out."

"Why would I stress her out? I don't understand."

Kelly looked like she'd said too much. "Forget what I said. You can go on up. If she decides to tell you, then the two of you can talk it out."

Confused and totally in the dark about their conversation, Gillian said good-bye and headed up the stairs in the studio that led to Piper's place. Once she knocked, it only took a few seconds for Piper to open the door.

"Hey! What are you doing here?"

Piper held the door open for Gillian to enter. Agnes strolled over and rubbed herself against Gillian's pant leg.

"Hi. I came by to talk to Kelly."

Piper's eyebrows raised. "What for?"

Gillian sat on the couch, and Agnes immediately took her place on her lap. "I wanted to ask her if she'd be interested in showing her art." Gillian told Piper about her friend's gallery. "I asked her to think about it, and there was no pressure."

"Wow, that would be great for her. She's so freaking talented."

Gillian pointed to her painting. "I know. Today, at the museum, I went to look at other Abstractionists, and I felt that Kelly's work was right up there with the best. It's a travesty that the whole world can't see it, never mind the greater DC area."

"That's so exciting, Gillian. Thank you for thinking of her for that. I was just about to order in. Care to join me?"

"Yes, what are we eating?" Two nights in a row of seeing each other, both at Gillian's doing. The newness of their friendship had

Gillian's adrenaline rushing, and she tried to keep her body from trembling.

"How's Thai?"

Gillian's mouth watered. "Yes. Chicken pad thai, please." She stroked Agnes's fur while Piper called in the order. She didn't know why, since that was only the second time she'd been in Piper's apartment, but she felt so comfortable and at home. Gillian asked Piper about other interesting things to see in the neighborhood. They talked about the other Smithsonian museums, what kind of art caught their eye, and who their favorite artists were. When the food arrived, they sat on the couch with their plates.

"How was your day?" Piper wrapped the noodles around her fork before eating.

"It was good. Everything is under control."

Piper laughed. "It is, is it? Great to hear."

Gillian joined Piper in laughing. "Yes, it is. My assistant, Maya, is studying to be a curator, working toward her PhD, so she's sort of my protégé. She takes care of a lot of business I normally would, which left me open to think about Kelly's work." Gillian took a bite of food despite the butterflies flittering in her stomach. She couldn't believe she was going to talk about this. "For some reason, everything about last night stuck with me."

Gillian felt her cheeks heat up, not meaning to admit that she'd thought about their time together. She played with her food in between bites, giving her something to do other than look at Piper. She felt Piper slide closer down the couch.

"What stuck with you?"

Gillian took a bite of chicken, not chancing a glance at Piper. Her breathing quickened, and her blood felt like it was rushing through her veins. "Dinner. Your corny joke." Gillian finally looked at Piper. "Our hug, and how good it felt."

Piper nodded but stayed in place. "Yes, that hug was quite something. Actually, everything. But I know you're not in a place to be anything other than friends, so I'll respect that."

Gillian nodded. "Thank you. But maybe I want to try a little more."

Piper's eyebrows raised. "More?"

Gillian nodded. "Maybe?"

Piper smiled and placed her hand on Gillian's, feeling that she wasn't quite ready if she was saying "maybe," so she decided to be the one to slow it down. "How about we get to know each other better? I mean, the only thing I really know is that you're a curator and you lost your wife. Do you want to tell me about her?"

Gillian stayed silent, and just as Agnes was about to jump in her lap, Piper took her plate and placed it on the coffee table. Gillian stroked her fur, calming her nerves, and giving her the courage to talk about Kate. It was like Agnes had become her new best friend and excuse to not look at Piper. She let out a deep sigh. "Kate was my wife. We met in high school, and I knew immediately that I would marry her. We had a great life together until she was killed in a motorcycle accident. That was two years ago, and it took a lot from me."

Piper slid even closer and squeezed her hand over Gillian's. "What drew you to her?"

Gillian laughed as she was remembering back to when she met Kate, and she almost felt like that teenaged Gillian again.

"I saw her in the hallway in high school, our sophomore year. She took my breath away. She was really good-looking, popular, athletic. I was the new girl at the school, but that didn't matter to her. She immediately made me feel welcome, and we became friends." Gillian continued with her story while Piper gave her full attention. Piper felt no jealousy, only sorrow that Gillian had lost her wife.

"What happened when she died?"

"She was riding her motorcycle on the back roads for one last ride before putting her bike away for the winter. She was hit by a driver who was texting. He swerved in front of her into her lane and hit her head-on. We were supposed to host her parents for Thanksgiving, but she wanted to go on that one last ride."

Piper's hair on the back of her neck stood up, and she felt her heart rate increase. "She died on Thanksgiving two years ago?"

Gillian slightly shook her head. "The doctors actually pronounced her brain dead on Thanksgiving, but we kept her on a ventilator until the next day. When the tests were complete and confirmed, we decided to donate her organs."

Piper's blood ran cold. It couldn't be. Could fate be that cruel? Did Piper have Kate's heart beating inside her, giving her life? A small sob escaped, and she covered her mouth.

"Piper? Are you okay?"

Piper shook her head then nodded. She couldn't talk to Gillian about this just yet. She needed to process then think about what it all meant. "Yeah, I'm okay. Just, you know, upset that you lost your wife." *And because you did, I'm alive.*

Gillian stood and grabbed her coat. "I'm glad I told you about her, but I'm mentally exhausted now, so I'm going to go home."

Piper nodded. "I'll walk you out."

They took the other set of stairs that led to the parking lot behind the shops, and Piper walked her to the sidewalk. Gillian turned to Piper and hugged her, neither of them saying anything, the only sound coming from the night life down the street. They broke apart, and Gillian kissed Piper's cheek.

"Thank you for asking about Kate. That meant a lot to me. It's funny, but you remind me a little of her the more I get to know you."

Well, hell. Gillian was already comparing her to Kate. "I appreciate you telling me. Text me when you get home so I know you're safe."

Gillian laughed. "I don't have your number." She handed Piper her phone so she could put in her contact info.

"There. Now you can text or call." Piper was proud of herself that her fingers held steady while tapping in her number.

"Good night, Piper." The soft look Gillian gave her made Piper's knees grow weak.

"'Night, Gillian." Piper stood on the sidewalk, watching Gillian until she turned the corner. Thoughts in her mind were swirling, and not from the kiss on her cheek that Gillian gave her. That should be at the forefront, but no, not tonight. Not with the information that Gillian gave her regarding Kate's death and organ donation, and the perfect timing of it all. Piper ran her fingers through her hair then over her face. "Fuck me."

She trudged up her stairs, her legs felt like her feet were in cement. Wasn't that just a kick in the pants? Her apartment still smelled like Gillian's perfume, or maybe it was on her sweatshirt. She sat on her couch, the same couch that potentially held promise earlier, but now held heartache, shock, disbelief. Piper patted her legs, welcoming Agnes onto her lap.

"Meow."

"Not now, Agnes." God, that was rude. She invited Agnes onto her lap then told her to stop talking. Rude.

The cat seemed to be aware of Piper's distress, and she burrowed into Piper's lap and started up her motor. She stroked Agnes's fur just as Gillian had done just a short time ago. Gillian and Kate were from this area. Piper knew this because of the years Gillian had been at the museum. Kate got in her accident on Thanksgiving, but Gillian had her organs donated the day after, which would be the exact day Piper got the call about the heart she'd later receive. She'd seen enough cop shows and read enough books with cop characters to know there wasn't such a thing as a coincidence. Not that she knew any real cops and TV shows were really fiction, but there was something to that. She had Kate's heart. She knew it. She knew it deep down in her…well…Kate's heart that was now hers. Piper was filled with restless energy, and she knew exactly what she needed.

She went to her bedroom and changed into her ratty clothes, the ones she wore when she was ready to get down and dirty with some clay. Her phone pinged, and she checked it to find a text from Gillian.

Thanks again for tonight. I look forward to seeing you soon.

Oof, what a night. *Me too.* What else could she say? There was so much to say, but she didn't know how.

Piper took the stairs that led to the shop and was surprised to find the lights on and Kelly standing in front of a blank canvas.

"What's up, sis?"

Kelly jumped and turned around. "Jesus, Pipes. Don't scare me like that." Kelly placed her hand over her chest.

Piper snorted and covered her mouth. "Consider it payback. What are you doing here?"

"Did Gillian tell you about her plan? About me possibly getting a show?"

"She did. You must be considering it if you're here late tonight."

Kelly smiled. "You know what? I *am* considering it. I have a few older pieces I've done, but I feel like my newer ones are so much better. I want to see how long it'll take me to produce a show-worthy painting, to see if I'm up to getting ready some really good pieces to show. What are you doing down here? Gillian gone already?"

"Yep." For once, Piper was speechless. She paced as she ran her fingers through her hair. She stopped, looked at Kelly looking at her, and nodded. "I'm gonna throw some clay."

"What's going on with you? You're acting weird."

"Am I? Am I acting weird? Because I'm feeling really weird right now." Piper continued to pace, and she started talking to herself. Well, silently, but she could still feel her lips moving as if she was speaking out loud.

"You're scaring me, Pipes." Kelly came over to Piper, grabbed her arm, and led her to a stool to sit. "What the hell is going on with you?"

"Gillian's wife died."

"Oh, that's awful. Poor thing."

"She died two years ago on Thanksgiving." Just saying those words made Piper nauseous. She clenched her jaw and tried to swallow back the bile.

Kelly bowed her head. "I can't imagine losing Drew. Especially around the holidays."

"Kelly." Piper stared at her sister-in-law and threw her arms up in the air. She scrubbed her face with her hands then let out a deep breath.

"What?"

"Gillian donated her wife's organs the day after. I think I have her wife's heart."

Moments ticked by while they stared at each other. Piper could almost see the wheels turning in Kelly's head, putting it all together.

"Are you fucking kidding me right now? If you're playing, it's not funny." It was Kelly's turn to pace, and Piper watched her as she processed the information.

"Do you think that would be something I'd make up? What the hell am I supposed to do?" Piper began pacing again, almost step in step with Kelly, and running her fingers through her hair after she took the rubber band out. She let out a growl and tied her hair back up.

"Okay, hang on." Kelly sat on the stool and grabbed Piper's hands. "Tell me what happened."

Piper told Kelly of her conversation with Gillian earlier, and also told her about the dill pickles in the mac 'n' cheese, and how Kate used to do that. "It's such a random food oddity, and it's only been a recent thing to me. What if it's because what Kate liked carried on over to me?"

"I'm assuming you haven't told Gillian about your heart transplant?"

"No. Things are so new right now, I didn't feel like it's something I should bring up just yet. I haven't even told her that I had a heart issue."

"Can you explain why?"

"Well, I don't want to scare her off. I mean, remember how I didn't want to get involved with anyone because I didn't want to have someone fall in love and then I might die? Yeah, that."

"Piper…"

She inhaled through her nose and closed her eyes. "I know it's my thing. But now, if she knows I have Kate's heart, would she want to be with me, or Kate?"

Kelly rubbed her forehead. "I see your point. But it's also not your responsibility to choose what Gillian wants."

"But what if it's Kate whose heart is beating in my chest?"

"Listen to me, little sis. You can't keep this a secret from her. She'd never trust you if she knew you lied to her."

"I'm not lying. I'm just not saying anything yet. If she gets to know *me* and likes *me*, then maybe I have an actual shot."

Silence filled the studio like a thick fog, and it was difficult for Piper to breathe.

"You can't keep this from her forever, Pipes. You need to tell her the truth."

"I will. I just have to wait for the right time."

Kelly hugged Piper, and they went their separate ways to produce their art. Not that there wasn't more to say, but she needed time to process everything and consider her options. Piper knew she had to tell Gillian, not only about her illness but of her transplant, and the strong possibility that it was Kate's. Of all the damn things that could keep them apart. She just needed a little bit of time so Gillian could develop feelings for Piper, and not think of her as just a vessel that housed Kate's heart.

CHAPTER TWELVE

M om, Dad, I'm here." Gillian removed her coat, hat, and gloves before entering the kitchen.

"Hi, sweetie. We're so glad you could come for dinner." Gillian hugged Gloria then Harold.

"Are you kidding me? I've been missing you and wanted to have some time with two of my favorite people."

"What's new, honey?" Harold handed Gillian a glass of wine while he sipped on his scotch.

Gillian took a deep breath and an even bigger gulp of wine. "I've kind of started seeing someone." Gillian had fretted over this moment for the past few days to the point of almost making her sick. Great, and now she was crying.

"Honey, why are you crying?"

Gillian sobbed and begged the tears to stop. She turned away from them to take a moment and wipe the droplets away from her eyes. She could do this. She had to do this.

"I loved Kate so much. So much that I couldn't see myself with anyone but her. And you know if she was still alive, another woman would've never been another thought. But I met someone recently, and we've started hanging out and have become friends. I think I might want to date her and see where it goes."

"Oh, Gilli, we would love for you to find someone that makes you happy. We wouldn't expect you to stay alone for the rest of your life. Tell us about her."

Gillian tried to control her breathing and her tears. She let out another deep breath. "Her name is Piper James, and she's my pottery instructor."

Gillian caught the look Harold gave to Gloria as well as his smile. Gillian laughed and already she felt lighter. "I know, teacher-student thing, but I'll remind you we're both adults."

Gloria smacked Harold in the stomach. "Don't pay any mind to him, honey. Tell us more."

"We've gone to dinner a couple of times, and I really enjoy her company. To be honest though, she reminds me a little of Kate." She pictured Piper rubbing her chin when in deep thought, as Kate had done so many times.

"How so?"

"Well, she loves pickles." She told them about the pickle dishes they've had.

Harold laughed. "Kate loved them with everything she ate."

"Right? And she also rubs her chin when thinking about something, which Kate did as well."

"Do you want us to meet her?" Gloria looked hopeful, and that made Gillian smile. Gloria and Harold were her parents by choice and by marriage, her own birth parents gone from her life. Their opinion meant everything to Gillian. They'd basically been her family since she was a senior in high school, and their love and advice had helped shape the woman she'd become. Well, Kate helped with that too.

"I think so, but not quite yet. We're still getting to know each other, but I didn't want to keep something so important from you."

"All right then. When you feel you're ready, you let us know."

"I will, Dad. Thank you." The relief Gillian felt was palpable, and she felt like she would collapse, like she had no bones in her body to keep her upright.

"Anytime, honey. By the way, we're very happy for you. Kate wouldn't want you to be alone for the rest of your life. And no matter what, you'll always be our daughter."

"That's how I feel, Dad. If whoever I decided to date didn't want me to continue to be in your life, they would be the one to go. You'll always be my family."

"Good. Now let's eat." Gillian grinned at her father-in-law's ability to always eat, even in a crisis situation, which was what Gillian felt that was.

❖

Saturday was finally here, and Gillian would get to see Piper. It had been a few days since they'd seen each other. No other texts between them other than when Gillian told Piper she was home. It had been so long since Gillian had dated anyone that she no longer knew the rules. She also was still working things out in her head, and the time away from Piper gave her one of the answers she was looking for, and that was she missed Piper. Regardless of what happened between them, Gillian knew she had a friend in Piper... maybe more.

A light snow was falling, so Gillian bundled up and carefully made her way to the studio. She wiped her shoes on the mat just inside the door. She looked up and saw Piper looking at her, amused, as Gillian removed her gloves, scarf, and coat.

"Cold out there?"

"Yes, and snowing, thank you very much. Hi, Kelly."

"Good morning. I'd like to talk to you after your lesson if you have some time."

"Yes, I'm free. I'll see you then."

Gillian made her way through the doors with Piper right behind her. She hung up her things and turned around. "May I help you?"

"I believe you can if you give me a hug." Piper stepped closer, and it sent a thrill through Gillian when Piper removed Gillian's hair from inside the collar of her shirt.

"Is that all?" Gillian's words came out husky, and her pulse thrummed through her veins.

"For now." Piper opened her arms and Gillian gladly stepped into them. Piper smelled like soap and a hint of lavender. They loosened their hold on each other but didn't quite let go.

"How have you been? We haven't talked in a few days."

"I know, I'm sorry about that. I've been in a creative mood, and when I wasn't working, I was throwing clay."

"Really? Can I see?"

"Sure. I'll show you after class. In the meantime, grab your smock. The other ladies should be here any moment."

Piper led Gillian and the other ladies through a lesson in making a bowl. The piece itself wasn't too difficult, but it would take more artistic talent to paint it to make it worthy of a place in Gillian's cabinet. If she did a good enough job of it, maybe Gillian would make it her new cereal or soup bowl. Piper taught them how to use a few of the tools, and Gillian was impressed with the simple design she etched onto the outer aspect of the bowl. Once their time was up, the ladies placed their work in the designated box that Piper would fire up in the kiln. Next week's class would be the final one of the group lessons they'd signed up for. That class would be painting the pieces they'd completed for glaze.

"Okay, let's see what you've done." Gillian had admired Piper's work, and now that they were growing closer, Gillian was excited to see what she'd done.

"Don't expect too much. They're still drying, so they're still a couple of weeks away from being complete." Piper pulled the pieces from the bin and placed them on a table for Gillian to study. She took her time studying each piece, admiring the etches and designs Piper had artistically implemented into her creations.

"Piper, they're beautiful. In my mind, I know the colors that would brilliantly accentuate them."

"Well, are you going to tell me?"

"Noooo. You're going to finish them, and when they're done, I'll let you know if you got it right."

Piper laughed. "Oh, the pressure you put on me. On another note, would you like to have dinner with me tonight?"

"Italian?" Gillian would have said yes, no matter what Piper wanted to eat.

"It's like you're reading my mind. How about I pick you up at seven?"

"How about we hit up that place a couple of blocks over? That way we can walk off our dinner. I'll pick you up at your place at seven."

"I like a woman who knows what she wants." Piper smiled, took her hand, and interlocked their fingers. They stood there, both watching their hands, then looked up and smiled at each other.

"I'm going to go talk to Kelly about the show. I'll see you later."

Gillian grabbed her belongings and went with Kelly into the office. She sat in a chair at a fold-up table that also was used as a desk, at least from what Gillian could presume. It looked like organized chaos. "I assume this is about my question the other night."

"It is." Kelly blew out a hard breath and shook her hands. "I discussed it with Drew and my sons, and they're all in favor of me doing it."

Gillian clapped her hands. "Oh, wonderful. I'm so excited for you. What made you say yes?"

"Honestly, it was the approval of my family. They've always come first, and they told me it's now time to put myself first. My boys are in high school, so they don't need me around as much. I mean, I'll be around, but I'll put together a studio at home so I'll still be there."

"All right. I'll call Elise on Monday and see what she says. May I take a couple of pictures of the paintings in the shop? Just to give her an idea of how talented you are."

Kelly's face turned red, and she looked away. "Are you sure my stuff is good enough? I mean, I've only been doing it as a part-time hobby. I've never been super serious about it."

Gillian waited until Kelly looked at her. "You have an incredible talent, and it comes through with every brush stroke. If I didn't think you had the talent, trust me, I wouldn't have said anything. I'm around beautiful art every day, and I would say your work is pretty comparable. You just haven't been discovered yet."

"I can't thank you enough, Gillian. This had always been one of my dreams, but once my kids were born, they became my focus, along with Drew. You're making one of my dreams come true."

Kelly wiped away a tear and smiled. Gillian came around the table and hugged Kelly.

"Just remember, I have to ask my friend if she'd be interested, but know that I'm going to sing your praises."

A knock on the door interrupted them, and Piper opened it without being invited.

"Whoa, what's going on here?" Piper entered with a big smile and no signs of jealousy.

"I'm going to have a show, Pipes. People are going to see my paintings."

"I'm so thrilled for you, Kel. It's very much deserved."

Kelly waved Piper over to join in on the group hug. Somehow, Gillian was the filling in a Piper-Kelly sandwich, and she wasn't mad that Piper was behind her, pressed up against her. Her entire body felt like it was on fire. The hug broke up, and Gillian was relieved and disappointed. She cleared her throat and grinned.

"Well, I need to get going." She took Kelly's hand and gave it a little shake. "I'll keep you apprised of what my friend says. And, you," she turned to Piper, "I'll see you at seven."

"Looking forward to it."

❖

"What's going on at seven?" Kelly's smile was so wide that Piper wasn't sure if it was from her potential show, or that she had a date with Gillian that night. Sometimes it was difficult to tell with her.

"We're going to dinner. Would you like to join us?"

"Are you nuts? You don't ask your brother and sister-in-law on a date with you and Gillian."

"Why not? It's called a double date."

"Yes, but do you really want her to split her time between the three of us? You two are getting to know each other."

"Good point. You're not invited after all." Piper threw her arm around Kelly's shoulders as they went back to the shop. "I'm really so excited for you, Kel. Your show is going to be a hit."

"You think?"

"I know." Piper loved all her siblings' spouses, but she'd always had a special connection with Kelly, and she couldn't love her more if she was her own flesh and blood.

Later that evening, Piper was just finishing getting ready, putting her earrings in when Gillian arrived. Piper opened the door to find her bundled in a warm coat and scarf, and Piper could hardly see Gillian's face.

"A little cold out there?"

"Just a smidge. Maybe we should drive. You look good by the way."

Piper took Gillian's hands and smiled. "I mean, you're all bundled up, but I'm sure you look good too." Gillian laughed, and the sound was music to Piper's ears. They drove the two blocks to the restaurant, and Piper was relieved Gillian suggested taking the car. The air was bone-chilling cold, so cold that it hurt her lungs to take a deep breath. Their dinner was delicious, followed by some sort of berry tart for dessert. On the way back to Gillian's, she placed her hand over Piper's, and they interlocked their fingers. Piper looked down and thought that it felt so good, so right, to have Gillian's hand in hers. Was that her thinking or Kate's? Piper didn't know. She'd like to think it was hers alone, that her attraction to Gillian was organic, and if she didn't have Kate's heart beating inside her chest, that she'd still be drawn to Gillian. What wasn't there to like? She was attractive, intelligent, artistic, kind. She was everything Piper wanted in a girlfriend. Maybe she would withhold her belief that she'd had a transplant that probably was Kate's heart to herself for now. She wanted to get to know Gillian more and see where this went.

"Do you want to come in for a little bit?" Gillian posed the question to Piper when they'd pulled up in front of Gillian's. That would give her an opportunity to know Gillian better by talking some more and also seeing the more personal side to her. Piper believed you could tell a lot about someone by the way their home was decorated.

"If you're sure, I'd love to."

Once inside, Piper took in the living room that was warm and inviting. There was a comfortable looking brown couch facing the fireplace with two matching chairs on either side. Piper walked to the mantel and looked at the wedding picture of Gillian and Kate. She felt Gillian come up beside her.

"That was on our wedding day."

Piper didn't have to look at Gillian to know she was wistful. Her voice spoke volumes.

"You both looked amazing. When was that?" Piper finally spared a glance.

Gillian smiled, but there was a hint of sadness to it. "About fifteen years ago. We were about thirty-three, thirty-four years old."

Piper returned her gaze to the photo. "So, you were together about fifteen years before you got married?"

Gillian laughed. "Yes. God, I feel so old now. It feels like we were just babies when we met."

"How amazing that you two had all that time together." If Piper was being honest, she was a little jealous that Gillian had so much time with Kate. She'd wished she'd known a love like Gillian and Kate had.

"Yes, it was amazing. I cherish the time we had together, and it was wonderful being married to my best friend. But she's gone now and not coming back. I know she'd never wanted to leave, but I also know that she'd never want me to spend the rest of my life alone."

Piper nodded then looked to the right. "Hey! That's my vase!" It was so exciting for Piper to see her work somewhere other than the shop or her parents' home.

Gillian laughed. "No, that's my vase. I paid for it and everything."

Piper hugged Gillian. "Thank you. I've never seen my work out in the wild before."

"More of your pottery should be out in the wild, as you call it. I meant it when I said your pieces are beautiful, and you should be charging much more than you are in the shop. Have you thought about showing? Maybe I can talk my friend into featuring you and Kelly together."

"Oh, no. No, no. Kelly deserves to have her own show. I'm just messing around with my work."

Still embraced, Gillian touched the tip of Piper's nose with her index finger. "Even if you are just messing around with your work, it's still gorgeous and deserves to be seen by a bigger audience."

"Do you know what I think is gorgeous? You." Piper's entire body was on fire, and she didn't need an extinguisher. She just wanted to combust right there from the heat shared between her and Gillian.

The air between them grew thick, their eyes locked until Piper's gaze dropped to Gillian's lips. Piper had dreamt of this moment, it seemed, for her whole life. She moved closer, closer, feeling her heart almost stop until she kissed Gillian. Their lips melded together, Gillian's soft and inviting for Piper's. Piper's heart then felt like it exploded. As the kiss deepened, Piper thought she'd lose her breath, but she wasn't about to stop the best kiss she'd ever had. Piper caressed Gillian's lips with the tip of her tongue until they opened, and she welcomed Piper's tongue into her mouth. Piper moaned and pulled Gillian closer until there wasn't an inch of space between them.

Piper felt Gillian's hand cup the back of her head and pulled her even more into her. Piper's hands started wandering on their own, it seemed. She no longer had any control of what her body did. Gillian was in control, and Piper was more than happy to be on the ride with her. Piper moved her hand up Gillian's back over her softer than ever could be imagined sweater, then moved it back down over Gillian's behind that was covered by her wool slacks. Piper gently squeezed, and Gillian pulled away, breathing hard. Gillian's skin was flushed, her lips swollen, and she looked so sexy.

"God, I'm sorry, Piper."

"Sorry for what? The kiss?" *Please don't say the kiss.*

"For pulling away. Definitely not sorry for the kiss. Wow! But I started to feel a little out of control, and I'm not quite ready for that. Can you forgive me?"

Piper shook her head. She was still trying to calm her body down and stop her head from spinning like a top. Whew, that was some kiss, and who knew how far they would have gone if Gillian hadn't put the kibosh on it.

"Nothing to forgive, I promise. I'm not quite ready to move so fast either. I like the pace we're going, getting to know each other, dating." Piper stepped closer to Gillian and cupped her cheek. "I really like you, Gillian. I look forward to knowing all of you eventually. We'll know when we're ready to take things further." She kissed Gillian gently on the lips, not to stoke the fire, but to promise more when the time was right.

"I really like you, too. Thank you for being so understanding."

Piper hooked her thumb toward the front door. "I'm gonna get going. Call me."

Gillian walked Piper to the door. "One more kiss before you go?"

Piper turned and smiled. "Happily." They slowly brought their lips together, and unlike last time, Piper kept her hands safely on Gillian's back. They ended the kiss with Piper giving Gillian a kiss on the tip of her nose. "I'll see you soon."

CHAPTER THIRTEEN

Gillian had talked to Piper on the phone on Sunday during one of Piper's breaks at work. Piper had asked if they could have lunch on Monday at the museum. She wanted to come into DC to see the new exhibit they were featuring. Gillian was proud of it, and she was excited to show Piper her work. Monday morning, Gillian pushed Piper out of her mind so she could get as much work done as possible so she could give Piper a personal tour. Gillian had already told Maya that Piper was coming by, and Maya made Gillian promise to introduce them.

At twelve thirty, Gillian's phone pinged with a text. Piper was just outside the café waiting for her. Gillian ducked into the bathroom near her office to check her hair and clothes and apply fresh lipstick. Knowing she'd see Piper that day, she wore a sweater that accentuated her breasts with just a hint of cleavage. The brown color matched well with her own brown hair and highlights. She was relegated to wearing wool slacks due to the cold weather, but they still looked really good on her if she was being honest. She spritzed a little perfume on her neck, dropped her things back in her desk drawer, and took the stairs to the first floor.

She stopped on the third step from the bottom and locked eyes with Piper. Ooh, there went the butterflies. She was so good-looking—somewhere between pretty and handsome. Gillian took Piper in, looking really good in black jeans, a black turtleneck, and black leather jacket. The monochrome-look fit Piper like a glove.

The closer Gillian got to Piper, the broader the smile filled Piper's face. It was an incredible feeling that she was the one that could put that smile on her face.

"Hi. You look fantastic."

Piper shook her head. "I can't find the proper word to describe you because beautiful is so overused and not enough. Exquisite. Yes, that's it. You're exquisite.

"Flattery will get you everywhere." Gillian finished the statement with a wink, and she knew it would not be difficult to continue this flirty banter with Piper, but she'd prefer to do it in a more private setting. "Come on, let's eat. I'm famished."

They grabbed their lunch and found a table with a gorgeous view of the courtyard.

"So, I drove here today instead of taking the Metro. May I give you a ride home when you're done with work?"

"I'd like that very much. Maybe we could grab takeout and have dinner at my place."

"Brilliant idea. Hey, what did the potter say when he destroyed his piece of art? That's just the clay it is."

Gillian covered her mouth as she laughed. Piper took a bite of her sandwich and grinned from ear to ear.

"Don't worry. I promise not to tell you too many corny jokes. I'd like to keep you around for a while."

"It just so happens I like your corny jokes." And she did. She'd never known anyone like Piper. She had a child-like quality to her, but there were other times, like when they kissed, where she was all adult, and Gillian very much liked that aspect as well.

"Really? Can you tell my family that when you meet them?"

"I'd be happy to."

Once they'd finished lunch, Gillian led Piper to the latest exhibit she'd put together that showcased a mixed bag of today's artists that represented many diversified communities. They spent ample time examining each piece with Gillian giving Piper information on all the artists, their work, and what they represented.

"I saw this when I was here last time, but to have you give me a private tour and the lowdown on the art is so much better. You really did an incredible job putting this together, and it's so important to get these new voices out into the world."

Gillian's chest warmed because that was exactly why she'd put this show together. She took Piper's hand and gave it a squeeze, silently letting her know that she knew Piper understood her vision. Once they'd finished the exhibit, Gillian took Piper to the second floor and showed her more exhibits she'd put together. After four hours of showing their art to Piper, Gillian felt exhilarated hearing Piper's views on certain pieces.

"Would you like to see my office?"

"Is that a euphemism?" Gillian laughed, and she actually felt like a schoolgirl with a crush. Almost like she felt when she met Kate in high school.

Gillian smacked her arm. "My assistant, Maya, wanted to meet you."

"Are you kidding? I'd love to see the space you occupy while coming up with your incredible ideas."

"You know, I could get used to all this flattery you're throwing my way."

"Good because I'm going to continue winding up to throw the pitch. That's a baseball reference in case you weren't sure."

Gillian laughed. "Thank you for that."

They reached the third floor where the staff offices were located. She spotted Maya looking out her door like she was on some kind of stakeout.

"Maya, can I help you with something?" Gillian knew exactly what Maya was doing, and she couldn't contain her smirk.

"Uh, no, not really." She stepped into the hallway and extended her hand to Piper. "Hi. I'm Maya, Gillian's assistant."

Piper took her hand and smiled. "Hello. I'm Piper James. So nice to meet you. Gillian tells me you're getting your PhD and want to be a curator. I think that's wonderful, and you're lucky to have Gillian in your corner."

Maya smiled, and maybe looked a little smitten, which Gillian found amusing.

"Anything I need to know? Sorry I've been gone all afternoon, but I was giving Piper a tour of some of the exhibits we've done."

"No, I got all my calls and emails done, and I had an idea of a new exhibit, but we can talk about that tomorrow."

"All right. Why don't you take off and enjoy your night."

"Yes, ma'am. Piper, it was really nice to meet you. I hope to see you again."

"Same here, Maya. Keep up the great work."

Gillian led Piper into her office and closed the door behind them. Gillian leaned against the door and looked at Piper's backside. She stopped and turned around, facing Gillian.

"Everything okay?"

"Yes, as a matter of fact." Gillian locked the door and moved closer to Piper. "Everything is perfect." Gillian placed her hand on the back of Piper's head and pulled her into her, kissing her hard and fast. Her lust had been steadily building since she first spotted Piper looking hot in her black clothes. Spending the afternoon with her, Piper's views on art, the intoxicating smell of leather mixed with Piper's cologne, had Gillian's pheromones on high alert. Now that they were behind closed doors, all alone, she couldn't hold back any longer. She slid her arms under Piper's jacket and embraced the warmth that met her hands.

When they finally broke apart, breathing hard, Gillian's forehead resting against Piper's, she continued to caress Piper's back. "I've been wanting to do that all afternoon."

"I'll see your afternoon and raise you since our last kiss. You've put a spell on me, Ms. Phillips."

"Is that right? Sounds like it might be dangerous." The words that came out of Piper's mouth made Gillian feel special. She'd been thinking of kissing her since the last time they'd kissed. Piper had been thinking about Gillian, and that made her feel special.

Piper kissed her, ramping up the heat. "It definitely could be. If I wasn't so well-behaved, I might have to clear a space off your desk for you to sit while I worshipped you."

Gillian fanned herself, her face and the area south on fire. "Oh, my."

"All right, stop touching me so I can behave. I want to get a good look at your office."

Gillian watched Piper move about her office, looking at the pieces of art on her walls, the books on her shelves, then she picked up the picture of Kate on her desk.

"This is a great picture of you and Kate."

"Yes, we took that on one of our trips to Provincetown. That was about four years ago."

"I've never been, but I hear Women's Week is an incredible time. Music, books, comedians. And I've heard it's a great town for art."

"It is. I think you'd really enjoy it." Gillian chewed her lower lip. "Can I ask you a question? Does it bother you to see pictures of Kate and me together, or for me to talk about her?"

Piper came around the desk and held Gillian's hands in hers. "It really doesn't. I know you still love her, and she was a huge part of your life. Just because she's gone doesn't make that go away. But I also believe that you have the capacity to love again. You can maybe fall in love with someone else and still love Kate."

Gillian draped her arms over Piper's shoulders. "That's very mature of you. And I really appreciate your understanding." Gillian kissed Piper gently on the lips.

"I mean, I can be even more mature if it means I get more kisses with you."

"Is that right? Prove it."

Piper tilted her head and licked her lips before leaning in and pressing her lips to Gillian's. With Piper having one hand on Gillian's cheek and the other on her lower back, pulling her closer, Gillian thought her legs would buckle. She offered up a dare to Piper, and she took it with gusto. She opened her mouth when she felt the tip of Piper's tongue brush her lower lip, and she moaned while their tongues danced and explored each other. After what wasn't long enough, their mouths separated, and Piper pulled Gillian into her body, hugging her while their chests heaved. That woman sure could kiss. Gillian never thought she'd experience another first kiss, but the other night proved her wrong. And while that one was amazing, it was also filled with nerves. That last kiss? Yeah, that was filled with excitement and lust. It was nice to know that she and Piper were more than compatible in the kissing department.

"So, uh, are you ready to go, or do you have some stuff to finish up?"

"What was that? I'm sorry, but my brain seems to have short-circuited."

Piper's smile was wide and her eyes were a shade darker than normal. "Is that right? That could be a problem. What should we do about it?"

Gillian placed her hand on Piper's chest and playfully pushed her away. "Just let me gather my things, and we can go."

When they exited the museum, Piper reached for Gillian's brown leather messenger bag and slung it over her shoulder.

"Would it be all right if I held your hand?"

Well, that was unexpected, but it gave Gillian a little thrill to know Piper wanted to hold her hand. She nodded and interlaced their fingers. The sky was inky and the air was cold enough so they could see their breath, but inside, Gillian felt warm. Hot, even. That wasn't something that she'd felt in such a long time. Her insides were warm for the first time in two years, and she was starting to feel hopeful.

"What would you like for dinner?"

"Actually, I made a big pot of chicken and vegetable soup yesterday, and I have a loaf of French bread if you're interested."

"I'm very interested. That sounds really good."

They got in Piper's car, and she turned on the heat full blast.

"Do we need to stop and get some pickles for your soup?" Gillian asked through laughter.

"Oh, funny lady." Piper tickled her, and Gillian had a difficult time trying to grab Piper's hands while laughing hysterically. "You are such a dill-light."

Gillian was out of breath by the time Piper ceased her tickle assault. "I'm just kidding."

Piper tried to look hurt, but her smile came through, and Gillian placed her hand on Piper's thigh as she drove out of the parking garage. Once they were on the road, Piper placed her hand over Gillian's.

"Tell me about your family."

Piper laughed. "My siblings are a mess. I'm just kidding. My parents live in Springfield, and my siblings all live within thirty minutes of them. In order, my brother Drew is the oldest. He's Kelly's husband and probably the one I'm closest to, although I adore all of them. Next is Rob and his wife, Julie. They're the ones with my niece Sam, who is the only one besides you that laughs at my silly jokes."

"Well, they may be silly, but they make me laugh, so please continue them."

Piper squeezed Gillian's hand. "Gladly. I'm the middle child, then Jon is next, and he's married to Laura. They have a son, Jon Jr., who's ten, and their daughter, Ashley, is twelve. My baby sis, Beth, is married to David, and they just told us they're expecting their first child, so we're all very excited for that."

"And Drew and Kelly have two sons, right?"

"Yeah, Andy is sixteen, and Caleb is fifteen. So, that's my crazy family. What about yours?"

Gillian took a moment to think how she was going to explain. "Well, I think I told you I'm not involved with my biological family anymore."

"I don't think so. What happened if you don't mind telling me."

"One day after school, Kate and I went back to my house to study for a geometry test we had the next day. We didn't really need to study all that hard since we were both getting good grades. It was just an excuse for us to spend time together. We weren't out to my parents or our friends, so whenever we could find time alone, we took advantage of it by kissing and touching each other. We were on my bed, then we started kissing." Gillian turned to Piper. "Are you sure you want to hear this?"

Piper squeezed Gillian's hand. "Only if you want to tell me, but I want to know everything about you, so if you feel comfortable continuing, please do so."

"Okay. So, we were making out, and she asked me to take off my shirt. She unbuttoned and unzipped my pants and had her hand inside my underwear when my dad walked in and saw us."

"Oh, shit."

"Yes, that pretty much summed up my thoughts. He yelled at Kate, accusing her of making me do things I shouldn't be doing. He kicked her out of our house, and when I told him that we loved each other, I thought he was going to have a stroke. He was a God-fearing man, very religious, and said two girls loving each other was perverted and a sin. He told me I could no longer see her. We fought and we screamed at each other; I was surprised none of our neighbors called the police."

Piper remained quiet but kept hold of Gillian's hand.

"I told him I was eighteen, legally an adult, and I could do what I wanted."

"Ooh, I bet that went over well."

A mirthless laugh escaped Gillian's mouth. "Oh, you have no idea. I ran upstairs, slammed my door, and cried until I had no more tears. I grabbed my suitcase out of my closet and packed it with as many clothes and essential toiletries that it would hold. I grabbed my coat and dragged my suitcase down the stairs. I told my dad that I was going to Kate's, and he couldn't stop me. I thought maybe he'd come around, say that we should talk about it, but all he said was that if I left, I was no longer a part of the family. I left without saying another word, and I walked the three blocks to Kate's house. When I rang the doorbell, her mom answered, saw my face and luggage, and she pulled me into her arms while Kate's dad took my suitcase inside."

Piper was silent, her heart aching for the eighteen-year-old Gillian that was kicked out of her home, out of her family just for falling in love with another girl. She was overcome with emotion that her own family not only accepted it, but that it was a non-issue.

"Wow. I don't know what to say. You haven't seen them since?"

"Not really. I went over there about a month later to pick up some more of my belongings, and I was hoping we could work things out. My mom answered the door, and at first it looked like she was relieved to see me, but then my dad came up behind her. He told me I wasn't welcome, and my mom's demeanor changed. He was the head of the house, and she did everything he told her to do, including disowning her eldest daughter."

"Gillian, God, that's awful. How could parents do that to their child?"

"I don't know. Thankfully, Kate's parents, Harold and Gloria, took me in. They became my family even before Kate and I got married."

Piper held Gillian's hand the rest of the way back to her house and tried to process everything Gillian told her. She was so close to her own family that she couldn't imagine them shunning her the way Gillian's parents had.

"Do you still want me to come in?"

Gillian turned to her when Piper had turned off the car. "Of course. You're going to love this soup."

Piper followed Gillian into the house and hung her coat on the rack over Gillian's. It felt strange to Piper that Gillian seemed so nonchalant about not having any contact with her family, but she supposed that it didn't affect her as much since it happened so long ago. Or maybe she was just good at hiding how she really felt about that.

They talked more about art, a safe and happy subject for them while Piper watched Gillian slice and butter the French bread and heat up the soup. After they finished eating, and Piper helped Gillian clean the dishes, they went and sat on the couch in the living room. Gillian told Alexa to play some jazz while they talked some more.

"Harold and Gloria sound like they're wonderful." Piper and Gillian sat next to each other and held hands.

"They really are. They helped me so much when Kate died. They helped me make the decision to donate her organs. I stayed with them for a while because I couldn't stand to be in our house without her." Gillian looked down at their intertwined hands and ran her thumb over Piper's. "I told them about you."

"You did?" The surprise hit her like a slap upside the head. "What did you tell them?"

"Well, I told them that you and I are starting to date. To be honest, I thought I would pass out from nerves. They've known me for a long time and welcomed me into their family without reservation. I've ever only loved their only daughter. Deep down, I knew they would be okay with it, but I was still scared."

"So, were they? Okay with it?"

"Yes. Very."

Piper wasn't aware that she'd been nervous as well as holding her breath until she felt a weight lifted off her shoulders. "Would it be weird to ask you if I could meet them one day? When you and they are ready?"

"I think that could happen."

Piper lifted Gillian's hand to her lips and kissed it. "Thank you for everything today. For the tour, for telling me about your family by birth and by choice, and for the delicious soup. Today has been a really great day for me."

Gillian kissed Piper's hand next. "It's been a really great day for me too."

"It's getting late and time for the beautiful curator to go to sleep."

Gillian walked Piper to the door and helped her with her coat. They drew closer until their lips met, soft, inviting, and a promise of things to come. Not a lot of heat that time, but a lot of comfort that wrapped around Piper like a warm blanket. She held Gillian tight so she could feel the same comfort Piper did.

CHAPTER FOURTEEN

How was your day at the museum?" Kelly was helping Piper restock the shelves first thing Tuesday morning. Piper didn't sleep well the night before, as her mind was buzzing with thoughts and images of Gillian. The more time she spent with her, the more she liked her. So much so, she wasn't interested in seeing another woman, and she'd hoped the same to be true for Gillian. Next time they spoke, Piper would talk to her about being exclusive. Not that she thought Gillian would be interested in dating anyone else, but she wanted to lock it in, so to speak.

"It was great. Gillian showed me the exhibits she'd done, and man, Kel, she's so talented. She gave me behind the scenes info on the artists and their work. I met her assistant who has visions of being a curator as well. Gillian is her mentor. Then Gillian and I had a hot make-out session in her office, then I took her home."

Kelly held up her hand. "Hold up there, little sis. Let's go back to the hot make-out sesh. How hot was it?" The smile on Kelly's face was cute; obviously, she was very excited that things were going so well with her and Gillian since she was the first one to push her to ask Gillian out.

"Sizzling. Smoking. Damn, it was hard to stop, but we've decided to take things slow. Plus, we were at her job, so, you know."

They continued their work, and Kelly continued. "Have you told her about your heart yet?"

Piper let out a deep sigh. "No, I think it's too soon for that. It's just not the right time."

Kelly stopped and turned to Piper. "When is the right time? When you're both getting naked to have sex, and she sees your scar? It's not exactly inconspicuous. You're asking for trouble, Pipes. You keep this from her too much longer, and she's going to be really upset with you."

"I know. I just have to figure out what to say and when."

The rest of the day, Gillian flooded Piper's thoughts. They hadn't made any future plans to see each other, but in Piper's opinion, tonight was as good as any. She pulled out her phone and pulled up Gillian's number. When the ringing went to voice mail, she left a message.

"Hey, there. I was wondering if you were free tonight, if you wanted to come over after work? I hope you're having a great day."

She replaced the phone in her pocket and welcomed a customer in the store. After a couple of hours, Piper pulled her phone back out to see if, somehow, she'd missed a call or text from Gillian, but still nothing. As the day went on, she tried not to worry, but she also didn't want to be that person who sent numerous texts or calls, wondering where Gillian was, and why she wasn't returning her call. She was probably just busy.

When seven came around, Kelly left and Piper closed up behind her. When the lights were off and the alarm set, she headed upstairs, feeling on edge from not having heard back from Gillian. She navigated her way to the kitchen, trying not to step on Agnes, who was weaving herself around Piper's legs and meowing up a storm, wanting her dinner two hours ago. Once she had Agnes squared away, she made herself a sandwich and plopped down in front of the television for a little mindless activity. A real estate show was playing, but Piper was scrolling her phone, reading news, catching up on social media, watching music videos—anything to keep her mind off Gillian.

They hadn't been seeing each other long, but Piper was developing strong feelings for Gillian. She was excited to see where things could go with Gillian, but also, she was frightened that she might lose it all, especially when she told her about possibly having

Kate's heart beat inside her chest. Since her transplant, Piper had tried to stay present in the moment, but there were times when she felt like she was living on borrowed time. She was just about to send a good-night text to her when there was a knock on the door. She opened it to find Gillian on her stoop.

"Hey, what are you doing here?"

Gillian stepped inside, and Piper closed the door behind her. Gillian opened her arms, and Piper stepped in.

"I'm so sorry I've been out of touch today. I forgot my phone at home like an idiot. I just got home a little while ago, and the first thing I was going to do was call you, but I decided to come over instead when I listened to your voice mail."

"I'm happy to see you, but you could've just called. You didn't have to drive over."

"That's the benefit of living only a few blocks away. I didn't have to deal with traffic or anything."

Piper laughed. "Come in and have a seat. Can I get you some water or juice?"

"Just some water is fine."

Gillian sat on the couch while Piper filled two glasses with water. She found Agnes in Gillian's lap when Piper sat next to her and placed their glasses on the coffee table. She leaned back and placed her arm behind Gillian.

"How was your day other than leaving your phone at home?"

Gillian giggled. "You know, you never know how attached you are to your phone until you don't have it. I didn't realize until I boarded the Metro for work this morning. By that time, it was too late. Other than feeling a little lost without my added appendage and missing your call, my day was good." Gillian leaned her head on Piper's shoulder and Piper felt the muscles in Gillian's shoulders relax. "How was your day?"

"Uneventful except for going out of my mind worrying why you hadn't gotten in touch with me." Piper chuckled when Gillian hugged her. "I don't want to be the person who's clingy and texting you to see why you haven't texted back."

Gillian placed her hand on Piper's thigh which sent the butterflies fluttering in her stomach. Just the simplest touch from Gillian could do that to her. It was thrilling and terrifying all at once.

"Just so you know, when you text or call, I will *always* return it…unless I leave my phone at home."

"That's very good to know. While we're on the subject, there's something I wanted to talk to you about."

Gillian sat up and looked at Piper. "Is everything all right?"

Piper squeezed Gillian's shoulder, pulled her closer, and kissed her forehead. "Better than all right. I know we're in the beginning of everything, but we never discussed exclusivity. I don't know where you are in your head, but I'm not interested in dating anyone but you. I just wanted you to know how I'm feeling about the subject."

Gillian turned her head and kissed Piper on her neck, sending her libido into the stratosphere. Something about a beautiful woman kissing her neck and making her feel like she meant something to said woman really stoked her fire.

"I'm not interested in seeing anyone other than you. I never thought I'd want to be with anyone after Kate died, couldn't imagine being with anyone else. But then we met, became friends and started to get to know each other. I'm glad you came into my life and gave me the chance to see what I could have missed out on. I'm hopeful for the path we're traveling together." Gillian tilted her head up so Piper could fully kiss her. They shifted their bodies so they were facing each other, tilting their heads so their lips would fully connect. They wrapped their arms around each other, forcing Agnes from Gillian's comfortable lap and meowing to make her displeasure known.

"Go away," Piper mumbled before reconnecting with Gillian. She didn't know how it was possible to be so connected with someone not only mentally but physically. Like their lips were meant for each other. Piper tried to push Kate out of her mind while she was kissing Gillian. She might have Kate's heart, but her lips belonged to her, and her only. Now would probably be the right time to tell Gillian about her heart before things went too far.

Gillian shifted until she was on her back and Piper was on top of her. Piper got lightheaded while kissing Gillian, and she had to pull back for a moment.

"What's wrong? Is it too much?" The look of concern on Gillian's face pulled Piper back to the present. Maybe now wasn't the right time to have that discussion. Piper couldn't think about anything other than kissing Gillian's swollen lips.

"No, everything is great. Too great that I'm feeling a little dizzy. No other woman had made me feel like that before, and I'm feeling a little discombobulated."

Gillian laughed, but she still seemed concerned, and she was still under Piper's body. "Do you want to stop?"

"Hell, no!" Piper shifted so she was fully on top of Gillian, her leg between Gillian's. Her center felt warm against Piper's thigh, and she wanted more. So much more that Piper felt like she was losing her mind. She moved her hand the length of Gillian's thigh, taking great care to keep her hand on the outer part rather than inner thigh that would lead to a place of pleasure, but also make it almost impossible to hold back. She moved her hand back to Gillian's waist and under her sweater, up the side of her body. Gillian's body started moving under Piper's, urging Piper to provide her with what she wanted. Piper skimmed the underside of Gillian's breast, under her bra until Gillian suddenly sat up, killing any further movement from Piper.

"Oh, gosh. I'm sorry." Gillian was breathing hard and her body was trembling.

"No need to be sorry, honey. It all felt so good, but we were practically at the point of no return." And now Piper was going to either have to take a very cold shower or take care of herself.

"I know. That's why I had to stop. I want you, Piper, but I'm not quite ready. I've never been with anyone besides Kate, which makes me nervous to be with anyone else, especially you. But I know when the time is right, it will be amazing. I hope you understand."

Piper pulled Gillian to her, holding her, rocking gently. "Of course, I understand. I'm sorry I took it so far, but you drive me crazy in such a wonderful way." Piper checked the clock and frowned. "I know you're only a few blocks away, but if you want to stay over, you can take my bed and I'll sleep on the couch." The thought of waking in the morning with Gillian in her apartment, sharing coffee and breakfast, left Piper really wanting Gillian to stay.

"No, I don't want to kick you out of your own bed. Besides, it'll be easier for me to get ready for work in the morning if I'm at home."

"Understood. Let me walk you out." The disappointment was palpable, but there was also a flood of relief that rushed through Piper. As much as Gillian turned her on, she didn't want to think like she was a teenaged boy. She wanted to be an adult, someone who was capable of being in control of her actions. And even though Gillian turned her whole world around, Piper wanted to make sure the time was right, and they were both on the same page.

Piper helped Gillian with her coat and walked her to her car. Gillian had started it to get the heater and defroster working but took her time hugging Piper.

"I'm sorry about missing your call, but I'm really glad we had some time together tonight. Call me tomorrow. I promise not to forget my phone at home."

Piper chuckled before she kissed Gillian good night. "I will. Be safe going home."

Piper stood in the parking lot until Gillian turned left onto the street that would lead her to her own home. Piper's heart was missing Gillian already, but her head was telling her to slow down. She'd decided to listen to her heart.

Chapter Fifteen

Gillian and Piper had seen each other every night that week with Gillian stopping by the store, even if for just a few minutes just so she could kiss Piper. She was trying to keep her head about her, but it was almost like she was addicted to Piper's presence. She couldn't seem to get enough of her, and much to her surprise, Gillian was falling quickly. She'd been with only one other woman, and if Kate hadn't died, she'd only be with one woman her entire life. They'd had a special relationship—one that was built on friendship, love, laughter, tears, dreams, and hard work. Marriage wasn't easy, but they worked at keeping things fresh. They'd gone on dates, tried new things, traveled to various places, and every day Gillian had spent with Kate made her fall more in love.

Since Kate's passing, not a day went by where Gillian didn't think of her or talk to her. However, over the past couple of weeks with Piper, her thoughts of Kate were lessening, and Gillian felt guilty for that. How was she supposed to keep Kate's memory alive while falling for Piper? It wasn't fair to any of them, but life wasn't fair, was it? She needed some group time with her ladies, so they'd planned on dinner at Heidi's for Saturday night. When she'd told Piper that she'd be spending Saturday night with her friends, Piper was nothing but encouraging, saying it was important to have time with friends. That Piper never seemed jealous or possessive of their time together made Gillian feel really good, but also maybe Piper was a little too good to be true.

Gillian arrived with a Caesar salad to go along with the lasagna Heidi was making. The other ladies brought dessert and appetizers. Although they frequently texted each other, they hadn't gotten together since Gillian had told them that she'd started dating Piper. She knew she'd be ambushed in the best possible way by her friends, wanting to know all the details, and she was prepared for it.

They gathered around the island in the kitchen with their drinks while the smell of Italian seasonings, garlic, tomato sauce, and mozzarella cheese filled the area.

"How are things with Piper?"

"Really well. We talked the other night and decided to be exclusive."

Jen coughed after taking a drink of her wine and nearly choked, making them all laugh. "Already?"

"Well, come on. I had no interest in dating anyone until Piper came along, so it was a no-brainer for me. She also hadn't dated anyone for a while."

"Why is that?" Amanda asked.

"You know, I'm not exactly sure. She just said she hadn't met anyone she was interested in."

"What I really want to know, is she a good kisser?" Heidi winked at Gillian before tapping her glass to Amanda's.

Gillian could feel her face grow hot and insides were swirling with the memory of kissing and touching Piper, and she fanned herself. "Sooooo good. She's pro level with her mouth and hands. Not that we're there yet, but when the time comes when we have sex, I can only imagine it's going to be off the charts."

Audrey set her beer bottle down a little too hard that made everyone look at her. "Be right back." Audrey left the kitchen with the others looking perplexed. Heidi was about to storm out after Audrey, but Gillian stopped her.

"I'll go." Gillian knew that Heidi sometimes had a problem with Audrey and her attitude. For the most part, they got along, but sometimes Audrey would act like she had a chip on her shoulder, and that aggravated Heidi.

Gillian saw the light on under the powder room door, and she could only guess that whatever set Audrey off, she was trying to calm down. Finally, Audrey emerged and stopped in her tracks when she saw Gillian.

"Come sit with me for a minute." Gillian grabbed Audrey's hand and led her to the couch. She continued to keep Audrey's hand in hers, and she turned to her. "What has you so upset?"

Audrey was silent and wouldn't look at Gillian until she squeezed Audrey's hand.

"Tell me."

"You're my best friend's wife. I don't like hearing about you kissing other women." Audrey's body was trembling, and when she finally looked at Gillian, she could see the tears welling in Audrey's eyes.

"Honey, listen to me. If Kate was still here, everything would be different. There would be no Piper. But Kate's gone. She wouldn't want me to spend the rest of my life alone, and deep down, you know that. I know that when you meet Piper, you'll like her."

"I don't know about that. She's trying to take what was Kate's."

Gillian let go of her hand and stood quickly, towering over Audrey who was still seated. "You listen to me. I'm not some piece of property that Kate owned. We were partners in every sense of the word, and we loved each other very much. And Piper can't take what I'm willing to give. So far, what Piper and I have is turning into something special, and I won't tolerate you acting like a jealous, petulant child. If you don't want to hear me talk about Piper, then you can just leave. But don't you dare talk to me like that again. Do we understand each other?"

The slight nod from Audrey wasn't much, but it was something. Gillian went back to the kitchen to find her friends whispering but stopped once they saw her. Gillian gulped down the rest of her wine and refilled her glass.

"Anything I need to know about?" Gillian looked at each one of her friends, and they shook their heads. "Good. So, where were we?"

"You were telling us how fantastic Piper is with her hands and mouth, and that you couldn't wait to have wild monkey sex with her." Heidi, Jen, and Gillian all laughed at Amanda's summary.

Audrey walked in looking like she'd been taken to task, which she had been. She looked at each woman as she apologized for her earlier behavior. "Gilli, I really am sorry. You were right about everything, and I'll try to be nice when we finally meet Piper."

Gillian raised one eyebrow.

"Okay, I *will* be nice to her."

Gillian opened her arms and Audrey stepped in. Gillian kissed her cheek, then wiped the lipstick she'd left behind on Audrey's skin. "Thank you." Gillian loved Audrey because she was Kate's best friend, but she wouldn't tolerate her disrespecting Gillian or her relationship with Piper.

"Speaking of, when do we get to meet her?"

"I don't know. I'll ask her next time I talk to her, but with the holidays coming, it'll probably be after. I'm not sure what her plans are, but I assume she'll go to her parents' house. She has a big family, and they're really close."

They enjoyed the rest of their evening having dinner and talking. Audrey spilled the beans about finally having a good first date that was going to lead to a second. Amanda and Jen were married, and Heidi was divorced with no interest in returning to the dating pool just yet. But when they all got together for friend night, no spouses were allowed unless it was a special occasion.

When they'd all said good night, Gillian called Piper once she was in her car. The sound of Piper's voice brought joy to Gillian, and she could feel her grin widening. She hadn't expected to experience that feeling again, but Piper was a special woman, and Gillian was excited to see how their relationship would progress.

"Hey. How was your dinner?"

"It was fun, mostly. Is it too late for company?" It was only nine o'clock, but she didn't want to stop by if Piper was winding down and getting ready for bed. She realized that her phone call sounded like a booty call, and she wasn't at all ashamed of it. She just wanted to see Piper.

"Never too late for your company. ETA?"

"About twenty minutes."

"I'll see you soon. Drive safe."

Drive safe. The fact those were Piper's last words told Gillian she was concerned for her safety and well-being, and she said them to Gillian every time they said good-bye. She took the time of the drive to reflect on her dinner with her friends, and that they wanted to meet Piper. They knew, maybe with the exception of Audrey, that Piper was beginning to be a very special part of her life. Her friends had her back. She knew that Audrey would eventually get over her misgivings. She understood where she was coming from—she was Kate's best friend, and she still carried the weight of Kate's death on her shoulders. Kate had called Audrey to invite her to ride with her, but Audrey had previous plans, so she declined. Audrey told her the night of Kate's funeral that she should've been with Kate, that maybe the accident wouldn't have happened. Gillian explained to Audrey they might have had to bury her too. The fact that the driver was texting while driving wouldn't have changed the outcome if Audrey had been with Kate. Gillian believed Audrey needed to seek counseling to help remove the monkey from her back, but that was Audrey's decision to make.

When Gillian arrived at Piper's, she practically ran up the stairs because she couldn't wait another second to see her. Before she could even knock, Piper opened the door.

"Are you psychic now?"

"I may have been pacing by the door and heard you take the stairs two at a time."

Gillian burst out laughing and threw her head back. "I did not! I took each stair, but it may have been quick."

"That doesn't matter. I'm just very happy to see you. Come in."

Piper closed the door behind Gillian and followed her to the couch. "Can I get you anything?"

"Yes. I'm in desperate need of your lips on mine."

"That's great because my lips just happen to want that."

They embraced like long-lost lovers, and if it had been a movie from the forties, Piper might have dipped her before kissing her senseless. Gillian was on the verge of collapsing from the intensity of Piper's kiss.

"Piper." Gillian whispered her name as she backed Piper to the couch. She fell on top of her, and the kissing intensified.

Piper sucked on Gillian's pulse point on her throat but released her before she could mark her. "I missed you so much." Piper claimed Gillian's lips again, using her tongue to enter Gillian's mouth. Their tongues wrestled until Gillian broke apart and sat straddling Piper's legs. Piper slipped her hands under Gillian's shirt and dug her fingers into her skin. It would be so easy to take Gillian to bed and make love to her, but she'd let Gillian set that pace, and she would follow wherever Gillian led them. They continued to kiss and touch each other, careful not to get things too hot to back away from, but Piper could feel herself falling further for Gillian, and she wanted their first time to be special, not a quick romp on her couch. She slowed down the kiss until she was able to stop completely.

"What's wrong?"

"Nothing is wrong. Just the opposite. I feel so good with you, and your kisses are driving me insane. But when the time comes for us to make love, I want both of us to be sure, and not just because we're horny."

Gillian laughed. "How do you know I'm horny?"

Piper cupped Gillian's cheek and smiled. "I don't know about you, but I'm about to explode. I don't want that to be on my couch. At least not for our first time."

Gillian lay on the couch and took Piper with her so they were facing each other. "How about we cuddle and kiss without the heat we seem to bring to them."

"I'm not sure if that's possible, but we could certainly try." A few moments went by before Agnes startled them by jumping on them, and Piper added in a few curse words. "That damn cat. I swear, she plots different ways to scare the shit out of me."

"Serves you right for leaving her alone. She needs a playmate."

Piper shook her head. "That's the last thing she or I need." Agnes sat on Piper's hip and looked down on Gillian and Piper like they were her peasants. "She already makes me feel like an inadequate cat mom. I don't need another cat to make me feel like that. My bruised ego can only take so much."

Gillian kissed Piper's nose. "Oh, poor thing. We can't let that happen. I wanted to ask you about the holidays. What do you normally do?"

"Well, we usually go to my folks' the day after Thanksgiving so we can all be together. My siblings usually go to their in-laws' on Thanksgiving. We also go there for Christmas Eve, then on our own for Christmas day. Since I'm the only single one, I usually spend the night and spend Christmas with my parents. What about you?"

"I spend Thanksgiving with my in-laws. When Kate was alive, we'd have Christmas Eve at our house by ourselves then go to her parents' for Christmas dinner. The past two years, I've spent both days with them because I couldn't bear to be by myself. But now that we're dating, if you'd like, we can spend some time together."

"I would love that." Piper didn't say it out loud, but maybe by then, they'd be ready to meet each other's parents. And she really needed to tell Gillian the absolute truth about her heart before she could learn about it from one of Piper's family members.

"On that note, I think I should be getting home. It's getting late, and you have to work tomorrow." Piper and Gillian rose from the couch and held hands as they walked to Gillian's car. Piper wrapped her arms around Gillian and kissed her passionately.

"I'll talk to you tomorrow, but text me when you get home so I know you're safe." Another night of Piper watching Gillian drive away to go home. She longed for the night when they would finally sleep in each other's arms.

Chapter Sixteen

"Mom, Dad, can you help me, please?" Gillian had her hands full with bags of food and scrapbooks. Harold opened the door and relieved Gillian of the packages.

"What on earth is all of this?"

"A few side dishes and a couple of surprises I've made for you and Mom." Gillian took off her tweed overcoat and black knit hat, and she hung them on the coat rack just inside the front door. She followed her father-in-law into the kitchen where Gloria was cooking up a storm.

"Hi, honey." Gloria offered her cheek when Gillian went to kiss her hello.

"I brought the green beans and yams for dinner, but I also made you both something, so when you can take a break, I'll show you your presents."

"Pour yourself a glass of wine while I mash these potatoes, then we can take a look at what you've done."

Gillian took her wine and bag of goodies into the living room where Harold was watching the Ravens lose to the Lions, as evidenced by his mild use of profanities. Gillian smirked, not really understanding how someone could get so upset with "their" team. It was just a game after all. But Kate used to do the same thing. Didn't matter what sport—basketball, football, baseball, soccer. Gillian would sit back in her recliner, reading her book while Kate watched the games. She'd look up only when Kate would scream, yell, or jump off the couch. Gillian would just smile and shake her head. Their interests had been so different, but somehow, they worked, and very well, thank you very much.

A little while later, Gloria came into the living room and sat next to Gillian on the couch.

"Harold, mute the TV and get over here."

He dutifully muted the game and sat on the other side of Gillian. She removed the two scrapbooks and placed them on the coffee table in front of them.

"Today is the two-year anniversary of losing Kate, and not a day goes by where I don't miss her with every beat of my heart. But I made a decision to stop mourning and start living my life again. With that will bring more concentration on the great times we had together. I've considered myself extremely blessed that a woman like Kate fell in love with me, and that you welcomed me into your family. I couldn't have asked for a better family than yours. With that said, these presents are a token of my love and appreciation to you both for always loving me."

Gillian opened the first book. When a sob came out of Harold's mouth, Gillian wrapped her arms around him and held him as he cried. She felt Gloria's arms wrap around her from behind. Gillian had a feeling that was how they'd react, and she'd prepared for it.

"Guys, it's okay. It'll all be okay. Kate will always be with us, but it's time to focus on all the great times we had together. Please, just look at the books." Gillian stood and grabbed their glassware and refilled their drinks. When she returned, Harold and Gloria were sitting next to each other on the couch, looking through the first book. She set the drinks in front of them then took a seat in Harold's recliner, content to sip her Pinot Grigio and watch them reminisce and laugh through their tears. Gillian knew in her heart that that was the night they would all begin to heal.

Gillian had brought her overnight bag with her so she could stay over and spend the next day with her family. Piper would be spending the next day with her own family. Gillian called Piper later that night when she was in bed.

"What are you wearing?"

Piper's laughter over the phone made Gillian giggle. Not very sexy when she was trying to make a little sexy talk.

"Nothing but a smile, baby. How was dinner?"

"It was nice. The scrapbooks I made got them emotional, but I feel like tonight was the time to start healing." Gillian had told Piper about her projects, and also what she planned to do to celebrate Kate, and Piper was all for it. She even enjoyed looking through the scrapbooks, and especially the pictures of Gillian throughout the years. It was so strange but refreshing that Gillian could be so open with Piper regarding Kate and their relationship. "What time are you going to your family's?"

"Early afternoon. I want to get a workout in the morning and do some cleaning. Or maybe I'll skip the cleaning and go down to the studio for a while."

"I didn't know you worked out. Do you belong to a gym?"

"No, I have everything I need in my spare bedroom—a stationary bike, weights, and a few other fun toys."

"Wow. I had no idea. Why didn't you tell me?"

Piper laughed. "Not exactly important, baby."

"Everything about you is important to me." It was. Gillian wanted to know everything about Piper whether it was a minor thing or major. She wanted to know it all.

"Damn it. You deserve a really big kiss for that one."

"And you know what? I'll take it, so exercise those lips of yours too."

"I can't wait to see you on Saturday. What did you want to do?"

"How about you come over, and I'll make us dinner. After, we can play a game, or watch television, or find something else to do."

"I can think of something else to do."

"Mmm, I just bet you can." Just the thought of that something else made Gillian feel her clit twitch, and a yearning came over her she hadn't felt in a long time. She thought that part about her was long gone. Apparently, it was just waiting for the right woman to bring it back to life. "Have a great day tomorrow, and I'll talk to you soon."

"Sweet dreams, Gillian."

Gillian hung up the phone and plugged it into the charger before sliding down further in bed until the comforter was just below her chin. It had been a good day with delicious food, remembering great times with Kate, then finishing up the night with a call to Piper. She would do her best to obey Piper's last comment and have sweet dreams.

❖

Piper and her family gathered the day after Thanksgiving as they always did. It was the second anniversary of her getting a new lease on life. Like the previous year, Piper felt a mixture of sadness and gratitude. Now that she was pretty sure who her donor was, she included Kate's name, as well as Gillian and her in-laws in her prayers. She'd closed her eyes and brought Kate's image to her mind. Yesterday morning, Piper had sent a text to Gillian, saying she'd be thinking about her and her in-laws all day. Gillian ended up responding via phone call, saying she'd talked to Kate when she woke up. Piper thought it was a great idea, that it would keep her memory alive. Gillian sounded like her normal self, and it helped ease Piper's mind that she was doing okay, or as well as could be expected.

Piper stood in the dining room looking out the sliding glass door that led to the back deck, thinking of Kate, Gillian, her own family, and how many lives changed two years ago.

"What are you thinking about, sweetheart?" Piper's mom stood behind her with her hands on her shoulders. Piper saw their reflection in the glass as light snow fell just beyond it.

"I'm thinking about Gillian today." Piper turned around and gave her mom a hug, and also checked to see if anyone else was lurking about. "Gillian and I have been dating, getting closer, and I really like her, Mom. But I recently discovered something that may keep us apart, and I'm not sure what to do about it."

"What is it? Do you feel comfortable telling me?"

Piper nodded and told her mom about Gillian and Kate, how Kate died, and her organs were procured the day after Thanksgiving.

"I think I have Kate's heart."

Piper's mom plopped down on the chair and cupped her face with her hands, disbelief written all over her face. "Have you told Gillian?"

"No. I'm not one hundred percent sure, but maybe ninety-nine-point-nine percent. I don't want to say anything until I'm absolutely sure."

"Is there a way you can find out?"

Piper shrugged. "I contacted the organization to see if I could find out the donor, but they said since I sent the donor's family a letter, it was up to the family to reach out. I'm in a holding pattern right now."

"Oh, my love. What are you going to do?"

"I don't know, Mom. Things are going so well between Gillian and me right now, and I want our relationship to grow. She's the first person who has sparked an interest since Sabrina left." Sabrina had been Piper's girlfriend, someone Piper was serious about, but when Piper's health worsened, Sabrina couldn't take it anymore, and she left. That was when Piper sold her townhome and moved in with her parents so they could help take care of her.

"What did Gillian say when you told her about your transplant?"

Piper turned and went back to standing in front of the glass door, not able to answer her mom.

"Honey, you haven't told her?"

She turned around to face her mom, feeling the tears form and threatening to spill. "I don't want to scare her off. I really like her."

The tears fell freely when her mom stood and wrapped Piper in her arms. "What if this information brings you closer? It's time to start taking some chances, love. If you can't be honest with Gillian, then you'll never have an honest relationship."

Piper nodded as she cried into her mom's shoulder. She knew she had to tell Gillian. She just had to wait for the right time.

CHAPTER SEVENTEEN

"Hey, Mom. How are you doing?" Gillian clutched her phone so hard she knew her knuckles were white. She'd left her in-laws' house a few hours before, but she'd been too chicken to talk to them about meeting Piper when she was face-to-face with them. She took the easy way out and waited until she was safe in her home to call them and talk to them about something really important. She didn't know how they'd react, and it was better for her own psyche if she didn't see their faces.

"We're good. We just saw you a few hours ago. What's going on?"

"I wanted to tell you that Piper and I are starting to get close. How would you and Dad feel about meeting her? She wants me to meet her parents, so we thought we could do both on Christmas day. What do you think?"

The other line was silent, and Gillian thought they'd lost their connection. "Mom? Are you still there?"

"Yes, honey. Sorry. I think we would like to meet her. What do you have in mind?"

"Are you sure? You seem hesitant."

"No, no, I'm sure. I knew this day would come eventually, but it'll be different to see you with someone other than Kate."

"You mean strange?" Gillian knew that would be a possibility. She'd been a part of their life for so long, had loved their daughter for even longer.

"No, I mean different. Dad and I are glad you've found someone you enjoy spending time with. How does she feel about meeting us?"

"Piper has been great about everything. Almost too good to be true if I'm being honest. She asks questions about Kate, about our time together, about you and Dad, but there's no sense of jealousy, only curiosity. I feel like I've lucked out in meeting her." That was so true. She'd heard stories from friends about jealousy and possessiveness they'd experienced, but she'd never had that with Kate, and now she didn't have it with Piper.

"In that case, we look forward to it."

Gillian let out a sigh of relief and felt like she wanted to cry. After Kate, Harold and Gloria were the most important people in her life. She would never intentionally do anything to hurt them, so the fact they were open to meeting Piper was a huge weight off her shoulders. At least for now. The actual meeting might be something else.

"Thank you, Mom. I can't tell you how much that means to me."

"Aw, honey, no need to thank us. We love you so much and want nothing but the best for you."

They said their good-byes with the promise to talk later in the week, then a whole new wave of nervousness swarmed Gillian. Christmas was quickly approaching, and she thought that might be a good time to meet the families. She would have to talk to Piper about that to see what she thought. What would Piper's parents think about her? She also wanted to find a small gift to bring them. Then there was Piper's gift. She had a feeling she would like it, but she'd hoped Piper wouldn't think it was too much.

When Gillian and Kate were teenagers and beginning to fall in love, it was easier. They essentially had no money, so they'd make each other cards, or give each other some silly cheap gift. If they wanted to get really romantic, they'd make mixed tapes for each other, but that hadn't lasted long since cassettes were overrun by CDs in the early nineties. But then they'd just write down the lyrics to some love song on pretty paper with little doodles, and that would be equally loved. By the time they were adults making good money, they knew what the other wanted and could afford it.

After Gillian finished her cleaning and laundry, she called Piper to tell her what time she could come over. Gillian got busy prepping dinner. She'd cut up lettuce, cilantro, tomato, and onion, and she put them in small containers in the refrigerator. She then mixed masa with chicken broth and a little bit of flour, and pressed out corn tortillas ready to fry, and she cooked ground turkey as the filling. Once the meat was almost done, there was a knock on the door. She opened it to find Audrey standing there.

"Hey, what a nice surprise. What are you doing here?"

"I wanted to come by and apologize again for my behavior lately. Can I come in?"

"Sure." Gillian opened the door wider and stepped to the side so Audrey could enter.

"It sure smells good in here. What are you making?"

"Tacos."

"With your homemade corn tortillas?" At Gillian's nod, Audrey stepped further into the house. "Want company for dinner?"

Gillian closed the door and took a deep breath, not knowing what Audrey's reaction would be based on her recent behavior. "Actually, Piper is coming for dinner, but if you'd like to stay, I'll set another place. That way you can finally meet her." Gillian tried her best to sound inviting, but she wasn't sure how successful she was.

Audrey nodded as she pulled her lips in. "I see. Well, I don't want to be a third wheel and interrupt your date."

"Audrey." Gillian tried to reach for her, but Audrey pulled her arm away and left Gillian's home. She stared at the closed door and shook her head. "So much for your apology." What in the world was going on with Audrey? She'd never acted like that until Gillian had mentioned Piper's name, and that they'd started dating.

Not five minutes later, Piper arrived, and Gillian welcomed her in her arms. Being held by Piper, Gillian felt cared for and protected, and right then, it was everything she needed. Audrey had been Kate's best friend for almost ten years before Kate died. Audrey's behavior would be understandable if Kate was still alive, but she wasn't.

"Well, this is a lovely welcome. It smells great in here, by the way."

Gillian turned into Piper's neck and inhaled. Something about her arms around her and the scent of Piper's skin had enabled Gillian to almost forget Audrey. "You smell good." Gillian said before kissing Piper's neck up to her jaw, and finally her lips. Gillian took her time showing Piper how much she missed her today.

"Come join me in the kitchen. I have to cook the tortillas and beans, then we can eat." She placed the beans on low then handed Piper a glass of sparkling water with a lemon wedge at Piper's request. She took a small sample of taco meat and held it to Piper's mouth.

Piper took a bite and closed her eyes. "That's delicious."

Gillian turned on her electric skillet and placed two tortillas in to cook. "Can I get your opinion on something?"

"Of course." Piper leaned against the counter, far away enough to not get in Gillian's way, but close enough to give Gillian comfort.

"Kate's best friend, Audrey, is still a part of my life. She often joins my three closest friends and me for our girls' night out, and I love her as Kate's best friend. But ever since I told the girls that we were seeing each other, every time we're together, Audrey gets an attitude." She flipped the tortillas then looked at Piper who was watching the tortillas in the skillet, but Gillian could almost see the wheels turning in Piper's head. She'd learned in the time they'd been dating that Piper would think before speaking. Gillian placed the tortillas in the warmer, then added two more.

"Maybe she's jealous because she has feelings for you." Piper ended the statement with a shrug.

"That can't be. I've known her for ten years. She's never acted like that."

"I could be talking out of turn, but hear me out. She thought of you all these years as off-limits because of Kate. Once she passed, maybe she was waiting for an 'appropriate' amount of time"—Piper used her fingers for air quotes—"before asking you out. Maybe she was waiting for you to say that you were ready to start dating. Maybe she was working up the courage to ask you out. But then we started hanging out, getting to know each other, then we started dating. She missed her window of opportunity, and she's mad." Piper took a drink of her water but continued to hold Gillian's attention.

"You think she likes me? That's absurd." Gillian added two more tortillas then stirred the beans on the other side of Piper.

Piper grabbed Gillian's hips and moved her over a little bit so they were standing in front of each other. "Is it? Why wouldn't she like you? You're smart, kind, beautiful, and down-to-earth. Anyone would be crazy not to be attracted to you. I'm just the lucky one that you like back." Gillian rewarded Piper's compliment with a deep kiss.

"You think I'm beautiful?" Gillian smiled and blushed when she asked.

"Yep. And smart, kind, and down-to-earth in case you missed those descriptives. I feel so lucky that you want to spend time with me."

Gillian kissed Piper again then pressed her forehead against Piper's. "I feel the same way about you." Gillian kissed Piper once more before finishing up with the tortillas. "Would you mind pulling the glass containers out of the fridge and putting them on the counter? We'll fix our plates buffet style."

Once they'd plated their food and took a seat at the round cherry wood dining table that was big enough to seat six, they'd started eating.

"So, what brought this up? About Audrey." Piper asked between bites of her first of two tacos.

Gillian told her what had happened when they were at Heidi's and again right before Piper arrived. Piper nodded as Gillian relayed the incidents while Piper finished off her taco.

"Does Audrey date currently?"

"Yes, she's on a couple of dating sites."

"Have any of them stuck?"

Gillian took a moment to recall. "Last time we all got together, she said she'd had a first date that would turn into a second date. So, you might be wrong."

"Uh-huh. Or she might be biding her time waiting for you."

Gillian placed her spoon down for her beans, quickly losing her appetite. "But I'm not interested in her, and I don't believe I've ever given any indication that I was."

"Baby, it's okay. It's not your issue, it's hers. If you feel comfortable, you could talk to her about it. I just don't want her upsetting you over something that isn't in your control."

Gillian reached for Piper's hand. "You know I'm only interested in you, right?"

"I do, but I'll never get tired of hearing it." Piper took Gillian's hand and kissed it before letting it go. "Continue eating. These tacos are amazing, and you've ruined me for any other tacos."

Once they'd finished eating and cleaning the kitchen, they settled on the couch to watch a movie. Even though they'd been seeing each other for almost a month, to Gillian, that was domestic bliss.

"I talked to Gloria earlier, and she's looking forward to meeting you."

"Oh, good. Mom and Dad are excited to meet you too. I'd like to give your in-laws a gift. What do you suggest?"

Gillian laughed. "I was stressing out what to get your parents earlier. It's so hard when you're meeting the parents for the first time."

Piper laughed along with Gillian. "As for my parents, how about a bottle of sparkling wine? We can have mimosas with breakfast." They'd decided that they would go to Piper's parents' house for breakfast on Christmas morning, then head over to the Phillipses' in the early afternoon.

"Perfect. Maybe a bottle of bourbon for my family. They like to have a drink at night while watching TV."

"Is it strange to be excited and nervous at the same time? I mean, I'm meeting your wife's parents."

"No, it's not strange at all, but it's going to be a different parent meeting, you know? Kate was their only child, and they welcomed me into their family when I was just eighteen. Harold and Gloria are extraordinary humans, and as much as they miss Kate, they want me to be happy."

"They do sound extraordinary. I guess I just want them to like me, or at least accept me as the woman you're seeing."

"Baby, they're going to really like you, just like I do." Gillian had been lucky to find a lasting love so young in life, but could she be so blessed that it could happen again for her? She wasn't sure how it happened, but she'd been finally able to open her heart to someone else who happened to be just at the right time.

CHAPTER EIGHTEEN

The chime on the door alerted Piper to a new customer, but when she looked up, she saw it was her friend Mallory.

"So, there you are. I thought you skipped town or something since I haven't seen you in a while. Hey, Kelly."

Piper laughed as she came around the counter to hug her old friend. "I know, I know. I'm an awful friend. I've been really busy lately, but that's no excuse. I miss our happy hours."

"She's been busy with her new girlfriend," Kelly explained in a singsong voice. "How are you doing, Mallory?"

"Apparently not as good as my friend here. Tell me about her."

Piper brought over a stool for Mallory to have a seat behind the counter with Kelly and her. "Her name is Gillian, and we've been dating for a little while. She's a curator at one of the Smithsonian museums, and she took a few pottery classes from me, which is how we met."

Mallory raised an eyebrow and looked around Piper to Kelly, and Kelly's own eyebrows moved up and down rapidly which made Piper roll her eyes. "Your pottery student, eh?"

Piper nudged Mallory. "Anyways, I really like her, and she seems to like me, but we're taking things slow, getting to know each other." The chime rang again, and Piper could feel her smile grow. "Speak of the devil, and the devil shall appear."

"Who do you think you're calling the devil?" Gillian came around the counter to where Piper was, and she greeted Gillian with a chaste kiss.

"I was just telling my friend about you. Gillian, this is my friend Mallory. Mal, this is Gillian."

Gillian offered her hand to Mallory, but she playfully slapped it away and gave Gillian a hug. The surprised look Gillian gave Piper made her chuckle. Once Mallory let Gillian go, she went and hugged Kelly. "What did Piper say about me?"

"Only that you've been dating a little while and how you met. I came by because Piper and I usually do happy hour on Wednesday nights, but she's been too busy to meet up. Now I know why." Mallory wiggled her eyebrows, and it made everyone laugh.

"Piper, why didn't you tell me? I wouldn't mind if you kept your weekly date with Mallory."

Mallory placed her arm around Gillian and looked at Piper. "I think I might like her more than I like you. Hey, Gillian? Why don't you and I start having our own happy hour, and we can leave Piper and Kelly here to work?"

The blush that filled Gillian's cheeks made Piper want to take her into the studio, away from prying eyes, and kiss her senseless. God, she was gorgeous. How did Piper get so lucky that Gillian wanted to be with her?

"Hey, you keep your mitts to yourself, Mal." Piper winked so Mallory knew she was kidding. "I promise to resume our weekly gathering after the holidays."

"I'll hold you to that. I gotta get going. I just wanted to stop in and surprise you." Mallory hugged Piper, Kelly, and Gillian before she started for the door. "It was really nice to meet you, Gillian. Feel free to join us anytime you like. Same to you, Kelly. I'll call you soon, Piper."

They all waved as Mallory left. "She's nice. How do you know each other?"

Piper kissed Gillian's cheek, finding it more and more difficult to keep her hands and lips to herself whenever Gillian was in her proximity. "We used to work together. She's a great lady and a great friend. Maybe after the holidays, we can have a gathering with your friends and mine."

"I'd love that. My friends are eager to meet you, but I want to keep you to myself for a little while longer."

"Aw, you two are so sweet, I think I might get cavities." Kelly stuck her finger in her mouth and pretended to get sick.

"Just for that, you can lock up. Gillian and I are going upstairs to have dinner." Piper kissed Kelly on the cheek then grabbed Gillian's hand and led her up the stairs to her apartment. "I made a small pan of chicken enchiladas this morning, so all I have to do is pop it in the oven for a little bit, and I'll make a salad, as well."

"I love that you're cooking for me. Even more, I love that you love Mexican food as much as I do."

"I mean, how can I say no to cheese, chips, and salsa?" They were met by Agnes, who started meowing the moment the door opened. "Yes, I know you're hungry. I'll get your food together right now, your highness."

Piper tended to Agnes then turned on the oven for the enchiladas. "Honey, you can turn on the TV if you want. I'm just going to make a salad really quick, then I'll join you."

Piper cut up the lettuce and vegetables then placed the bowl of salad in the fridge. All she could think about was joining Gillian on the couch, which helped put a pep in her step. She poured Gillian a glass of wine. She kept a couple of her favorite bottles on hand for nights like this. She took the glass of wine and water for her and joined Gillian on the couch. She tapped her glass to Gillian's. "Here's to us."

"To us." Gillian took a sip then placed her glass on the coffee table. "Come here." Gillian took Piper's face in her hands and pressed her lips to Piper's. She'd been thinking about kissing Piper all day long, making it a very long day, indeed. It was almost like Piper's lips had become Gillian's drug, and she was completely addicted to them. Gillian pressed Piper onto her back on the couch and lay on top of her. Their kiss deepened, Piper moved her tongue with Gillian's, and Gillian could feel her pelvis begin to move against Piper's. She let out a whimper as she felt her clit swell and her panties get wet. She slid her hand under Piper's shirt and traced her fingers along her smooth skin until she reached Piper's breast, and she squeezed her nipple between her index finger and her thumb. Piper moaned, and it encouraged Gillian to go further.

She moved the shirt up to expose one of Piper's bra-covered breast, and she bit her erect nipple. A noise that sounded like a raging river rushed through her head as she sucked harder, making Piper buck under her. She wanted to strip them of their clothing and properly attend to Piper's breasts and her center. Piper's hands gently pushed her away, leaving Gillian breathing hard and discombobulated.

"What's wrong?" Gillian had difficulty getting her words out through her gasps.

"The oven. Dinner. The timer went off and dinner's ready."

Gillian sat up and gathered her hair behind her neck and tried to calm her breathing. "Yes, dinner. Right."

"Sorry, baby. Let me just take out the enchiladas, turn off the oven, and I'll come right back. We can resume where we left off."

Gillian let out a deep breath. "No, that's okay. I'm famished, so dinner sounds really good right now." Eating enchiladas would give them time to cool down and recover their normal breathing. Gillian almost felt like a teenager again with her make out sessions with Piper. She was glad they were waiting to sleep together, but it might be getting close, otherwise Gillian would go crazy with need.

Piper cupped her cheek and kissed her sensually, slowly. "Are you sure?"

"Ha! No, I'm not sure, but it's probably for the best right now. You just drive me crazy when you kiss me, that I don't want to stop, and it makes me want to do a lot more."

Piper kissed her again, a kiss that ratcheted up Gillian's libido, and she was about to tell Piper to just turn off the damn stove and return to the couch so she could finish what she started.

"I promise, when the time comes, it will be worth the wait."

Piper's words to God's ears, Gillian thought as she followed Piper into the kitchen to plate their food. If they didn't make love soon, Gillian thought they might just spontaneously combust. But what a way to go.

CHAPTER NINETEEN

Piper pulled into Gillian's driveway on Christmas morning. The sky was gray, the air was frigid, and there was a fresh dusting of snow on the ground. It was a white enough Christmas, and her first with Gillian. Her second with Kate's heart. She needed to tell Gillian about being the recipient of Kate's heart, but she hadn't found the right time. She promised herself she'd do it before the new year. She grabbed the box that Kelly was nice enough to wrap because if left to her own devices, the gift would've looked like it was wrapped by a five-year-old. Kelly also wrapped the gift she would give to the Phillipses'. Piper owed Kelly for being so creative with gift-wrapping. She rang the doorbell and waited for her girlfriend to answer the door. The word wasn't something she'd thought she'd ever use again for herself, but she was ecstatic she was wrong about that. She was also grateful for having a persistent and meddling family that pushed her into asking Gillian out. When Gillian answered the door, Piper felt her insides grow warm. That gorgeous woman standing before her was her girlfriend, and she felt damn lucky.

"Merry Christmas, sweetheart. Come in before you catch yourself a cold."

Piper handed Gillian her gift. "You look amazing." Piper felt she had to say the obvious before she wrapped her arms around Gillian and kissed her. The kiss lasted forever, or probably just a minute, but Piper wanted it to continue. If they hadn't had such a big day planned, Piper would be content to sit on the couch making out with her *girlfriend*. It was crazy to Piper how hard she'd fallen for Gillian in such a short amount of time. She'd like to believe it was all her doing and not because she had Kate's heart. "Merry Christmas to you."

"I'm ready to go unless you wanted to open your gift first."

"Mmm, I think we should open them when we get back. That way we can take our time."

Gillian kept her arms around Piper's neck and leaned back. "I really like that idea of taking our time."

Piper felt her entire body heat at the double entendre, and her imagination went to a place where it had no business being now before they met each other's parents. "I can't wait."

Gillian grabbed a nice bottle of sparkling wine with a red bow tied around the neck off the entryway table once she returned from placing the gift Piper brought her on the coffee table.

Piper whistled. "That's a really nice gift right there." Piper pointed to the bottle she knew to be pretty pricey. "They're going to love it." Piper held the bottle so Gillian could put on her coat, and they made their way to Piper's car.

Piper had a station on that was playing Christmas music, and Gillian sang along to some of the words. Piper joined in even though she had a terrible singing voice, but what the hell? So far, it was a great day. "Hey, Gillian, what do you call Santa when he stops moving? Santa Pause." Piper shimmied her shoulders as she resumed singing and Gillian laughed. Once they regained their composure, they spent the rest of the drive talking about their Christmas Eves with their respective families.

When they finally arrived at Piper's parents' house, she spied them peeking out the living room window. She nudged Gillian and pointed to the window. "Aren't they subtle?"

Gillian laughed and placed her hand on Piper's thigh. "I think it's cute. Come on, I'm excited to meet them."

Piper met Gillian on the sidewalk and held her hand as they made their way to the front door. The door opened once they reached the stoop, showing how excited her parents were to meet

Gillian. They'd been wanting Piper to find someone to spend her life with, and even though they'd been together a short time, Piper could actually see that happening.

"Gillian, it's so nice to finally meet you. I'm Debra and this is Richard. Are you a hugger? Can I give you a hug?"

Gillian acted delighted as she smiled and accepted a hug from first Piper's mom, then her dad.

"I come bearing gifts. Piper said a bottle of sparkling wine could be used for mimosas with breakfast."

"Wonderful. Let's come in and get acquainted."

Piper led Gillian to the couch in the living room followed by her dad. Her mom joined them after she'd put the bottle in the refrigerator. Piper had warned them to not get too personal. She had already told them about Kate and about her having Kate's heart. The only other person who knew was Kelly, and she'd made her swear not to tell Drew. He was the biggest gossip of her family, and if he knew, it wouldn't be long before the others knew what he knew.

"Piper tells us you're a museum curator at one of the Smithsonian museums. That must be very interesting and rewarding."

Piper squeezed Gillian's hand and silently thanked her dad for the softball question.

"That's right. I've been doing it for quite a while, but I really love the creativity it gives me. I also work with a lot of wonderful and talented people."

"Piper said you took some pottery classes from her. She tried to teach us, but we were awful. We have no idea where she got her artistic ability." Piper's mom beamed at her like Piper was her pride and joy. Which she was. She already knew she was her mom's favorite and teased her siblings about it every chance she got.

"Piper is extremely talented. In fact, I scolded her shortly after we'd met because the price tags on her pieces of art were too low. As far as teaching pottery, she's an excellent instructor and very patient with us novices."

"Come on, you picked it up pretty quick." Piper addressed Gillian then her parents. "She has the ability and capability of being very good if she wants to stick with it."

The look Gillian gave her made Piper smile. Her cheeks and neck always turned red when given a compliment, as Piper learned early on when they'd first started dating.

Over a country breakfast of biscuits and gravy, scrambled eggs, bacon, sausage, and mimosas to wash it all down, they continued to get to know each other, and Piper couldn't have asked for a better first meeting. Gillian had asked Piper's parents how they met, how long they'd been married, and they talked about Piper's siblings and her childhood.

"She was very athletic growing up, playing soccer and softball. Did she tell you she went to college on a softball scholarship?"

"Why, no, she didn't." Gillian looked at her with a mock glare. "Holding out on me? You didn't tell me you played sports."

"That's because I don't anymore. I gave up playing to concentrate on art."

Piper's dad shook his head. "She was so much fun to watch play. If it wasn't for her heart, she'd probably still be playing recreationally."

Piper could feel the blood drain from her face, and she felt light-headed. God damn it. She didn't want to tell her just yet. She hoped Gillian didn't see the warning glare she'd given her dad.

"What's wrong with your heart?" The look of concern on Gillian's face made Piper want to cry. She didn't have any specific answers ready for her, and she struggled for an explanation.

"Nothing anymore. I had an illness that gave me some issues, but it's better now." She'd hoped that would appease Gillian because she really didn't want to tell her the entire truth in front of her parents, and especially before she went to meet Kate's parents. She shot her dad a look that told him to change the subject.

"Yeah, she's better now. And a terrific artist, don't you agree, Debra?"

"Oh, yes. Come with me, Gillian. Let me show you some of the pieces she's gifted us. I can show you some of her childhood pictures as well."

"Why do you hate me so much, Mom? Don't show her what I looked like when I was a kid. Gillian, believe me when I say I outgrew those hairstyles and braces." When they were out of earshot, Piper looked at her dad. "Dad! Why'd you say that? You know I haven't told her yet."

"I'm sorry, kiddo. I completely forgot. We were talking about sports, and my mouth just kept going."

"No more talk of my heart. I'll tell her about it soon." Piper needed to think of damage control in case Gillian asked her more questions about it.

"I promise, but you need to tell her, honey. You can't keep this from her."

"I know. I'm just waiting for the right time." Piper thought back to *all* of the right times she could have told Gillian, but she ended up chickening out.

When her mother and Gillian returned to the table, Piper decided to get back on the topic of art and steer the conversation away from herself.

"Mom, did Kelly happen to mention that Gillian talked a gallery owner friend of hers into getting Kelly a show?"

Gillian held up her hand. "All I did was show Elise some pictures of Kelly's paintings, and she agreed to a meeting with Kelly. She brought in some of her work, and Elise booked her on the spot."

"Yes, she did tell me. That was very kind of you to do that for her."

"I offered Piper a joint show, but she turned it down."

"Honey, why did you do that?"

"I don't know. I guess I wanted Kelly to have her own show and be in the spotlight. She deserves to have her own glory."

Gillian grabbed Piper's hand and looked at her adoringly. "You are so sweet. Is she always this sweet?"

"Hmm, sometimes, except when she gets together with her brothers and sister, then the gloves come off with all of them. They drive me crazy sometimes, but since I birthed them, I guess I have to put up with it."

They all laughed, and Piper hated to cut the visit short, but they had to be on their way to see Gillian's family.

At the door, Piper's mother hugged Gillian. "It was so nice to meet you, and we hope to see you again soon." She then hugged

Piper and whispered in her ear. "I really like her, and seeing the way you two look at each other brings me great joy, my love." They hugged Piper's dad, and they were on their way to the Phillipses'.

"So, what did you think?"

"Your parents are great. I felt right at home there, and they're very open and friendly. I see where you get your warm personality from."

"Thank you. Anything I should know about Harold and Gloria before we get there?"

"No, they're warm and open like your parents. You'll like them."

Piper popped a mint into her mouth, more to produce saliva to her Sahara Desert dry mouth. It had been a really, really long time since she'd met a lover's parents. But these weren't just any ordinary parents. These were the parents of Gillian's deceased wife. The woman whose heart beat inside her chest. Jesus! Could life get any more complicated?

When they arrived, they were greeted much like Piper's parents greeted them. "It's nice to meet you, Mr. and Mrs. Phillips. Merry Christmas." Piper handed a bottle of bourbon to Harold and the wrapped gift to Gloria.

"It's nice to meet you too, Piper. You didn't have to get us anything, and please call us Harold and Gloria. Come in, you two."

Just like at Piper's parents', they gathered in the living room. Piper wiped her hands nervously on her pants, trying to keep her palms dry. She knew how much Harold and Gloria meant to Gillian, and if they didn't like her, she wasn't sure if Gillian would stay with her. But also, because they were so special to Gillian, Piper wanted them to like her.

"Should we open the present now?" Gloria smiled at Piper, and it helped quell her nerves.

Harold turned the bottle over in his hand and looked contemplative. "I don't know. You don't think it's too early to drink?"

The eyeroll Gloria gave had them all laughing. "I meant this one," she said as she pointed at the wrapped box.

"Of course. I hope you like it."

Gloria carefully unwrapped the present while Gillian and Harold looked on. Piper hadn't told Gillian that she was giving her parents a piece of her pottery. It had been one of her favorites, and she didn't want to put it out in the store for purchase. But something told her that the vase should go to them, so she dusted it off, packed it carefully, and had Kelly wrap it. Now that she was in their living room, the vase would look wonderful in there.

Gloria removed the vase, and Gillian gaped at her. "Where have you been hiding that?"

"Piper, this is gorgeous. Did you make this?"

Piper nodded and turned to Gillian. "I've been holding onto it for something special. I didn't want it going to a stranger." She then turned to Harold and Gloria. "I know we just met, but Gillian has told me so much about you and Kate, I feel like I know you, and I wanted you to have it."

Gloria got up and gave Piper a hug, but not just a thank you hug. She held Piper close for a few moments, and Piper felt a lump form in her throat. When Gloria finally released her, Piper could see the wetness in her eyes. Harold smiled at Piper after he studied the vase.

"Really great work, Piper. We love it, and I know exactly where it should go." Gloria nodded, obviously on the same wavelength as her husband. He went to a built-in bookshelf in the corner of the living room that Piper hadn't noticed before. He rearranged some things that Piper couldn't see since he was standing in front of it. He stepped aside once he placed the vase down. Piper joined him and discovered the shelves were devoted to family pictures of Harold, Gloria, Kate, and Gillian. She picked up a picture of Kate that looked similar to one in Gillian's home. Piper placed her hand over her heart and tried to compose herself. She wondered how Harold and Gillian would react when they realized she had their Kate's heart.

"I'm honored. Truly," Piper said as she patted her heart and blinked back her tears.

"Whew, I don't know about anyone else, but I could use a glass of wine. Anyone else?" Piper, Gillian, and Harold raised their hands. "Harold, come help me bring glasses to the girls."

Once they were alone, Gillian kissed Piper on the cheek. "Are you all right? That was a very kind thing to do, sweetheart. For Dad to put it on the family shelf means they already like you."

"Trust me, I felt the significance of the placement. That's why I got so emotional." She felt her mouth quiver as she smiled. She never expected the emotions to hit her so hard, but there they were, and she'd own them like a damn warrior.

Harold and Gloria returned with four glasses of a deep red wine, and Piper immediately liked the taste of the Merlot that was handed to her. Harold held up his glass to toast.

"Merry Christmas, and welcome to our home, Piper. We hope this is the first of what will be many gatherings."

"Thank you. I look forward to it."

❖

Gillian and Piper returned to her home after what Gillian thought to be two very successful meetings with each other's parents. When Harold added the vase Piper gave them to the family shelves, she thought she'd lose it. She had to bite the inside of her cheek to keep from crying. She felt that was a sign of not only how special Gillian was to them, but that anyone she considered special, Harold and Gloria did too. Those shelves contained pictures that were mostly of her and Kate, but some of them had Harold and Gloria, or the four of them together. On the ride home, Piper said how much she liked them, but most of the time she was quiet, almost reflective. At least that's what she told Gillian. It had been a big day for them, and Gillian felt so much for Piper at that moment that she wanted tonight to be even more special. The emotions that ran through her made her want to weep for joy. She felt Kate looking over them all day, approving of everything that happened.

"Would you like some hot apple cider to drink while we open up our presents?"

"Oh, yes. That sounds delicious. You don't happen to have caramel ice cream syrup, do you? Put that on the rim, and it's like drinking a caramel apple."

Gillian shook her head and laughed. "As a matter of fact, I do. That's how I was going to make it. Kate and I used to drink it when we opened presents."

The look on Piper's face was the first time she'd shown any kind of emotion other than understanding when Kate's name was mentioned. Not that Piper had an indifference to Kate or their marriage, but she was always even-keeled. Now, she almost looked spooked.

"Honey, what's wrong?"

"Nothing really. Do you think about the things Kate and I have in common? Is it strange?"

"Sometimes I do. It freaked me out in the beginning, especially your love for pickles." Gillian smiled, and Piper felt a smidge better. "But it doesn't anymore. You and Kate have some similarities, but you're your own woman. One I like very much and am so grateful I met."

Gillian wrapped her arms around Piper who seemed to relax the longer they held each other. "I'm going to fix our cider, so go make yourself comfortable."

As Gillian moved around the kitchen, she wondered what was really bothering Piper. Sometimes she felt like Piper was an open book, and there were times where it felt like she was holding something back. Bells should be clanging in her head and red flags should be flying, but they weren't. She was just going to have to trust her gut and her heart.

She entered the living room to Christmas music on low and a few candles burning. It was a very romantic scene, and all her previous thoughts flew away like Santa Claus on his sleigh.

Piper took her mug and Gillian sat on the couch next to her. They clinked their mugs and took a sip.

"Merry Christmas, Gillian. This has been a wonderful day."

"I agree, sweetheart. And the night is only beginning." The smile on Piper's face and the gleam in her eyes made Gillian set both mugs down and take Piper in her arms and kiss her like there'd be no tomorrow. Gillian had intentions, and it involved a lot of kissing, even more touching, and naked bodies.

"Let's open the presents first, then I have another one for you to open in the bedroom."

Piper's eyes went narrow and dark. "Let's open these now so we can get to the other in your room."

Gillian handed Piper a flat box that was medium sized. Piper unwrapped the gift and opened the box to find a framed print of Georgia O'Keeffe's *Red Canna*. Piper had mentioned to Gillian while at the museum that O'Keeffe was her favorite artist and that she loved *Red Canna of 1924* because of the shades of orange, red, yellow, and lavender that just seemed to burst like fire and flames.

"Oh, Gillian, this is beautiful. This is my favorite O'Keeffe."

"I know. You mentioned it when we were at the museum, but the time you spent standing in front of the original, explaining how it made you feel alive and that you wanted to live life to the fullest. I figured this would be a good reminder to do just that."

Piper placed the print down on the table and took Gillian's face in her hands before she placed a passionate kiss on Gillian's lips, and nearly saw stars from the intensity. Gillian eased up and tried to get her senses back to normal.

"Okay, your turn." Piper handed the gift to a still dazed Gillian who needed a moment to gather her wits and realize what was going on. She opened the present and she pulled the vase from the box that Piper had showed her the previous week, but wasn't finished yet. The vase was painted in different hues of green, blue, and gray that all blended into each other, and it truly took Gillian's breath away.

"Were these the colors you imagined for this piece?"

"Yes, sort of. But what you did with them exceeded my imagination. You're an absolute artistic genius with pottery, painting, colors, and glazing. I couldn't have asked for a more beautiful gift."

"Not more beautiful than you, Gillian. These past weeks have been incredible, and so much more than I could've imagined."

Gillian stood and held out her hand for Piper to take. She led them upstairs to her bedroom and turned on the lamp on her nightstand. She returned to Piper, took her in her arms, and kissed her. She tilted her head, and when she opened her mouth to accept Piper's tongue, she felt a flood of wetness immediately in her underwear. It was a regular occurrence whenever she and Piper kissed and touched each other. The butterflies in her stomach felt like they were about to take off and carry her with them. Gillian moved her hands along Piper's back under her sweater and over her smooth skin. The nerves threatened to take Gillian over. She'd never had sex with anyone other than Kate, and tonight would change that. She wanted Piper to make love to her. It was time for both of them to take their relationship to the next level. Her parents' approval was almost the equivalent of giving her permission to move on. She'd never forget Kate, but tonight was the time to further her relationship with Piper.

She took the hem of Piper's sweater and lifted until Piper raised her arms and allowed Gillian to discard the sweater. She stepped back to take Piper in, and that's when she saw the long vertical scar along Piper's sternum. She held her hand out, afraid to touch it, knowing the feel of scar tissue would make it real.

"Piper? What is this?"

Piper had a decision to make. Be vague about having surgery, or go into detail about what really happened. At the moment, she chose what she felt was right.

"I had an infection in my heart, and I needed surgery to fix it. But I'm fine now. I follow my doctor's orders, I take medicine to keep it healthy, and I eat a mostly healthy diet. It's nothing to worry about, honey. I promise."

Gillian traced the scar with her fingertips, the touch tentative and a slight look of fear on Gillian's face. Piper knew she needed to diffuse the situation.

"I didn't want to fall in love with a woman, and she with me if there was a possibility I could die. But Kelly reminded me that we never know how long we have, that even the healthiest person could die."

"Like Kate."

Shit. But Gillian wasn't wrong. Piper took Gillian's hand in hers and gave them a little shake. "Exactly. If you knew in the beginning that she would die in an accident, would that have deterred you?"

"No. I loved her and the life we spent together."

"Exactly. The important thing to remember is that you two had a lovely life together. I wish for your sake, and that of Harold and Gloria, that Kate hadn't died, even though it would've meant I'd never had the pleasure of knowing your kisses or your touch. I would never want you to go through that. But the point is that we're here now, alive, and I don't know about you, but you mean so much to me, and I'm really hoping our relationship continues to grow and blossom."

Gillian continued to hold Piper's hand and look her in her eyes, paying attention and taking in everything Piper was saying.

Gillian sighed. "You're right. We don't know how much time we have, but I also care so much about you that I want to continue to see where this goes."

Piper took Gillian into her arms and held her until she felt Gillian start to relax. "I believe it's my turn." Piper winked and slowly lifted Gillian's shirt over her head and added it to her own sweater on the floor. She then unbuttoned Gillian's trousers and slowly slid the zipper down, letting the pants pool at her feet. Gillian kicked them off after toeing off her shoes and stepping out of them. She then returned the favor for Piper, and once they were both naked except for their underwear and bras, they stepped back from each other and simultaneously took the other in.

"You're beautiful, Gillian, and this seems like a dream come true for me." Piper closed the distance and cupped the back of Gillian's head before her lips met Gillian's. She felt her heart rate increase and her legs grow weak. They moved their way to the bed, and Piper moved so she was on top of Gillian. "I feel like I've waited a lifetime for this moment with you."

Piper leaned in and kissed Gillian thoroughly. During that time, Gillian unhooked Piper's bra and she sat up enough to take it off. Gillian raised her hands to cup Piper's breasts, and when Gillian pinched her nipples, her underwear became damp. Piper hurriedly removed the article of clothing then removed Gillian's, and her scent hit Piper, making her mouth water. Piper pushed Gillian's bra up over her breasts, and she took a nipple into her mouth, lightly sucking and biting, making Gillian writhe under her. She took her time with one breast then the other. Piper kissed her way down Gillian's torso, going as slow as she could even though all she wanted in that very moment was to taste Gillian and bring her to climax.

She continued moving her way down, kissing and nibbling, and licking around Gillian's sex. Gillian started to squirm, encouraging Piper to take Gillian's swollen clit into her mouth and suck it in. She moved her mouth and tongue up and down Gillian's shaft, then moved lower to dip her tongue into Gillian's opening. In and out, thrusting in and out, then moving a little north to use her tongue to flick Gillian's clit. Gillian's moans made Piper pull Gillian's clit back into her mouth. When Gillian's hand went to the back of Piper's head, pulling her in closer and harder, Piper sucked Gillian in until her body froze, and she cried out Piper's name.

"Keep going, Piper. Keep going. God, that feels so good. You're going to make me come again."

Gillian's words urged Piper on until she was able to bring Gillian to a second orgasm. Once Gillian's clit softened in Piper's mouth, she kissed her way back up Gillian's body until her mouth met Gillian's. They spent a good amount of time kissing, Piper moving her tongue against and around Gillian's.

"That was amazing, baby. And if you give me a moment to recover, I'll gladly reciprocate."

Piper ran her fingers through Gillian's lustrous hair, kissed her forehead, each cheek, the tip of her nose, then finally her lips again. "Take your time, love. That was perfect and I don't mind reliving it in my mind."

Gillian laughed before latching her lips on Piper's neck, then licking a drop of sweat off her skin. Before Piper knew what was happening, Gillian flipped Piper onto her back and straddled her pelvis while removing her bra. She leaned down until her nipple was just above Piper's mouth. Gillian grabbed her breast and moved it around Piper's lips, teasing her, making her chase it until she was able to suck Gillian's nipple into her mouth. Gillian reached behind her and stroked Piper's sex while she moved her pelvis back and forth over Piper's lower stomach, coating her skin in her wetness. Piper moved her center, chasing Gillian's fingers.

"Baby, please don't tease me. I need to come."

Gillian's fingers entered Piper's sex, in and out, then spread more of her wetness over Piper's clit. Piper felt like she'd explode with a few more strokes, but Gillian moved her fingers back inside, curling her fingers upward. Piper's orgasm came barreling like a train exiting a tunnel at full speed.

"God, I'm coming."

When Piper cried out, Gillian came shortly after. Piper put her hand between her legs, squeezing her clit to bring out the rest of her orgasm as Gillian collapsed on top of her. Once her spasms ended, she let out a deep sigh, completely sated.

"I know this isn't the ideal time to ask this, but is Agnes okay?"

Piper burst out laughing, pulling Gillian closer to her. "She's spending the night with Rob and Julie. My niece, Samantha, adores Agnes for some reason. Her parents are contemplating getting a cat, but they're doing a test drive with Agnes. If Sam can make it through the night without torturing Agnes, then she might be in the running for her own cat."

"I hadn't really planned on us making love for the first time tonight, but it appears it was meant to be for them to take my cat for the night. I'm yours to do what you want." Piper spread her arms and legs, inviting Gillian to do whatever she wanted with her.

"Oh, the possibilities are endless."

Gillian moved down Piper's body, licking and kissing almost every damn inch of her skin, and Piper wasn't mad that she was taking it slow now. "Take your time, baby. We have all night."

Chapter Twenty

C̶an you take a look at these? The show's coming up, and I want to make sure they're decent." Kelly grabbed Piper by the hand and led her to a curtained off area in the studio where she had her latest canvasses. Piper took a careful study of the four pieces Kelly had created, lingering to take in the colors and shapes. She shook her head in awe of what her sister-in-law could create. She was so freaking talented. Kelly could create so much more than what Piper could imagine.

"They're perfect, sis. You're going to kill this show. Your time for fame is arriving at the station." Piper hugged Kelly, holding her tight and being so grateful that she had such a wonderful person in her life that wasn't just family, but also a great friend. "Elise will be thrilled."

"Thanks, Pipes. It's all I've been concentrating on lately. Thanks for picking up extra time at the store so I can paint."

"No problem. Anything I can do to help, I'm all in."

"How are things going with you and Gillian? How'd the family meeting go?"

Piper squinted her eyes and studied Kelly. "How did you know, and how much do you know? And more importantly, who else knows?"

Kelly laughed and patted Piper on her shoulder. "As far as I know, only me. Your mom knows you and I are close and that I know Gillian, as well. She told me that they absolutely loved her."

Piper relaxed and smiled. "Yeah, she's pretty incredible." Piper told Kelly about meeting Harold and Gloria, and how they placed her vase on the family shelf. That still choked up Piper when she thought about it. Kelly put her arm around Piper's shoulders but said nothing. Nothing needed to be said. Kelly knew everything and was the only one who did other than her parents.

"So, um, big news. Gillian and I spent the night together on Christmas night."

Kelly's mouth dropped along with her arm off Piper's shoulders. She blinked a few times before speaking. "There are so many things I want to ask, starting with how was it?"

Piper's heart felt like it swelled and grew warm. "Incredibly amazing. It was tender, loving, sexy, nonstop."

"Pipes, I'm so happy for you. I really like seeing you two together. So, the second question is, I suppose she saw your scar. How did you explain that?"

Piper looked away, unable to meet Kelly's eyes and tried to find something to divert her attention. "I told her I needed surgery to get better."

"Huh. So, you told her you got a transplant?"

"Uh, not exactly those words."

"Yeah, I got that. You need to tell her, Piper. The longer you keep it from her, once she finds out, it might not be something she could forgive you for. Are you willing to risk that?"

"No, and I know what you're saying. I promise I'll tell her soon. I think I might be falling in love with her, Kel. I don't want to lose her."

Kelly hugged Piper. "I hate to tell you this, sis, but you're already in love with her. And if I had to guess, she's right there with you. If you tell her now, there might be a chance that she'll be able to get over you holding that from her. I'm just stating my opinion, if Drew had withheld something from me, my ability to forgive would depend on why and for how long he kept the secret."

Piper nodded. She knew what she needed to do. "We're going to the parents' for the New Year's Eve party. You, Drew, and the boys are going, right?" It had been a long-standing tradition to have a party at their parents' on New Year's Eve. They did a pot luck, danced, and played games all night. There wasn't a better way to bring in the New Year than being with her loved ones.

"You know we wouldn't miss it. Even the boys are excited, and they don't get excited about being with the family." Kelly rolled her eyes and made Piper chuckle.

"Do me a favor and try and keep the siblings from rushing Gillian and overwhelming her. The Jameses can be a lot."

"True, but they're a good lot. They'll love her because you do."

"Not to mention the fact that she's absolutely wonderful. She's perfect for me, and I can't believe how lucky I am that she likes me too."

"Don't underestimate yourself, Pipes. You're a pretty great catch yourself, so the two of you are both deserving of each other."

"Have I ever told you that Drew totally married up? You're a saint to put up with him." Piper knew Kelly knew she was joking because she loved all of her siblings.

"All right, let's get to work. Time to open shop."

❖

Piper pulled the chicken breasts out of the oven as Gillian knocked then let herself in.

"It smells great in here."

Piper placed the tray on the stove and removed the oven mitts before kissing and hugging Gillian.

"Mmm, you smell good." Piper kissed Gillian's neck and nipped at the skin just below her earlobe, making Gillian squirm and giggle.

"Flatterer." Gillian grabbed Piper's face and kissed her like she missed her. "Do we have to eat now, or can the food wait?"

Piper smiled against Gillian's lips. "What did you have in mind?"

"Well, I'm hungry for you. Does that suit you?"

Piper laughed and led Gillian to her bedroom. "Why, yes. Yes, it does."

They'd seen each other just yesterday, but now that they'd made love, they were hungrier for each other and couldn't get enough of each other. They'd rid each other of their clothes before falling onto Piper's bed. Once they were naked, Piper took her time worshipping every inch of Gillian's gorgeous curves and smooth skin. As she got closer to Gillian's sex, Piper's mouth watered at the thought of tasting her. Piper teased Gillian's clit with her tongue and sucked it into her mouth until it grew hard. Gillian placed her hand on the back of Piper's head, but she had no intention of leaving until she brought Gillian to climax. She took her time teasing Gillian, sucking, stroking her with her tongue, kissing around her clit, and sucking her back in. Every time Piper felt Gillian on the precipice, she pulled back, wanting to make it last. She knew her torture would be returned, but if it was up to Piper, she'd remain where she was for hours.

"Stop teasing me and let me come." Gillian's voice was husky and strained, and Piper didn't know if she'd ever heard anything sexier. Gillian's need and demand spurred Piper on to finally bring Gillian to orgasm when she slid two fingers into Gillian's opening while she stroked her clit from base to tip. Gillian screamed out and grabbed Piper's hair to pull her in closer, then pushed her away when she couldn't take anymore.

Piper climbed back up and held Gillian in her arms, peppering her face with kisses as Gillian recovered. The mixture of Gillian's scent of her skin and the smell of sex made Piper crave more of her. She moved her lips to Gillian's and took her time thoroughly kissing her, making them both moan from pleasure.

"That was amazing, Piper, but remember that saying about paybacks, because you're about to get yours."

The chicken long forgotten, they spent the rest of the night in bed pleasuring and loving each other, and Piper couldn't have wanted anything more. Food meant nothing to her when she had a gorgeous, incredible woman in bed next to her, curled into her side, warm and sated. Since Gillian had taken the week off from work between Christmas and New Year, they were able to enjoy being with each other every night. Piper fell asleep knowing she could really get used to that.

CHAPTER TWENTY-ONE

Piper knocked on Gillian's door and was taken aback when she answered wearing a deep burgundy sweater and black trousers. The sweater was tight enough to show off all her delicious curves but respectable enough to wear around children, which is what she'd be in the company of that night. Gillian was about to meet every single member of Piper's family, and Piper knew that everyone would absolutely adore her. But still, her palms were wet and her heart raced. She knew everything would be fine, but that would be a very important night.

Piper wrapped her arms around Gillian before kissing her hello. "You look beautiful. Maybe my parents would excuse us for not attending their party, and we could have our own little private party here." Piper kissed her again while moving her hands down to squeeze her ass.

Gillian laughed as she playfully pushed Piper away. "Not on your life. I finally get the chance to meet all of your family. I'm not wasting my opportunity to learn every cute thing you did as a child growing up."

They arrived at the Jameses' house with music playing and loud voices as Piper opened the door. She turned to Gillian. "Are you sure about this? It's not too late to change your mind."

Gillian cupped Piper's cheek and leaned in for a chaste kiss. "I'm looking forward to bringing in the new year with you and your family, so stop being a chicken."

"Okay, you asked for it. But quickly, why does the person who runs Times Square feel like a failure? He always drops the ball." She grabbed Gillian's hand and pulled her into the living room with the sound of Gillian's laughter following them. "Okay, you turkeys. The party can get started!"

Piper and Gillian were swarmed by all of the James family. Greetings were delivered to Gillian like she'd been part of their lives for years instead of meeting most of them for the very first time. Debra and Richard hugged Gillian and whisked her away from Piper, introducing her to Piper's siblings, their spouses, and kids. The whole debacle took about twenty minutes before she was able to hand Gillian a glass of Merlot. She clinked her own glass to Gillian's. "Happy New Year, honey."

"Almost, but it's looking good. Can I request a kiss from you at midnight to bring in the new year?"

"Always. I look forward to it and more."

They sat on the couch and watched all the kids participate in a dance competition that wasn't really a competition at all because they always received the same score cards of "ten" that all of the adults held up, thrilling the younger kids that they could earn the same score as their older cousins.

Piper left Gillian on the couch so she could fix them a plate of food. She smiled when she found Samantha sitting on Gillian's lap, fiddling with her necklace.

"Are you Aunt Piper's girlfriend?"

Gillian laughed at the unguarded curiosity of Piper's youngest niece, Samantha. "Yes, I am. Did she tell you about me?"

Sam shook her head, not looking at Gillian, obviously more interested in the necklace she was wearing. "My momma and poppa talk about you, and I hid so they couldn't see me, but I heard them. I'm glad you're Aunt Piper's girlfriend. You're pretty."

Gillian placed her hand on Samantha's tiny back and rubbed it. "Thank you. I think you're very pretty too. And very nice."

"Aunt Piper got a new heart. Did you know that?"

"Really? I didn't know she got a new heart. I knew that her heart was sick but got better."

Samantha nodded. "She was really sick. I heard Momma tell Poppa that if she didn't get a new heart, she would have died. I cried because she's the best aunt, and she tells funny jokes."

Gillian felt almost sick to her stomach that Piper had been so sick, but also that she'd kept that from her. In her opinion, that would have been something very important to know. She took a deep breath to quell the nausea. "Yes, I think her jokes are very funny too. Do you remember when Piper got her new heart?" Gillian's own heart was racing as if she was about to receive a devastating blow. Why didn't Piper tell her she received a new heart? She told her she had a bad heart, that she had surgery, and now it was better. But that's different than having an actual new heart. She had a sudden desire to run and find Piper and demand she tell her everything.

Samantha nodded. "It was Thanksgiving. I promised to save dessert for her when she came home with her new heart. She told me she'd never miss another holiday because of the special person who gave her the heart."

Samantha jumped from Gillian's lap when Piper returned and handed the plate to Gillian. Samantha took advantage of Piper's empty lap and hopped up into Piper's arms. Sam's little arms wrapped around Piper's neck.

"I see you met my favorite six-year-old. You weren't telling Gillian stories about me, were you?"

Samantha nodded, making Piper laugh. "I told her that you got a new heart so you can have lots of holidays with us."

Gillian swore she could see the blood drain from Piper's face, making her more curious to find out exactly what happened. If what Samantha said was true, why didn't Piper tell her she received a new heart instead of just telling her that she had surgery? When Piper had told her about her heart surgery on Christmas night before they made love, Piper made it sound like it was a procedure like an ablation or something. Receiving a donor heart was a lot different. Extremely serious. And Samantha said it happened at Thanksgiving, but what year?

Gillian lowered her voice and leaned closer to Piper. "I think we have to have an honest conversation later."

When Piper closed her eyes before giving a slight nod, Gillian knew there was going to be a heavy shoe dropping later.

❖

Stupid, stupid, stupid. Kelly warned her, she kept telling her she needed to be honest with Gillian about her heart. Piper had planned on telling her soon. What she hadn't planned on was her six-year-old niece spilling the beans before she had a chance. That wasn't true. She'd had plenty of chances, she'd just been too chicken. Well, the time had come. Piper only hoped Gillian would forgive her for keeping that from her. As if mutually agreed upon, they both kept up a good and friendly front for the sake of Piper's family. But the longer it festered with her throughout the night, the more stressed she felt. Finally, Piper quietly talked to her mom and told her the short version of what happened.

"I think we should go so Gillian and I can talk about this, but I want to try to sneak out of here before anyone realizes."

Piper's mom hugged her. "I hope for both of your sakes that you can figure out if you indeed have Kate's heart, and that you can both move forward together."

"I hope so too, Mom. And thanks for your help."

A few minutes later, Piper's mom called everyone into the family room so she could say a few things. That gave Piper and Gillian the opportunity to slip out without anyone noticing. She felt awful for leaving without saying good-bye to her family, but that would have to take a back seat to how she felt for withholding vital information from Gillian.

It was a very quiet, very long ride back to Gillian's. She tried to ask a few questions, but Piper explained to her that she'd prefer to wait until they got back to her place so she could give Gillian her full attention, which was the least she could do.

Once they were seated in the living room each with a glass of water, Piper started one of the hardest conversations she'd ever had.

"I wasn't completely honest with you about my heart condition." Keeping eye contact with Gillian when Piper felt ashamed was hard.

Damn hard. "At first, my reason for withholding that information was that I didn't want to bring that to the table when we were first getting to know each other. In fact, I hadn't planned on getting involved with anyone because I didn't think it was fair to the other person when I didn't know how long my life would be. Then I met you, and you took my breath away. I was instantly attracted to you, and I wanted to get to know you better. Then you told me about Kate, and I especially didn't want to have you go through losing anyone else. But the more I got to know you, the more I liked you, the more afraid I got to tell you in case you didn't want to be with someone who had a heart transplant."

"Piper, I can understand how that would frighten you, but did you ever take me and my feelings into consideration? How I would feel that the first woman I started dating after my wife died would have an increased chance of dying early as well?"

"I did, I promise. But I talked to Kelly about it, and she said that none of us knew how much time we had, even the healthiest of people."

"So, you talked to Kelly about this?"

Piper nodded, and Gillian's face grew red. That couldn't be good. "What I really need to tell you is so hard." Piper took a big drink of water, only prolonging the inevitable. The huge lump in her throat was making it impossible to swallow the water, and it ended up going down the wrong pipe, making her cough. Once her fit was over, she tried again. "I received my donor's heart the day after Thanksgiving two years ago. I think I have Kate's heart."

Gillian shook her head and blinked several times. "I'm sorry. What did you say?"

"I mean, it tracks, right? Her organs were harvested the day after Thanksgiving, and I went in for surgery that night. I was having Thanksgiving dinner the actual day after with my family when I got the call. I honestly thought that would be my last holiday with them, I was so sick. And when I was in the hospital getting prepped, I had so many mixed emotions—I felt hopeful for my health to get better, and I'd be able to live a lot longer, but I also grieved for my donor and their family."

Gillian got up and paced the living room, muttering to herself so low, Piper didn't know what she was saying. Gillian stopped in front of the fireplace, picked up their wedding picture, and stared at it with her back to Piper. Piper wrung her fingers, waiting for Gillian to say something.

Gillian placed the frame back on the mantel and turned to face Piper. "Is that all the proof you have?"

Piper shrugged and held out her hands. "I mean, there's my love for dill pickles in macaroni and cheese, which is a new development."

"You also like grape juice, which is way less common than orange, apple, and grapefruit juice."

Piper stayed silent and let Gillian work it out in her head. The longer Gillian stayed quiet the faster Piper's heart raced. "I wrote a letter to the donor's family, but I had to send it to the donor organization, so I don't know what happened to it." Finally, Gillian looked at her.

"Would you mind giving me some time? I have a lot to process and think about."

"Of course." Piper placed her arms on her legs and grabbed her head. How could she let that happen? Why didn't she just tell Gillian in the beginning and laid everything on the table before she started falling for Gillian.

"Piper."

Piper looked up, hoping to see forgiveness in Gillian's warm brown eyes.

"Could you please leave? I need time by myself."

"Oh, yeah, of course." Piper stood and started to go to Gillian to kiss her good night, but Gillian's body language told her a kiss would definitely not be welcome at that point. Piper hung her head as she headed to the door and donned her coat. She took one last look at Gillian, afraid that that might be the last time she ever saw or spoke to one of the most remarkable women she'd ever had the pleasure of knowing. And loving.

CHAPTER TWENTY-TWO

The moment Piper left, Gillian went directly to her bedroom and took out a large envelope out of her nightstand. It contained notes and letters from some of the recipients of Kate's organs. Her hands shook as she took them out and held them in her lap. She hadn't read any of them, fearing it would rip her heart right open. Harold and Gloria had read them then placed them in the envelope for Gillian if she ever wanted to read them. She shuffled through the pages, interested only in one particular letter at that time. Piper's name appeared on one of the pages, and Gillian gasped. Her pulse raced as she placed the other letters on her bed.

My name is Piper, and because of your loved one's generous donation, my diseased heart was replaced with a healthy one. I had an illness that infected my heart, and I was in heart failure. I wanted you to know how much I appreciate you and your family, and I will say a prayer for you every day.

I wanted to tell you a little about myself. I'm the third of five kids in my family, and I have five nephews and nieces. I love art and creating it. Prior to me being in heart failure, I used to teach art at a community college. I'm not sure if I'll go back to teaching when I'm fully recovered or do something else, but I now have the opportunity to decide. I promise I won't take one day for granted, and I will give thanks to you and your loved one every day. Thank you again, and I wish you peace.

By the third time reading the letter, Gillian's tears fell freely down her cheeks. She grabbed a tissue off the nightstand and blew her nose. How was it possible that the one woman she wanted to date actually had Kate's heart? How would she tell Harold and Gloria? The day they agreed to donate Kate's organs came rushing back to Gillian's thoughts.

Gillian, Harold, and Gloria hadn't left Kate's bedside all night, and they were present when the doctors performed more tests to conclude that Kate was, in fact, brain dead. Gillian sat next to the bed holding Kate's hand. Her skin was still warm. She could still feel the pulse in her wrist. It didn't seem right that her heart was still beating, but she was clinically dead. She knew Kate's heart was still beating because of the respirator. The doctor told her they'd keep her on it to keep the oxygenated blood flowing to her organs. The beeping of the machine and whooshing sound of the respirator had become white noise to her in the otherwise quiet private room.

Gillian looked out the window to see the sun starting to rise, starting a new day, Gillian's first day of the rest of her life that she'd have to live without the love of her life.

"Mom, Dad, are we sure about this?"

Harold and Gloria sat on the opposite side of the bed holding Kate's other hand. They both continued to look at her barely recognizable face, covered in abrasions and bruises, but nodded their agreement. Gillian pushed the nurse's call button, and when the nurse entered the room, Gillian asked her to get the doctor. When he finally arrived, Gillian told him they were ready to say good-bye. They'd actually never be ready, but the longer they waited might put someone else's life in jeopardy. Gillian stood, followed by Harold and Gloria. She cupped the sides of Kate's face and studied it one last time. She pressed her lips to Kate's forehead and let them linger. That would be the last time she'd ever kiss her wife.

"I love you so much, and I will always love you. Thank you for the love and life you gave me. Until we meet again, my love, you will always be in my heart." She waited for Kate's parents to say good-bye then gathered to hug each other and mourn. Once outside the room, the doctor spoke to them quietly and again explained what the next step would be.

"I'm very sorry about Kate, but from the bottom of my heart, thank you for donating her organs. You'll help a lot of people because of that. Someone from the hospital will be in touch with you to help you through this. In the meantime, I want to ask you to stay with her for now. When we take her to the operating room, I'd like for you all to go with us."

Gillian nodded, and the three of them walked back into the room and took their previous places. She had no idea why the doctor would want them to accompany them, but she was grateful to have just a little more time with her wife. Sometime later, Gillian wasn't sure how long because time had just seemed to stop, the doctor came in with a few more people, all with serious looks on their faces.

"Ms. Phillips, Mr. and Mrs. Phillips, it's time." Gillian nodded, and she stood off to the side with her in-laws as the doctor had suggested. They released the brakes on the gurney and wheeled Kate out to the hallway with Gillian, Harold, and Gloria following behind. When they turned the corner, there were so many people lined up against the walls, most dressed in scrubs. The doctor turned to them. "When we have a donor like Kate, we like to honor them and their family for their generosity, to let them know how important of a decision they had to make during an indescribable time in their life. From all of us, thank you." All of the hospital personnel that lined the walls began clapping, some with tears in their eyes, as they guided Kate's gurney down the hall, to the operating room where Kate would save or help other people. Gillian and Gloria hooked their arms through Harold's as they followed Kate down the hall. When they reached the doors, they stopped and allowed Kate's family to say good-bye for the last time.

Gillian kissed Kate's hand. "I love you. I've always loved you, and I always will. Thank you for being the best wife, the best friend, the best everything to me."

They wheeled her through the doors, and just like that, Kate was gone.

Gillian sat on her bed holding a framed picture of her wife, rocking back and forth while crying. She had a difficult time reconciling that her wife's heart was inside the woman who was now her girlfriend. That might explain why there were things Piper did that reminded her so much of Kate. That wasn't what attracted her to Piper though. Her looks, sure, but also her love for art, her kindness, and how could she forget her corny jokes? But the fact remained that Piper knew, and she kept it from her. Lying wasn't something Gillian would tolerate from anyone, but especially her girlfriend.

She needed to tell her in-laws about what she learned. The letter from Piper to the donor's family confirmed that she guessed right. She would have to wait until the morning since it was way past midnight. In the beginning of the evening, Gillian felt hopeful of where things were going with Piper. She was meeting her entire family, and they were going to bring in the New Year with a kiss and end the night by making love. Instead, she would end the night falling asleep in her clothes on her bed clutching the picture of Kate to her chest. *If* she could fall asleep.

The next morning, Gillian took a quick shower, threw on some sweats and a baseball hat, totally abnormal attire when she was leaving her house, but at this point, she just didn't care. She didn't feel she could put off the conversation she needed to have with her in-laws for even a minute. She quickly knocked on the door before entering just to give them a head's up that she was there. When she walked into the house, it was still dark. Gillian hadn't bothered to pay attention to the time, but their grandfather clock that had been in their family for generations showed it was only seven thirty. She had to admit that that was pretty early, especially on New Year's Day. She made herself at home and started a pot of coffee while she rummaged through their cabinets and refrigerator. She'd decided to make breakfast rather than sit idly by thinking about Piper having Kate's heart beat inside her chest.

Gillian pulled the biscuits out of the oven, plated the bacon, and turned off the burner that cooked scrambled eggs. She poured herself a second cup of coffee and had her back to Gloria when she came in.

"Honey, what's going on?"

Gillian gasped and hot coffee splashed on her hand, and she set the now half empty cup on the counter before holding her hand under cold running water. She turned around to see Gloria dressed in a house coat with a worried look on her face. Coming over that early in the morning was unusual, and it must have worried her. That was the last thing Gillian wanted to do, but she was flying blind with her feelings. Gillian burst into tears, finally releasing the feelings of conflict she'd felt since Piper left the night before. She practically ran into Gloria's arms.

"Honey, what is it?"

Gillian sobbed while Gloria held her tight. When she was finally able to catch her breath, she told Gloria what she'd learned last night. "On Christmas night, I saw a scar that ran down Piper's chest. When I asked her about it, she said she had to have heart surgery, but she was vague, said that she had an infection, but she was better now. Well, that wasn't the whole story, as I learned last night from her niece of all people. She said her aunt Piper had a new heart, and when she found out what Samantha said, she got very quiet, and we ended up leaving the party early. When we got back to my house, Piper told me that she had to have a heart transplant. Then she dropped a total bomb and said she received the transplant the night after Thanksgiving. She was convinced that she had Kate's heart."

Gloria stepped back from Gillian and looked like she couldn't believe what Gillian had just told her. Gloria reached back and blindly grabbed the edge of her kitchen counter, opened her mouth, then shut it again, probably not knowing what to say. And why wouldn't she be speechless? Gillian felt the exact same way the night before when Piper told her about her heart.

"Oh, my gosh." Gloria covered her mouth with her shaking hand.

"I wasn't sure what to think when I found out, but after Piper left, I pulled out the letters you'd given me from the recipients. I found the one from Piper.

"I had forgotten about those. Are you sure? They can only give their first name. No other identifiable information is given."

"I'm sure, Mom. She identified herself as Piper, not exactly a common name. She said she was the third of five children, and that she loved art. Plus, she has a few quirky tastes that Kate had. I had always thought she felt familiar to me, and now I know why."

Gloria kept her arm around Gillian's shoulders and led her to the couch in the living room.

"I don't know what to do."

"About what exactly?"

"I told Piper to give me some time. I can't wrap my head around this. To start, she said she'd known for a few weeks that she had Kate's heart, or so she thought. But she kept it from me. So, the fact that she'd kept this huge news from me for three weeks is what really upsets me. How can I trust her if she kept this a secret from me? What other secrets would she withhold? Also, is it her that likes me and cares about me, or is it Kate? Are Piper's feelings for me even hers? This is what kept me from sleeping most of the night."

Gloria stayed quiet and continued to rub Gillian's back while she leaned forward with her arms on her legs. The continuous movement eased the pressure in Gillian's chest.

"Do I smell bacon?" Harold arrived in his bathrobe and hair, what little he had left, sticking in all different directions. The sight made Gillian burst out in laughter because honestly, she wasn't sure if she had any more tears to shed.

"Harold, go get dressed, and I'll be right in." Gloria hugged Piper before standing. "Go warm up breakfast, and we'll meet you at the kitchen table."

Gillian went to the kitchen and reheated the food, then brought it to the table along with three cups of coffee and the various condiments they'd want for their food. Just as she set the silverware down, Harold and Gloria emerged from their bedroom, and Gillian was greeted with a bear hug from Harold.

"Mom told me everything. I don't know what to say."

Gillian hugged him back and kissed his stubbly cheek that was filled with brown and gray whiskers. "Yeah, it's been a bit of a shock. You're lucky I waited this long to come over. I thought about ringing the doorbell at two this morning when I knew I wasn't going to get a full night's sleep."

"I'm so sorry, pumpkin."

They sat down and buttered their biscuits, and Harold added ketchup to his eggs. Gillian and Kate always teased him about it, but that morning, the consistency of his actions calmed Gillian. It felt as if everything yet nothing had changed. The consistency Gillian got from her in-laws had always been her safe haven. She could count on them for anything and everything.

Gillian was falling in love with Piper, and she loved everything about her, but the fact that she lied and withheld information from her, important information, she didn't know if she could forgive that. That hurt her to the core.

Once the dishes were washed, and they reconvened to the living room, the tension grew thick again.

"What do you want to do, Gilli? Do you love Piper?"

Gillian nodded. "But she lied to me, Dad. To all of us. She came to your home, and she didn't say anything. She just kept it to herself, knowing she had Kate's heart beating inside her."

"Yes, but try to see it from her perspective. Once she'd realized she thought she had Kate's heart, maybe she thought you'd only want to be with her because of that."

Gillian felt her mouth open, but no words came out. She stood and paced the living room while she thought about what Harold said. She stopped and looked at him, incredulous to that thought.

"That just came to you? You've known about this for a minute, and that's what popped into your mind?"

Gloria stood and held her hand up. "Hang on, Gillian. You have no right to talk to your father like that. I know you're upset and confused, but you watch what you're saying. We love you. We love Kate, and we miss her more than we could ever say, but I won't put up with you speaking to us like that."

Gillian started crying again and went to Harold, wrapping her arms tightly around him. "I'm so sorry, Dad. I didn't mean it."

"I know, honey. We're all off-kilter right now. Don't worry about me."

"I will always worry about you and Mom. You took me in when my own birth parents disowned me. I owe you everything, not just because of that, but because you always supported Kate and me, and you're my family. I love you both so much."

Gloria came over and wrapped her arms around both of them. "We love you, too, honey. I'm sorry I was so hard on you, but I want you to know we love you and want to help you any way we can. When you brought Piper over on Christmas day, we saw how much you both cared for each other, and there's nothing we want more than for you to be happy."

"If Kate was still alive, this wouldn't even be an issue." Gillian wiped the tears off her cheeks.

"Of course, it wouldn't. But Kate's gone, and she's not coming back. You deserve to find love again, and even though you and Piper hadn't been dating for very long, we could tell you both care for each other. Wouldn't it be worth it to hear what she has to say and see if you could work it out? There'll never be another love like what you and Kate had. But what you and Piper could have might be different, but just as special."

"What your mom is trying to say is that you'll always be our daughter, whether you choose to forgive Piper and be with her, if you find someone else, or if you decide to be by yourself. We don't want that for you, and if I had a vote, I'd vote for you to give Piper a chance to explain."

Back on the couch with Gloria, Gillian wiped her eyes then her nose with the tissue Gloria handed to her. "I promise to think about it. I love you both so much, and no matter what happens, you'll always be my family."

Harold threw his arms up in the air and flashed a goofy grin. "Well, happy freaking new year."

When Gillian left her in-laws, she called Heidi to see if she could come over. Heidi and Gillian had been best friends since childhood, and Heidi had always been Gillian's voice of reason. She trusted her other friends too, but Audrey was someone she wouldn't tell just yet. She'd been a bit hot-tempered lately whenever she spoke of Piper, and if she mentioned that Piper also had Kate's heart, Gillian couldn't even guess how Audrey would react.

Heidi led Gillian into the living room and handed her a mimosa. "You sounded like you could use this. What's going on?"

Gillian went through the story again, which she still had a difficult time believing even though she had an actual letter from Piper proving it was true. When Gillian finished, Heidi let out a heavy breath then downed her entire glass. She got up without saying a word, walked out of the living room, and returned with the bottle of sparkling wine to refill her glass. She sat next to Gillian on the couch and wrapped her arms around her.

"I don't know what to say. That's one of the craziest things I've ever heard. How are you dealing with this?"

"Honestly? I'm not sure. I'm shocked about her having Kate's heart, but I'm angry that she withheld it and lied to me. How can I trust her if she'd lie to me about something so big?"

"I'm not sure, Gilli. I agree that's a pretty big lie. Did she tell you why she didn't tell you when she first suspected she had Kate's heart?"

"Yes, she said in the beginning, she didn't say anything about her even having a heart transplant because we were getting to know each other. Then she said she was afraid I wouldn't want to be with someone who had been so sick after I had lost Kate. Even on the night we had sex for the first time, and I asked about her scar, she said she had to have surgery. That would've been the perfect time to tell me the truth. Or she could've told me when we decided to be exclusive. There were plenty of opportunities for her to tell me, but instead I learned it from her little niece."

Heidi rubbed Gillian's leg. "Do you think that you'll be able to forgive her?"

Gillian felt the tears well in her eyes, and she looked up and blinked rapidly, trying to stop the tears from falling. It was a futile attempt. She shook her head. She was so tired of crying. "I don't know. I have a lot of soul searching to do."

"Have you told the others?"

"No, I wanted it to be just you for now. Amanda and Jen, I wouldn't mind knowing, but the way Audrey's been behaving lately, I have no desire to tell her."

"Yeah, she's been a little crazy lately."

"Do you think Audrey has feelings for me?"

"What? Why would you ask that?"

Gillian shook her head again. "Piper suspected Audrey might have feelings for me since she'd get so mad whenever I mentioned Piper's name. I never thought about it until Piper mentioned it."

Heidi shrugged. "I mean, it's possible. There were times when she seemed a little too overprotective, and her behavior lately could indicate she's jealous."

"Jesus. How did my life become such a damn soap opera? Doesn't this sound like something you'd see on *Days of Our Lives*?"

Heidi laughed and refilled their glasses. "All that's missing is an evil twin sister that's a serial killer and is framing you for all the murders."

"Shut your mouth. The day's not over yet."

"Speaking of, what are your plans for the rest of the day?"

"Well, let's see. Since I told Piper I needed time to think, I don't have anything going on. Why?"

"How about we spend the day under a blanket snacking on cheese and crackers and watching action movies?"

"I say you have yourself a date." Gillian was already feeling a little better. She still had no idea what she was going to do about Piper, but she didn't have to make any decisions that day.

CHAPTER TWENTY-THREE

Piper, what are you doing?" Piper was standing at the window of the store pretending to watch the snow fall, but what she was really doing was looking for any signs of Gillian, hoping she'd finally come see her and let Piper explain everything and ask for forgiveness. It had been a week since Piper tried to call Gillian, but she'd told Piper that she wasn't ready to talk just yet. She understood. It was a pretty big bomb she'd dropped, but the ball was now in Gillian's court. Piper just had to be patient and hope that she would be forgiven. Since then, it'd been radio silence. Not seeing her, not talking to her was making her nervous and irritable. She'd snapped at Kelly once, but Kelly pretty much threatened her and shut her down.

Since then, Piper had tried to keep herself busy with work and pottery, but all of her pieces were only worthy of the trash can. Even Agnes was keeping her distance.

"I'm just watching the snow fall. Is that a crime now?"

She felt Kelly's arm around her waist and her chin on Piper's shoulder. "Still haven't heard from her?"

"No. She said not to contact her, that she needed more time to think."

Piper walked back behind the counter. There hadn't been a lot of foot traffic because of the snowstorm that threatened to dump almost a foot of the white powder.

"Why don't you go home before the roads get too bad? There's not much going on here, and if by chance we get a customer, I can handle it."

"Are you sure? I can stay and keep you company."

Piper felt like a complete ass for being so cranky. She hugged Kelly and kissed her cheek. "I'm so sorry for the way I've been acting. I just miss her so damn much. You were right, that I should've told her in the beginning. Why didn't I listen to you?"

"Pipes, you had your reasons for keeping it from her, but Gillian deserved to know. Also, keep in mind that you've had weeks that you've known about this. She's known for a week. Give her time to catch up. I'm hoping she forgives you because you two really care about each other."

"I love her, Kel."

"I know you do, sweetie. And I'm sure she loves you too. Hey, why don't you just lock up and go upstairs to chill? Watch some TV or read a book. Take care of you."

"Yeah, I might as well. The shop closes in an hour anyways. Last I checked, there wasn't much street traffic. Be safe going home, and text me so I know you made it safely."

"I will. I love you, sis. Everything's going to be all right."

"I love you too, and I hope you're right."

Once Piper saw Kelly get in her car and drive off, she turned out the lights and locked the door to her store. She was still feeling restless, and going upstairs to binge-watch a show wouldn't help. The only thing that would keep her mind off Gillian was throwing clay. She took off her button-down shirt and wore only her bra before she donned her smock. She put some clay on the wheel after she gathered all the necessary tools, and she got to work. She worked hard to keep Gillian out of her thoughts and put all her mental energy into her pottery. Three hours later, she finally had the piece she'd been trying to complete that she'd had in her mind. She made that piece for Gillian, and when it was complete, she'd deliver it along with her heart. Piper only hoped that Gillian wouldn't turn either away.

❖

Gillian had been spending more time at work since returning after the holidays. She'd tried to immerse herself in her work to keep her mind off Piper, but she kept finding her way back in. It had been two weeks since she'd last spoken to Piper, and Gillian missed her more than she ever thought possible. But then she'd recall the big lie, and she'd get upset all over again. Would she be able to ever trust Piper to tell her the truth and be honest with her regarding important events and information? Would she be able to forgive her? She had to admit that she did appreciate Piper keeping her word about giving Gillian time to think, even though she was miserable from not talking to her, holding her in her arms, kissing her, making love to her.

Gillian woke early on Saturday morning after a restless night's sleep. All of her nights seemed to be restless. Since the first time Gillian and Piper slept together, Gillian loved having Piper in bed with her, to curl up against, listen to her heart beat. Being in an empty bed made Gillian feel lonely. She didn't want just anyone in her bed. She wanted Piper.

Gillian never thought she'd be interested in any other woman after Kate died, but once she'd given herself permission to start dating again, Piper showed up and eventually took her place in Gillian's heart. Not only did Piper interest her, but she ended up falling for her.

There was one thing Gillian had been meaning to do but had put it off as long as she could, and now she needed to talk to Audrey. "Hey, are you free tonight? I need to talk to you about something, and I'd really like your input."

"Of course. Name the time, and I'll be there."

"How about six? I'll make us dinner."

Gillian picked up a photo of Kate and sat on the couch. She spent a few moments studying Kate's face—every angle, every freckle, every laugh line around her eyes. She was such a beautiful woman inside and out. Never a day went by that Gillian didn't feel completely loved by her wife.

"Honey, I don't know what to do. I really loved spending time with Piper, and I really liked her family. I don't know if the fact she has your heart is a bonus or hindrance. Obviously, bonus because of you, Piper was able to recover from heart failure, and she's able to have a wonderful life doing the things she loves and able to see her nieces and nephews grow up. Her family is loving, friendly, open, and funny. I know her parents would get along so well with Mom and Dad. The problem I'm having trouble with is that she does have your heart, and she lied to me about it. She didn't say it, but sometimes I wonder if she thought if I knew, that I'd want to be with her because she had your heart. That's crazy, right? I mean, I was freaked out at first that she ate some of the same quirky things you used to eat, and some of her mannerisms were the same as yours. But that's where the similarities ended."

"There are so many things I adore about her, the first of which is she's not jealous of you and me. She'd never expressed any ill will when I'd talk about you or when she'd look at your pictures that I have all over the house. She told me that you and I had a beautiful life together and that we were lucky to have had a love so strong. She hasn't been trying to compete with your ghost. She let me take it slow, at a pace that was comfortable for me. You're never coming back, but that doesn't mean I'd stop loving you. I don't think she'd want me to stop. I think she trusted me to be able to love both of you."

Gillian shook her head that had been quite the mess for the past two weeks. There were some days when she just wanted to hide under the covers, that if she didn't set foot into real life, that everything would go back to how it was. Not as far back as to when Kate was alive. As much as she wished she was still alive, she'd grown to know that everything happened for a reason. It was the journey Gillian was supposed to be on. Maybe Piper was brought into her life so she could see that she could love again, and that life was better when one spent it with someone they not only loved, but also really liked. Someone who would treat her with love and respect, would make her laugh, would wipe away her tears, would stay up late making love, and wake up early to make love again. Piper had certainly done that.

Later that evening, Gillian opened the door to find Audrey standing there holding a bouquet of flowers. She handed them to Gillian, but stood on the stoop waiting to be invited in.

"These are beautiful, Audrey. You didn't have to."

"Yes, I did. It's the least I could do after the way I've behaved."

"Come in. Can I get you a beer?"

"Sure." Audrey took off her coat and followed Gillian into the kitchen. "It smells good in here. Can I help with anything?"

"No, everything is almost done. Let's go sit in the living room. I have something to tell you."

"Okay." Audrey drew the word out and looked nervous, eyes wide and wringing her hands.

"I learned something about Piper that has me on edge, and I felt that you should know since Kate was your best friend."

Audrey's body started rocking back and forth—subtle, but Gillian noticed. Audrey always did that when she was nervous.

"When Kate died, her parents and I decided to donate her organs. It's something we'd talked about, but never applied as organ donors. Some of the recipients wrote us letters telling us about themselves and why they needed a transplant. Once of those letters was from Piper. She received Kate's heart."

"Excuse me? The woman you're dating got Kate's heart?" Audrey stood and paced the living room, running her hands through her short black hair. "How? How did this happen?"

"How did what happen? Piper obviously matched. She was in heart failure, but Kate saved her." Gillian was getting tired of watching Audrey pace. "Could you please come sit down?"

"When did you realize this?"

Gillian felt the blush creep up her neck into her face. She'd kept that information from Audrey just as Piper had kept it from her. But Audrey wasn't her girlfriend and wasn't Kate's wife, so Gillian didn't feel obligated to tell her. She decided to because Audrey had been Kate's best friend.

"About two weeks ago. When Piper told me that she thought she received Kate's heart, I had a hard time believing it too, but after she left, I took out the letters we got from the recipients of her organs, and there was one from Piper. I know it to be true, but I'm still having a hard time believing it."

Audrey ran her hands through her hair again. "Why are you telling me this? Do you think I'd want to be friends with her because of that? You told me you thought I'd like her, but I never could, and I never will."

"Why is that?" Gillian withheld that she hadn't talked to Piper since that time because that was none of Audrey's business.

"Because." Audrey resumed her pacing, clearly agitated.

"Because is not an answer." Gillian watched Audrey go through her paces.

"She's trying to be Kate, to take over her life."

"What in the hell are you talking about? Why are you acting this way?" Gillian stood in front of Audrey and put her hands on Audrey's shoulders to hold her still. "What are you talking about?"

"You should be with me, not her. I'm the one you've known longer. I'm the one who was there for you when you were grieving for Kate. I'm the one who loves you, not her." Audrey moved so fast that before Gillian even knew what was going on, Audrey was kissing her hard. Audrey's arms tightened around Gillian, and she tried to enter Gillian's mouth with her tongue. Gillian finally got her wits about her, and she pushed Audrey away so forcefully, Audrey almost lost her balance.

"What the hell do you think you're doing? Don't you ever touch me like that again!" Gillian wiped her mouth with her sleeve as if that would erase what happened. "You listen to me, you jerk. I'm not interested in you being my girlfriend, and I never have been. I've never given you any indication that I was interested in you other than friendship. Get out of my house, and don't contact me again unless you're willing to be just friends. There will never be anything between us except friendship, and if you can't accept that, then I wish you well. You think about that before you talk to me again." Gillian grabbed Audrey's arm and led her to the front door. Gillian threw Audrey's coat at her and opened the door. She couldn't even look at Audrey. She'd never been so angry in her entire life.

"Gillian, please."

"Get out, Audrey. I'm not kidding. Get out and think about what I said." Once Audrey stepped over the threshold, Gillian slammed the door behind her and locked the door just in case Audrey had any ideas of returning.

Gillian stormed into the kitchen to find the soup she'd made boiling over the rim of the pot. She turned off the burner and took the flowers that Audrey had given her and threw them in the trash. She grabbed a dish towel and bit down on it while she screamed. Tears fell as she continued to muffle her screams. She felt violated by Audrey's invasion of her personal space and kissing her without permission. She had the urge to call Piper, knowing she'd come right over and comfort her, but it wouldn't be fair to Piper since Gillian still had no idea if she could forgive her. As if she was summoning Piper, Gillian received a text from her. She checked her phone and sobbed when she saw the simple message.

I miss you.

Oh, God, she missed Piper so much. Why did she have to lie to her? Gillian wished she had the ability to forgive and forget, but she'd never been that way. She wouldn't and couldn't leave Piper hanging with no response.

I still need time, but I miss you too.

Chapter Twenty-four

One month. It'd been one month since Piper had seen Gillian, and she was beginning to think she'd never see her again. Piper felt like she'd been ghosted. How much time did Gillian actually need to know whether or not she could forgive Piper? She hoped Gillian would forgive her, but either way, Piper wished Gillian would make up her mind already so she could stop living in limbo. Piper would break her promise tomorrow to hold communication with Gillian. Regardless of what happened, Piper needed to get on with her life, either with or without Gillian. Tonight was Kelly's first show, and Piper would give it all of her attention. It was a huge opportunity for Kelly to get her name and talent out into the world, and nobody deserved it more than Kelly.

Piper put the finishing touches of makeup on her face then put on her jewelry. It had been quite some time since Piper had gotten dressed up, and she felt good about herself. It was amazing how some nice clothes, makeup, and jewelry made Piper feel good, feel worthy. She was a nice person who made a big mistake. If Gillian couldn't see that, then maybe it was time for Piper to move on. She sighed. She wanted to move on, all right, but with Gillian by her side.

Piper fed Agnes dinner, rubbed her cheeks a few times, then grabbed her coat. "No wild parties, no drinking, you got me, Agnes?" Her meow told Piper she understood. Piper was excited to see her family tonight, also a little nervous. She hadn't seen them since New Year's Eve, but the next day she'd sent a group text to her siblings about what happened between her and Gillian. None of them said anything about how stupid Piper had been, so she was grateful for that. Once some more time had passed, she'd be expecting them to rib her good-naturedly because that's what they did—they teased each other, but only when they knew it would be taken only as teasing. But so far, nothing. She wasn't sure if that was a good or bad thing.

She walked into the gallery, and she thought she'd tear up. All of the people who were mingling were there to see Kelly and her artwork. Piper took her coat off and laid it over her arm as she made a beeline to Kelly and Drew.

"You guys! This is amazing!"

"Pipes, I feel like I'm going to throw up. What if I don't sell anything? What if I'm a complete failure?"

Piper put her hands on Kelly's shoulders and looked her straight in the eyes. "What if you sell everything and are a complete success?"

"Piper's right, honey. This is the best work I've ever seen you do. I may not know a lot about art, but I know everything about my wife, and she's a winner."

"Damn it, Drew. Don't make me cry and screw up my makeup."

Piper chuckled and kissed Kelly and Drew on their cheeks. "I'm going to look around and say hi to the fam." She picked up a bottle of water and headed straight to her parents who were talking to Rob and Julie.

"Hey, everyone. How's it going?" She got hugs from her family.

"It's a pretty good turnout, I think," her mom said. "I can't believe how wonderful Kelly's pieces came out."

"Yeah, she's been working on the colors, angles, and strokes. Her creativity just smashed through the walls. So, where are the others?"

"Beth and David couldn't make it. Beth's been having awful morning sickness."

"But it's nighttime." Piper's mom smacked her arm, making Piper rub the area.

"You know darn well that it can hit any time of the day or night. Beth is going to Facetime in a little bit so we can show her around. Jon and Laura are around here somewhere."

"Okay, I'm going to go look around, and I'll catch up with you later."

Piper took her time studying each piece, in awe of Kelly's creativity. She looked at the price tags the gallery owner, Elise, placed next to each piece and nearly choked at how much she was charging. It was so much more than what they charged for the pieces in their store. She could almost hear Gillian's voice telling her she told her so, that they priced too low. A wave of sadness came over Piper, and she felt her shoulders slump. She had something really good with Gillian, and she majorly screwed up. Well, she was done feeling sorry for herself, and she was done waiting for Gillian to make a decision. She would show up at Gillian's door tomorrow morning and lay everything on the table. She'd apologize, she'd tell her she'd never withhold anything from her again, and most importantly, she'd tell her how much she meant to her, how much she loved her.

She finally ran into Jon and Laura and talked to them until Elise called for everyone's attention. When the din of conversation finally died down and everyone looked at Elise, she spoke.

"Thank you everyone for coming tonight. A dear friend of mine brought this woman to my attention." Elise reached her hand out and Kelly took it. "She told me about a gifted artist that I needed to see, and when she showed me a couple of pictures of Kelly's work, I knew she was right. Kelly James is an abstract artist that is from this area. She'd been a hidden gem, but that changes tonight. It will be my mission to get everyone in the art world to know who she is. Ladies and gentlemen, may I present to you Kelly James."

The applause grew louder as Kelly's face grew redder. When Kelly wiped away a tear, Piper felt her own tears form. She was so damn proud of Kelly, not only for her art, but she knocked it out of the park with being a wife and mom. She and Drew were happily married, and their sons were awesome human beings who gave Piper hope for the future.

"Thank you. I'd like to first thank my husband and my sons for being so supportive of me." Piper hadn't even seen Caleb and Andy before, but there they were wearing nice slacks, button-down shirts, and ties and looked sharp with their hair slicked back. Those two young men were going to break a lot of hearts as they got older, but they'll also help change the world for the better.

"I'd like to thank my family for being here and always being so supportive." Kelly's parents and sister were standing next to Piper's family, blowing her kisses.

"My sister-in-law, Piper, has been my best friend and partner in crime when it comes to art. I'm so lucky that I get to spend my days with her running our store, laughing, and joking with each other, and not only having the opportunity to create my own work, but also teach others how to sketch and paint."

"And finally, I'd like to thank Gillian Phillips for talking Elise into giving me a chance to show my work. Please, wander around, and if you have any questions, I'm available. Thank you all again for coming out tonight."

Piper felt a ball of anxiety take place deep in her gut, and her pulse raced when she heard Gillian's name. Was she there? She stood on her tiptoes to scan the crowded room. She weaved in and out of the patrons looking for any sign of Gillian's presence, but she wasn't there. She walked over to Kelly and interrupted a conversation she was having with a potential customer.

"I'm sorry, sir, just one moment." Piper turned to Kelly and lowered her voice. "Is Gillian here?"

"No, honey. At least, I don't think so. I just thanked her because she was a big part of this night. I have one more piece of advice for you."

Piper stood silently waiting for Kelly to finish.

"Go get your woman. Both of you need to move on from this, and do it together. Go make her talk to you."

"I planned on doing it tomorrow."

"No, you do it now. Leave here, don't stop anywhere, and head straight to her house. You both have had enough time dicking around. Go apologize, promise you'll never lie to her or hurt her again, and plead for her to take you back." Kelly kissed Piper's cheek then shoved her in the direction of the door to the gallery.

Kelly was right. Enough time had passed. As her dad always said, it's time to poop or get off the pot. On the drive over to Gillian's, Piper rehearsed what she'd say to her. She just hoped that Gillian could forgive her, and they could move forward together.

When she arrived, there were two cars in Gillian's driveway that Piper didn't recognize. Maybe she should come back tomorrow. She sat in her car with the engine running, hot air blowing from the vents, drumming her fingers on the steering wheel. No, she'd talk to her now. She got out of her car and pocketed her keys as she walked to the front door before she lost her nerve. She rang the doorbell and waited. When Gillian didn't come, she knocked hard on the door. It finally opened and a woman stood there that Piper didn't know.

"Can I help you?"

"Uh, yes. Is Gillian home? I'm Piper."

"Oh, hello. It's so nice to meet you. I'm Heidi, Gillian's best friend. Would you like to come in?"

"I-I don't want to interrupt your gathering. Could I just have a moment with Gillian?"

"Sure. She's in her bedroom changing. Come on in." Heidi grabbed Piper's hand and led her into the kitchen, or maybe the lion's den given the inquisitive looks on the other two women's faces. "Ladies, this is Piper. That's Amanda, and that's Jen."

"Oh, my gosh. It's so nice to finally meet you. Have you come to ask for Gillian's forgiveness?"

Heidi laughed and gripped Piper's arm tighter, maybe hoping their friend didn't scare her away. "Jen, give her a break, and don't be a bitch."

Piper shifted her weight from one foot to the other. She wasn't expecting to meet Gillian's friends tonight, but to be honest, a month without talking to her, Piper had no idea what Gillian had been doing, or who she'd been hanging out with. She figured Gillian had told her friends about Piper and the falling out they'd had. She could only imagine what they thought of her, but at that moment, they seemed genuinely happy to meet her. Well, except for maybe Jen, but she was so sweet about asking if Piper was ready to grovel.

Heidi moved closer and spoke softly. "Before Gillian returns, the three of us are trying to talk her into listening to what you have to say, and to stop ignoring you. Are you planning on lying to her again?"

Piper shook her head quickly. It was so strange talking to Gillian's friends about what happened between them, like it was a betrayal of her and Gillian's private affairs. "I promise to never lie to her again."

Heidi, Amanda, and Jen looked her up and down, sizing her up, and Piper felt like she'd been under their microscopes, laid bare for them to examine. "Okay, you hurt her again, and you'll wish you never came here, do we understand each other?"

"Absolutely." And just like that, Piper appreciated those women and their fierce protection of their friend.

"Piper?"

Piper turned around to find Gillian looking more beautiful than Piper had ever seen her, and it made her want to weep at her beauty.

"Gillian, I'm so sorry for interrupting. I wanted to talk, but I didn't know you had company."

"I thought I told you I wasn't ready to talk yet." Piper could see Gillian tremble. She wasn't mad at Piper, she was afraid, which made Piper even more determined to make it up to her.

"You did, but that was a month ago. We need to talk so we can either move on together, or go our separate ways. I hope to God that we can move on together."

Gillian nodded. "We're just about to have dinner, but I promise I'll call you tomorrow."

Piper would rather get their conversation out of the way, but she understood. She was the one who'd showed up unannounced. "Good enough. I'll talk to you tomorrow." Piper looked at Gillian's friends and nodded. "Ladies, it was nice to meet you. Sorry for interrupting." The last thing Piper saw before turning to leave was all three of Gillian's friends giving her the thumbs up. That boosted her confidence that they wanted Piper and Gillian to end up together. She saw herself out, hopeful for her conversation with Gillian tomorrow.

❖

"Oh, my, Gilli, Piper is something else. She's hot."

Gillian rolled her eyes at Amanda. Leave it to her to notice the obvious. "She's so much more than her good looks, you know." Even though Gillian had thought about Piper every day, not seeing her for so long reignited the fire for her that she thought had been extinguished. Amanda wasn't wrong. Piper was hot. And funny. And kind. And a great kisser. And an amazing lover. She was understanding, not jealous of her marriage to Kate or her relationship with her in-laws. Piper loved Gillian's family and they adored her right back. They had a love for art in common, and now pottery. Gillian was surprised how much she enjoyed throwing clay, and she wanted to keep doing it, maybe even get her own wheel to do it at home.

The doorbell rang, and Gillian's heart thudded in her chest at the thought of Piper returning. She couldn't decide if she was relieved or disappointed to find a man standing in front of her holding two bags of Chinese takeout. She signed the credit card receipt and took the food after thanking him. She took a moment to shake off her mistake of hoping it would be Piper on the other side of the door, and she plastered on a smile and forged excitement.

"Food's here." She placed the containers on the counter along with serving spoons and forks so they could dish out their plates. They refilled their glasses before taking their seats at the table.

"I'm surprised Audrey isn't here. Did she have a hot date or something?"

Gillian and Heidi glanced at each other, since Heidi was the only one Gillian had talked to about the night Audrey tried to kiss her. Heidi shrugged as she took a bite of food, indicating it was Gillian's story to tell. Gillian took a sip of her wine and cleared her throat.

"Audrey won't be hanging out with us for a while, if ever again. She felt she was entitled to my affections now that Kate was gone."

Amanda and Jen looked at each other at the same time, eyes open wide, jaws dropped. Then they looked at Gillian at the same time. It was almost comical how in sync they were with their timing and expressions, like they were identical twins.

"I'm sorry. What did you say?"

Gillian relayed the story of what happened when she invited Audrey over to tell her that Piper had Kate's heart. Gillian had called Amanda and Jen the day after she told Heidi so they were all caught up on that front. Gillian felt a little bad that she didn't tell them all at the same time, but Heidi was her Ride or Die, as Heidi often said.

"That little bitch." Jen's eyes narrowed, and she looked good and mad. Normally, Jen was the quiet, more subdued one of the group, but get her riled up, and look out. She turned into a wind-up toy that bounced along the surface. "How dare she make a move on you. Besides being with Piper, you've never given any indication that you were interested in her." She took a moment and looked at the others before she set her gaze back on Gillian. "Did you?"

"No!" Gillian felt almost as outraged then as she did when Audrey tried to kiss her. "I've never felt anything but friendship for her as Kate's best friend. The only one I've ever been remotely interested in kissing is Piper."

"Speaking of that gorgeous woman, when are you going to forgive her?" Heidi took a bite of her orange chicken after asking the question, nonchalantly changing the subject.

"Mmmm, Heidi's right. It was one infraction. You need to forgive her." Amanda twirled chow mein around her chopsticks as she spoke. "Do you honestly think that what she did was malicious?"

The room got quiet as Gillian's friends practically shoveled food into their mouths and gave Gillian time to think. Her appetite diminished, and she pushed her plate away.

"No, she doesn't have a malicious bone in her body. Piper is one of the kindest people I've met. And the more I think about it, I understand her reasoning. We were both fragile in this relationship; her having a heart transplant and not sure if her life would be shortened, and me, having lost my wife. I mean, what are the chances that the first woman I'm interested in dating received Kate's heart?" Gillian wiped the tears from her eyes that had recently returned as constant companions.

"Hear me out because this might sound crazy. But what if Kate orchestrated this?" Jen shrugged and pointed to Heidi and Amanda with her now empty chopsticks that had recently held a large plump piece of shrimp that she'd lost her grip of. "You said it yourself, Gilli, that you're constantly talking to Kate and could almost hear her voice talking back. Have you asked her if she's had a hand in this?"

"N-no, not really." That was absurd, right? That Kate would've brought Piper and Gillian together? Maybe not. Before Kate passed, Gillian didn't believe in hearing from loved ones that crossed over, but now she craved it. Even with Gillian moving on and dating Piper, she was still looking for Kate's approval and advice. It had helped quell her loneliness, to talk to Kate, even talking to her about Piper. But as Gillian and Piper grew closer, she noticed she was talking to Kate less. It was almost as if Gillian knew Kate was looking after her and didn't need the play-by-play of her life anymore. When Gillian and Piper grew closer, Gillian was talking to Kate less, but since trouble brewed between them, she'd started talking to Kate more. It comforted Gillian to know Kate would always be with her, watching over her, and making sure she didn't get too deep into anything she couldn't handle. Gillian could handle Piper. That she was certain of. She'd talk to her tomorrow, and she'd move on with or without Piper. But moving on with Piper was what she was hoping for.

CHAPTER TWENTY-FIVE

Piper had another restless night's sleep, a common occurrence since her unwanted break from Gillian. She kept berating herself for lying to Gillian, and she often played out in her mind the night she discovered Piper's surgery was more serious than she'd let on. She imagined if she'd been honest with her to begin with, where they'd be at in their relationship currently. She also thought of when she'd finally had the opportunity to talk to Gillian and apologize, the two options Gillian had were forgiving her and them starting over, or saying good-bye for good. The latter made her sick to her stomach and gave her serious anxiety, which wasn't good for her health. But today, it would be resolved, one way or another. Gillian had texted Piper to say she'd be over mid-morning, and Piper had spent the time rehearsing once more what she'd say.

When there was a knock on the door, Agnes arrived before Piper did, obviously thinking the guest would be for her. Piper shooed Agnes away so she wouldn't escape. Her heart beat wildly as she ran her hands over her chest then shook them out. When she opened the door, she thought her heart would stop beating on the spot. She'd just seen Gillian the night before, but her beauty always made Piper feel like she was seeing her for the first time. Time stood still and the air grew thick, making it nearly impossible to breathe.

"May I come in?"

"Oh, yes. Of course." Piper stepped to the side and once Gillian crossed the threshold, Agnes was rubbing against her leg like a little furry hussy. "Agnes, leave her alone. Can I get you something to drink? Water or juice?"

"No, I'm fine." Gillian headed to the couch and Piper followed her like a little puppy.

Piper decided to just rip the Band-Aid off and get right to it. "Gillian, I am *so* sorry for lying to you about my heart. What I felt was right at the time was in fact, the absolute opposite of right. At first, I didn't want to tell you about my condition because we were just starting to get to know each other, and if things didn't work out, then you didn't need to know. Keep in mind that you're the first woman I've dated since I got sick. I was seeing a woman for over a year, someone I thought would be someone I'd marry someday. But when I was in the beginning of heart failure, she broke up with me, said she didn't want to have to take care of me. She made me feel like I'd be a burden.

"When I had the transplant and finally recovered, I didn't think I'd ever date anyone again for fear of being a burden. Then I met you, and I was instantly attracted to you, like I was being pulled in your direction like a magnet. Then we kept running into each other, and I got to know you a little better through the pottery lessons. It didn't take me long to become smitten."

The small grin on Gillian's lips gave Piper the courage to continue. She wanted nothing more than to take Gillian's hand in hers while she told the rest of the story, but it was too soon, so she kept her hands to herself.

"You told me about donating Kate's organs and when I realized the timing, I should have said something to you and we could have worked it out together, but fear took over, and I thought the last thing you'd want was to get involved with someone who had a potentially fatal condition after losing Kate so young, but especially if I'd had Kate's heart. I realize now that I should never do your thinking for you, that you're a grown woman who can make decisions for yourself. I definitely should've told you the night we made love for the first time. You seeing my scar should have been the segue in to me telling you the absolute truth."

Piper couldn't go on without some sort of contact with Gillian, so she took a chance and reached for her hand. The fact that Gillian didn't pull away, and in fact, intertwined their fingers gave Piper the courage to finish.

"I promise I was going to tell you after the holidays. I know that doesn't make it better, and it's a really lousy excuse. But, Gillian, I would never intentionally hurt you. I would do everything in my power for you to never be hurt again. I love you, Gillian. I think I've loved you since the first night I met you standing in front of my store. And if you give me another chance, I swear to you that I'll never lie to you again, and I will spend every minute of every hour of every day showing you that I love you, and that you can trust me. Please, Gillian, please give me another chance."

The tears that fell from Gillian's eyes gave no indication of what Gillian's answer would be, and the silence was deafening. Piper let go of Gillian's hand, and she cupped her face, wiping the tears away with her thumbs.

"Baby, please. I love you so much." At that point, Piper wasn't ashamed to beg for Gillian's forgiveness. She'd do whatever she could to win her back.

Gillian nodded, but said nothing, and Piper was still hanging on by a thread. "What does your nod mean? I need words, baby."

Gillian's laughter was the sweetest sound Piper had ever heard. "I forgive you."

"You do?" Piper's voice was higher than a prepubescent boy's.

"Yes, but I swear, Piper, if you ever lie to me again, there won't be another chance."

Piper quickly stood and pulled Gillian up with her, and she wrapped her arms tightly around Gillian, and took in everything she could—the smell of Gillian's skin, the soft swell of her breasts pressed up against Piper's, the thick, silky hair that Piper had wound her fingers around.

"I promise to never lie or hold anything back from you again. I love you so much."

"I love you, too, Piper."

"Oof." Those sweet words finally undid Piper, and she held onto Gillian even tighter as she sobbed uncontrollably, the stress released the tension in her chest, allowing her heart to beat again. She took Gillian's hand and placed it over her heart.

"You feel that? Every beat of my heart is for you."

"I've missed you so much, Piper. This past month has brought a lot of reflection on my part. I think you're right that if I had learned about your heart troubles early on before we even started dating, I definitely would have kept you in the friend zone. If that had happened, I'd never have known how it felt to be loved by you."

"I've been beating myself up since you learned the truth that I wasn't honest with you about everything when you first told me about donating Kate's organs. As a recipient, I wasn't privy to anything about the donor. I was able to write a letter, but I had to send it to the organization affiliated with the hospital, and they forwarded it to the family."

"Yes, I found it and read it. After you left that night, I pulled out a large envelope that contained letters from the people who benefitted from the organ donations. I hadn't read them before, but Harold and Gloria did, and they gave them to me for when I was ready. I read your letter that night, and I felt like I got to know you better. I had no idea that you used to teach art at a community college. Have you thought about returning to that?"

They were now sitting on the couch holding hands, and Agnes was curled up in Gillian's lap.

"I've thought about it, but honestly, I love owning the store and working every day with Kelly. Besides, I still get to teach art, just on a smaller scale."

"On New Year's Day, I sat in bed and read the rest of the letters we'd received. It was amazing to learn how many people Kate helped, and it helped me realize that even though she died, she helped a lot of people, not just stay alive, but improved the lives of the recipients."

Piper nodded and squeezed Gillian's hand. "It was an extremely unselfish act and generous gift that all of you were able to provide. Um, I'm not sure how you'd feel about this, but would you be interested in listening to Kate's heart?"

Gillian covered her mouth with her shaking hand while nodding.

"I'll be right back."

Piper returned a minute later with a purple stethoscope she'd bought last week. She'd planned on going to Harold and Gloria's to apologize for not telling them the truth when she met them and offer them an opportunity to listen to it. She still wanted to do that, but now she could have Gillian go with her. She handed the instrument to Gillian to fit in her ears, then she placed the flat part of the diaphragm over her heart. The moment Gillian heard the heart beat was evidenced by her eyes widening then tears forming. Gillian placed her hand over Piper's chest so she could feel the steady beat while she listened to it.

"Oh, God, Piper." Gillian smiled through her tears. "I can't believe I get to hear her heart beat again."

"You can listen to it anytime you want."

Gillian took the stethoscope out of her ears and handed it back to Piper. "Are you sure? You won't think it's weird? It won't make you feel bad?"

"Of course not. I know how much you loved her, and if she was still living…"

"You wouldn't be."

"Well, that's not necessarily true. There could've been another donor, but it wasn't looking good. What I was going to say, that if she was still living, she'd still be here with you and her parents. But she's not, and because of that, I'm able to continue living. However it happened that our paths crossed, I'm grateful for you. At first, for your friendship. Now, for your love. You've given my family and me the greatest gift, and in return, I want for you to listen to Kate's heart beat inside my chest. It'll remind you how much she loved you, and now how much I love you."

They were both crying now and holding each other tightly, Agnes long gone, not having any time or tolerance for the humans moving around.

"Do you think Harold and Gloria would want to listen?"

Piper felt Gillian nod then she leaned back and wiped her tears. "I'm glad I decided not to wear any makeup today. I'd look like a complete mess right now."

Piper cupped Gillian's face. "You look beautiful. I'll always think you're beautiful whether you have makeup on or not. Whether your hair is styled, or you have bedhead."

Gillian laughed and shook her head. "When did you want to go see them?"

"Would now be all right? I've been wanting to go and apologize for not being honest with them. I bet they hate me."

Gillian shook her head. "That couldn't be further from the truth, my love. After they got over the shock, they understood why you hadn't said anything. They do like you, and I know they'd appreciate the gesture. Let me just call them to make sure they're home."

Once they confirmed Harold and Gloria would be home, they gathered their coats and the stethoscope, and they were on their way. Gillian hadn't told them of the surprise, only that she and Piper made up and that Piper wanted to talk to them.

When they arrived, Harold and Gloria pulled Piper into a group hug, and Piper felt the tears sting her eyes.

"We're so glad you and Gilli made up, Piper."

That made Piper cry harder, and she tried to apologize through her sobs. "I-I'm s-s-o s-sorry."

"Shh, no need for that. Let's go sit down."

Gillian wrapped her arm around Piper's waist and guided her to the couch. Once Piper got her emotions under control, she apologized for not telling them that she suspected she had Kate's heart.

"That wasn't something I wanted to withhold from you, but I wanted to tell Gillian in private first. Whether or not Gillian and I got back together, I had plans of coming over to apologize. I also wanted to give you something only I could give, but you can have it any time you want." Piper pulled the stethoscope out of her coat pocket. "Would you like to hear your daughter's heart?" Piper stood in front of Harold and helped him fit the earpieces into his ears. She put the diaphragm over her heart. When Harold heard the beats, he burst into tears. Seeing a grown man cry always made Piper cry, but that time, she remained still. She placed her hand on his shoulder and rubbed it. After a few minutes of listening, he removed the scope and hugged Piper hard.

"I can't tell you how beautiful that sound was. Thank you for that."

Piper nodded and kneeled before Gloria. "Your turn, Ms. Gloria." She got everything situated, and like Gillian, Gloria placed her hand over Piper's heart, and listened to her daughter's heartbeat. Gloria didn't cry. She closed her eyes and smiled the entire time, giving Piper a sense of peace. That had been one of the most emotional days Piper had ever had, but she'd do it over every day to bring Gillian, Harold, and Gloria the gift of hearing their loved one's heart beat again.

When Gloria removed the stethoscope from her ears, she cupped Piper's face, and kissed her on the mouth. It took Piper by surprise because the only one she allowed to kiss her on the mouth was Gillian and her parents. But because she was Kate's mom, and Gillian's mother-in-law, she welcomed it.

When she returned to Gillian's side on the couch, she clasped her hands together as if she was about to pray. "I told Gillian earlier that because of your and Kate's generous gift, I get to continue living my life. I want you to know that every day since I received Kate's heart, I've prayed for her, and for all of you, that you were able to find peace. I'm luckier than most because not only do I know my donor's family, but that I'm able to love them as well. I know we haven't known each other long, but Harold and Gloria, I love you, and you will always be a part of my family and me."

Gloria reached for Harold's hand and they smiled at each other. To Piper, it looked as if a peaceful feeling flowed between them, and it was magical to observe.

"We love you too, sweetheart. Thank you for keeping Kate alive for us. You will always be a part of our family, as well."

When they made their way back to Piper's apartment after picking up takeout, they dished out their plates with sushi rolls, edamame, and a bowl of udon, and sat at the small dining table Piper had in her apartment. They talked about Kelly's gallery show the previous night, and Piper told Gillian she was mentioned by Kelly when she was thanking people.

"I was sorry to miss it, but I figured you and your whole family would be there, and I wasn't sure if my presence would make everyone uncomfortable."

Piper chuckled and took a bite of her rainbow roll. "When Kelly thanked you, I stood on my tiptoes, scanning the entire gallery for you. When I asked her later if you'd been there, she said no, but it was time for me to go talk to you and get us worked out. She practically kicked me out of the gallery." Gillian had reached for Piper's hand and kissed it, letting her lips linger.

They finished dinner and got the leftovers packed up in the fridge.

"Um, I don't know what your plans are, and I know you probably have to work tomorrow, but I'd really love for you to spend the night. I just want to hold you in my arms tonight, feel your body next to mine, and know it's not a dream—that it's reality, and we belong to each other."

"I think I can show up a little late tomorrow morning." Gillian closed her eyes and relished the fact that she and Piper had made up and that Kate might have had something to do with it.

Piper and Gillian began undressing once they reached Piper's bedroom. Piper had no intention of making love that night—she just wanted to hold Gillian in her arms as they slept. But Gillian appeared to have different ideas, and Piper would never deny her anything. Gillian got into Piper's bed and held her arms out to welcome Piper. She settled on top of Gillian and began kissing her, gently at first, but then their passion ramped up, and their kissing became hungry, hands exploring, hips moving. Piper slid her hand into Gillian's sex and pressed two fingers deep inside, stroking in and out, in and out, curling her fingers to hit that special spot.

"Oh, God, Piper. Just like that. Keep going. Show me how much you love me." Piper kept moving in and out, faster as Gillian began to pant, breathless, then her whole body stiffened as she cried out Piper's name. Gillian's body shuddered and came to a rest. Piper stilled her fingers, then stroked Gillian's clit and held it there until the spasms ceased.

"That felt so damned good." Gillian's breaths were heavy and fast. "I've missed you so much."

"I've missed you too, baby. But I'm not done yet. I want you to know just how much I love you and cherish you."

Piper moved her way down Gillian's body and lifted her legs over Piper's shoulders. She moved her tongue around Gillian's clit, licked up her juices, then sucked her clit into her mouth. She increased the pressure until it grew hard once again. She tried to take it slow, draw out Gillian's pleasure, but when Gillian grabbed Piper's head and pulled her closer, Piper gave her what she wanted. Gillian's body grew taut as she cried out Piper's name for the second time that night. Piper lay next to Gillian and gathered her into her arms.

Gillian attempted to lift her hand. "My turn."

Piper chuckled. "You can hardly move your arm. Just relax and let me hold you. We'll have plenty of time together, love." For the first time in a month, Piper felt like the weight of the world had been lifted off her chest, and she could finally breathe.

"I love you, Piper."

"And I love you, Gillian.

EPILOGUE

Now, Harold and Gloria, I want to warn you that my family can be very rambunctious and loud, but I promise they're good people."

Piper's parents had already met Harold and Gloria a couple of times for dinner with Piper and Gillian, and they got along really well. But they were now about to meet the whole family and have Thanksgiving together, as usual with the James family, the day after. The day before, on actual Thanksgiving, Piper joined Gillian at Harold and Gloria's for dinner. Piper would have to work out extra hard the coming week, but it would be so worth it. Harold and Gloria had welcomed Piper into their family, and there wasn't anything she wouldn't do for them.

"Sweetheart, we're excited to meet everyone, so stop worrying." Gloria linked her arm through Piper's as they headed to the front door.

"Okay, but if you need a quiet space, let me know." Piper opened the front door to her parents' house, and the noise seemed to be at a respectable level for now. The first to greet them was Samantha. She was now seven and getting too big for Piper to lift into her arms.

"Aunt Piper, Aunt Gillian!" Samantha gave them each a hug then turned to Harold and Gloria and stuck her hand out. "Hello, I'm Samantha James."

Piper and Gillian stifled their laughs because Sam did exactly as they taught her how to introduce herself.

"Well, hello, Samantha James. I'm Harold Phillips, and this pretty lady is my wife, Gloria."

Samantha shook their hands. "Pleased to meet you. Let me introduce you to the rest of our family." Sam took Harold's hand and led them all into the living room. Harold and Gloria gave each other amused looks as Piper lowered her voice. "We're trying to get her to stop being such a wallflower."

"Everyone, can I have your attention?" Sam cupped her hands around her mouth to make her voice louder. "This is Harold and Gloria." Sam turned around to look at them. "Who are you again?" Sam whispered.

Everyone laughed as Harold announced they were Gillian's parents. Everyone knew that already, but it still made Samantha feel like a grown up. Piper took over and introduced them to her siblings, their spouses, and their kids after her mom and dad greeted them. Sam ran over to Piper's youngest sister, her husband, and their baby.

"And this is Charlotte. I used to be the baby of the family, but now Charlotte is. Isn't she so cute?" Sam smiled large and gave Charlotte a little tickle under her chin, making her laugh. The baby made Sam forget all about them, and they went around mingling with the James family. Piper wrapped her arm around Gillian's waist and kissed her on the cheek.

"What a difference a year makes."

Gillian leaned into Piper. "Indeed. And what a wonderful year it's been."

Next weekend, Piper was going to officially move in with Gillian, and they would decorate the house for the holidays. Kelly and Piper decided to rent out the upstairs apartment to their one other full-time employee who was also an up-and-coming artist in their community. Now that Kelly's paintings were in demand, she wanted to devote more time to her painting, which she also did at the shop's studio.

"All right, everyone, time for dinner." Once everyone was seated, Richard stood and held up his glass, and everyone else followed suit.

"This is a special day for us. We have the privilege of welcoming Gillian, Harold, and Gloria into our family. Because of their generosity, our Piper is celebrating her third Thanksgiving with the heart that belonged to their beloved Kate. We celebrate the lives of two extraordinary women, Kate and Piper, and their love for Gillian. Happy Thanksgiving, and here's to many more holidays together."

The entire family, Phillips and James, stood and clinked their glasses together. Piper and Gillian looked at each other and smiled, sure that Kate was with them and smiling, looking over them. Piper could feel her with every beat of her heart.

About the Author

KC Richardson attended college on a basketball scholarship, and her numerous injuries in her various sports led her to a career in physical therapy. Her love for reading and writing allows her to create characters and tell their stories. Her second novel, *Courageous Love*, was a Golden Crown Literary Award finalist in the Traditional Contemporary Romance category. She and her wife live in Southern California where they are trying to raise respectful fur kids.

When KC isn't torturing/fixing people, she loves spending time with her wonderful friends and family, reading, writing, kayaking, working out, and playing golf. She can be reached at kcrichardsonauthor@yahoo.com, on Twitter @KCRichardson7 and on Facebook.

Books Available from Bold Strokes Books

Coasting and Crashing by Ana Hartnett. Life comes easy to Emma Wilson until Lake Palmer shows up at Alder University and derails her every plan. (978-1-63679-511-9)

Every Beat of Her Heart by KC Richardson. Piper and Gillian have their own fears about falling in love, but will they be able to overcome those feelings once they learn each other's secrets? (978-1-63679-515-7)

Grave Consequences by Sandra Barret. A decade after necromancy became licensed and legalized, can Tamar and Maddy overcome the lingering prejudice against their kind and their growing attraction to each other to uncover a plot that threatens both their lives? (978-1-63679-467-9)

Haunted by Myth by Barbara Ann Wright. When ghost-hunter Chloe seeks an answer to the current spectral epidemic, all clues point to one very famous face: Helen of Troy, whose motives are more complicated than history suggests and whose charms few can resist. (978-1-63679-461-7)

Invisible by Anna Larner. When medical school dropout Phoebe Frink falls for the shy costume shop assistant Violet Unwin, everything about their love feels certain, but can the same be said about their future? (978-1-63679-469-3)

Like They Do in the Movies by Nan Campbell. Celebrity gossip writer Fran Underhill becomes Chelsea Cartwright's personal assistant with the aim of taking the popular actress down, but neither of them anticipates the clash of their attraction. (978-1-63679-525-6)

Limelight by Gun Brooke. Liberty Bell and Palmer Elliston loathe each other. They clash every week on the hottest new TV show, until Liberty starts to sing and the impossible happens. (978-1-63679-192-0)

Playing with Matches by Georgia Beers. To help save Cori's store and help Liz survive her ex's wedding they strike a deal: a fake relationship, but just for one week. There's no way this will turn into the real deal. (978-1-63679-507-2)

The Memories of Marlie Rose by Morgan Lee Miller. Broadway legend Marlie Rose undergoes a procedure to erase all of her unwanted memories, but as she starts regretting her decision, she discovers that the only person who could help is the love she's trying to forget. (978-1-63679-347-4)

The Murders at Sugar Mill Farm by Ronica Black. A serial killer is on the loose in southern Louisiana, and it's up to three women to solve the case while carefully dancing around feelings for each other. (978-1-63679-455-6)

Fire in the Sky by Radclyffe and Julie Cannon. Two women from different worlds have nothing in common and every reason to wish they'd never met—except for the attraction neither can deny. (978-1-63679-573-7)

A Talent Ignited by Suzanne Lenoir. When Evelyne is abducted and Annika believes she has been abandoned, they must risk everything to find each other again. (978-1-63679-483-9)

All Things Beautiful by Alaina Erdell. Casey Norford only planned to learn to paint like her mentor, Leighton Vaughn, not sleep with her. (978-1-63679-479-2)

An Atlas to Forever by Krystina Rivers. Can Atlas, a difficult dog Ellie inherits after the death of her best friend, help the busy hopeless romantic find forever love with commitment-phobic animal behaviorist Hayden Brandt? (978-1-63679-451-8)

Bait and Witch by Clifford Mae Henderson. When Zeddi gets an unexpected inheritance from her client Mags, she discovers that Mags served as high priestess to a dwindling coven of old witches—who are positive that Mags was murdered. Zeddi owes it to her to uncover the truth. (978-1-63679-535-5)

Buried Secrets by Sheri Lewis Wohl. Tuesday and Addie, along with Tuesday's dog, Tripper, struggle to solve a twenty-five-year-old mystery while searching for love and redemption along the way. (978-1-63679-396-2)

Come Find Me in the Midnight Sun by Bailey Bridgewater. In Alaska, disappearing is the easy part. When two men go missing, state trooper Louisa Linebach must solve the case, and when she thinks she's coming close, she's wrong. (978-1-63679-566-9)

Death on the Water by CJ Birch. The Ocean Summit's authorities have ruled a death on board its inaugural cruise as a suicide, but Claire suspects murder and with the help of Assistant Cruise Director Moira, Claire conducts her own investigation. (978-1-63679-497-6)

Living For You by Jenny Frame. Can Sera Debrek face real and personal demons to help save the world from darkness and open her heart to love? (978-1-63679-491-4)

Mississippi River Mischief by Greg Herren. When a politician turns up dead and Scotty's client is the most obvious suspect, Scotty and his friends set out to prove his client's innocence. (978-1-63679-353-5)

Ride with Me by Jenna Jarvis. When Lucy's vacation to find herself becomes Emma's chance to remember herself, they realize that everything they're looking for might already be sitting right next to them—if they're willing to reach for it. (978-1-63679-499-0)

Whiskey and Wine by Kelly and Tana Fireside. Winemaker Tessa Williams and sex toy shop owner Lace Reynolds are both used to taking risks, but will they be willing to put their friendship on the line if it gives them a shot at finding forever love? (978-1-63679-531-7)

Hands of the Morri by Heather K O'Malley. Discovering she is a Lost Sister and growing acquainted with her new body, Asche learns how to be a warrior and commune with the Goddess the Hands serve, the Morri. (978-1-63679-465-5)

I Know About You by Erin Kaste. With her stalker inching closer to the truth, Cary Smith is forced to face the past she's tried desperately to forget. (978-1-63679-513-3)

Mate of Her Own by Elena Abbott. When Heather McKenna finally confronts the family who cursed her, her werewolf is shocked to discover her one true mate, and that's only the beginning. (978-1-63679-481-5)

Pumpkin Spice by Tagan Shepard. For Nicki, new love is making this pumpkin spice season sweeter than expected. (978-1-63679-388-7)

Rivals for Love by Ali Vali. Brooks Boseman's brother Curtis is getting married, and Brooks needs to be at the engagement party. Only she can't possibly go, not with Curtis set to marry the secret love of her youth, Fallon Goodwin. (978-1-63679-384-9)

Sweat Equity by Aurora Rey. When cheesemaker Sy Travino takes a job in rural Vermont and hires contractor Maddie Barrow to rehab a house she buys sight unseen, they both wind up with a lot more than they bargained for. (978-1-63679-487-7)

Taking the Plunge by Amanda Radley. When Regina Avery meets model Grace Holland—the most beautiful woman she's ever seen—she doesn't have a clue how to flirt, date, or hold on to a relationship. But Regina must take the plunge with Grace and hope she manages to swim. (978-1-63679-400-6)

We Met in a Bar by Claire Forsythe. Wealthy nightclub owner Erica turns undercover bartender on a mission to catch a thief where she meets no-strings, no-commitments Charlie, who couldn't be further from Erica's type. Right? (978-1-63679-521-8)

Western Blue by Suzie Clarke. Step back in time to this historic western filled with heroism, loyalty, friendship, and love. The odds are against this unlikely group—but never underestimate women who have nothing to lose. (978-1-63679-095-4)

Windswept by Patricia Evans. The windswept shores of the Scottish Highlands weave magic for two people convinced they'd never fall in love again. (978-1-63679-382-5)

An Independent Woman by Kit Meredith. Alex and Rebecca's attraction won't stop smoldering, despite their reluctance to act on it and incompatible poly relationship styles. (978-1-63679-553-9)

Cherish by Kris Bryant. Josie and Olivia cherish the time spent together, but when the summer ends and their temporary romance melts into the real deal, reality gets complicated. (978-1-63679-567-6)

Cold Case Heat by Mary P. Burns. Sydney Hansen receives a threat in a very cold murder case that sends her to the police for help where she finds more than justice with Detective Gale Sterling. (978-1-63679-374-0)

Proximity by Jordan Meadows. Joan really likes Ellie, but being alone with her could turn deadly unless she can keep her dangerous powers under control. (978-1-63679-476-1)

Sweet Spot by Kimberly Cooper Griffin. Pro surfer Shia Turning will have to take a chance if she wants to find the sweet spot. (978-1-63679-418-1)

The Haunting of Oak Springs by Crin Claxton. Ghosts and the past haunt the supernatural detective in a race to save the lesbians of Oak Springs farm. (978-1-63679-432-7)

Transitory by J.M. Redmann. The cops blow it off as a customer surprised by what was under the dress, but PI Micky Knight knows they're wrong—she either makes it her case or lets a murderer go free to kill again. (978-1-63679-251-4)

Unexpectedly Yours by Toni Logan. A private resort on a tropical island, a feisty old chief, and a kleptomaniac pet pig bring Suzanne and Allie together for unexpected love. (978-1-63679-160-9)